SILENT'S TEACHER

SILENT'S TEACHER

Peggy Winnett

Visit the author at http://www.silentsteacher.com

Library of Congress Control Number:		2015910512
ISBN:	Hardcover	978-1-5035-8242-2
	Softcover	978-1-5035-8243-9
	eBook	978-1-5035-8244-6

Print information available on the last page.

Rev. date: 10/02/2015

To order additional copies of this book, contact:
Xlibris
1-888-795-4274
www.Xlibris.com
Orders@Xlibris.com
709967

CONTENTS

PART I
Fall Term
1992

Chapter 1 3

Chapter 2 6

Chapter 3 10

Chapter 4 14

Chapter 5 17

Chapter 6 21

Chapter 7 24

Chapter 8 28

Chapter 9 31

Chapter 10 34

Chapter 11 37

Chapter 12 40

Chapter 13 47

Chapter 14 50

Chapter 15 55

PART II
Spring Festival
1993

Chapter 16..61

Chapter 17..64

Chapter 18..70

Chapter 19..78

Chapter 20..83

Chapter 21..90

Chapter 22..98

Chapter 23..101

Chapter 24..106

Chapter 25..112

Chapter 26..116

Chapter 27..120

Chapter 28..124

Chapter 29..128

Chapter 30..132

PART III
Spring Term
1993

Chapter 31..137

Chapter 32..144

Chapter 33..149

Chapter 34...153

Chapter 35...159

Chapter 36...163

Chapter 37...167

Chapter 38...170

Chapter 39...172

Chapter 40...177

Chapter 41...179

Chapter 42...184

Chapter 43...188

Chapter 44...190

Chapter 45...195

Chapter 46...199

PART IV
Summer
2003

Chapter 47...203

Chapter 48...207

Chapter 49...209

Chapter 50...214

Chapter 51...219

This Book is dedicated to

Jim P. Spencer

Turns out that writing remains a solo activity. But once something is down on paper, helping hands of all kinds reach out to add the polishing that brings the story to its completion.

These are the people who helped this author along the way. My thanks go out to them for their valuable contributions.

Jean Zimmer, copy editor and compassionate guide.

Claire Jenison, eagle-eyed proof-reader. Nice going, Claire.

Paul Shepard who kept me on the straight and narrow where details of Chinese cultural practices were concerned.

Mary Grace who provided a piece of vital technical information.

Diana Tindall who accepted the assignment of reading one of the parts and providing helpful commentary.

Matthew Shilvock of San Francisco Opera who pointed me in the right direction.

Lori Harrison of San Francisco Opera who gave so generously of her time in order to answer the questions I posed.

And to the Monday morning writing group who provided weekly feedback, so that they know the story as well as I do, my heartfelt thanks for all the encouragement and thoughtful insights: Sasha Berman, Candy Carlisle, Fred Shea, Cie Simurro, Billy Lynch, Ed Orzechowski, and Lucy Greenburg.

For the cover artwork, I wish to thank Em Jollie for the elephants and thank Clara and Kenny Cheung for the Chinese calligraphy.

PART I

Fall Term
1992

CHAPTER 1

The day the postman brought the letter to the house, the snow was starting to melt and puddles of water dotted the bare ground between the boundary fence of their yard and the unpaved road beyond. Ning happened to glance up from the concrete slab that served as a washing area adjacent to the eastern end of the house; she was sitting on her haunches washing piles of vegetables to be cooked later. She saw him take giant steps here and there to avoid stepping in the deepest of the water holes. His pace slowed as he approached their mailbox. By the time he was placing the letter in the box, she had already stood up and started advancing toward the road.

When Ning actually had the letter in her hands, she did not immediately rip it open. No, she took her time, savoring the moment. Last December, she had taken a two-hour bus ride to a nearby city. It was the day known all over the People's Republic of China as *gaokao*. Along with a hundred and ninety-nine other students seeking admission to a university, she had sat for an exam that lasted six hours with one break for a meal served in a cafeteria. Everywhere in China students finishing high school were taking identical exams, far more exam-takers than places to admit them. Ning, however, had felt confident throughout the exam. It was only now, on this March day of the melting snows, at the sight of the official government seal, that some stirrings in her were tugging at her wall of confidence.

She quickly entered the house to take up a small knife and slit open the envelope. Yes, her confidence had been well-placed, yes, she was invited to become a student in August at a university. In school, English was her best subject, so she was being sent to a university that specialized in foreign languages. She slipped on her heavy shoes and warm quilted jacket, folded the letter neatly into an inner pocket, and ran off to the market to share the news with her mother.

The market lay in the center of the town. It was at the intersection of the main road and a road that ran out toward the ceramic factory, the one industry established in this primarily agricultural region. Her mother's workplace was in the market compound. She worked for the master tailor of the town. He had a little shop huddled under the corner of the corrugated tin roof that covered the market. The tailor had taken on the woman as a helper, but soon her expertly turned out items brought in customers who specifically requested her work. Ten years ago, she had to give the tailor fifty per cent of what she earned. Today, she turned over only twenty percent. She had learned the value of her work and could bargain as well as the next person. This was a necessary asset in a woman whose husband was dead.

It was late morning when her daughter came by. The morning shoppers had come and gone. The shallow wooden bins that displayed produce, grain and legumes were not as fully stocked or as well arranged as they had been a few hours ago. Market women slouched on stools behind their bins, counting the badly soiled bills that comprised the morning's earnings, separating the *fen* and *jiao* from the larger denominational *yuan*. There would be time for them to replenish their stocks to be ready for another wave of buyers in the late afternoon.

The market gave off pungent smells, what with the live fowl in cages plus the live fish swimming about in buckets of water that could barely contain them. When a customer bought a chicken or a duck, the bird was generally slaughtered right there and then. Fish and fowl were sold near the fresh meat counter, which occupied one long side of the market not far from the corner tailor's shop. The combination of smells was a feature of the market that Ning always noticed, though her mother didn't seem to know what she was talking about if her daughter mentioned it.

Today Ning barely registered the smell of the market as she entered. She was preoccupied with her news. Ning crossed hurriedly from the entrance to the shop. She saw her mother bending her head close to the work at the machine on the table in front of her. Her mother looked up as she entered. No words were spoken as Ning retrieved the letter from her pocket and handed it over. Her mother read it quickly and handed it back to Ning. The jubilation that they would share over the contents of the letter was to be expressed only later in the privacy of their home.

Ning wished she could tell her father the news. She still remembered him, though not as clearly as she would have liked: it had been ten years since he died. Her mother liked to speak of him, to tell her about their earlier life together. They'd both been raised in this town so they'd met as school students. They knew before they were eighteen that they would want to marry and that their families would approve. But he was burning with ambition to continue his education past high school, so they postponed their wedding. He'd completed only two years when he was ordered to leave university and report to a labor camp for "reeducation." It was the late 1960s in China, a time when higher education and professionalism were demeaned, belittled, despised. Life in the fields and factories was proposed as the ideal, good for the State and good for production. Her mother had waited for him. He was gone for three years. They married within three months of his return. Their daughter wasn't born until 1975.

Back in the house, Ning took out the photo taken on their wedding day. Her mother had preserved this photo during the times when it was not safe to display it, by concealing it between the cardboard pieces backing the picture of Chairman Mao, a picture that was prominently displayed on a wall in their home. In the couple's photo, you saw a faintly smiling woman standing shoulder to shoulder with a deadly serious man. They seemed to be of equal size. Her mother's square shoulders were on a level plane with the sloping shoulders of her father. An oval face with solemn eyes looked out at Ning. She stared at the photo.

She whispered aloud, "Father, I'm going to make you proud."

CHAPTER 2

When Hanna Hobbs returned from the interview, she kicked off her shoes and ran a bath for herself. She'd bathe and change into her comfies before settling down to the computer to write the necessary letters. She wanted to do it this very day while the suggestions made during the meeting were still fresh in her mind. Then she could go to the post office first thing in the morning.

Hanna was completing study to become qualified to teach English as a foreign language. When instruction began, she had no idea where she might want to go to do this teaching. Then, life provided a pointer. She attended the showing of a foreign movie at a film festival in town, a film recently produced at a Beijing studio. Hanna left the screening knowing that China was going to be her first choice. Here, she'd lived in the San Francisco Bay Area most of her life, had gone to school with students of Chinese descent and learned to eat with chopsticks before she was twelve, but she'd never had any desire to go to that country: rather formidable, she'd thought.

Today, January 6, 1992, Hanna kept her appointment with the officer in charge of educational matters at the Chinese Consulate. She'd explained her academic and employment background to him. He'd been most encouraging. He, himself, had done graduate study in the U.S. and was strongly in favor of student — teacher exchanges between countries. Hanna departed from his office with a short list of universities in China that might be hiring English teachers in the near future.

When the tub had filled and her clothes had been shed, Hanna stepped into the waiting warmth. Once fully submerged, she let her shoulders and head slide back until they rested against the rim of the tub. Because she'd moved a little too quickly, a strong ripple effect threatened to send water over the edge, but the water finally settled without spilling. Hanna took several long, slow, deep breaths.

She let her eyelids lower until they nearly closed. The warmth of the water encased the flesh of her body and moved into the porous hollows of her bones. Ah … bliss. A lassitude came over her. Her thoughts wandered. I wonder if I'm doing the right thing, she mused. I have my doubts. It's just that I feel I have to do something, something that will change the direction of my life. I'm not young, but I'm not old either! I'm just stale, flat, in a rut. I've liked my work at Community College, but I want to get out in the world and meet a few people, experience life in a different way. Still, Ben thinks I'm crazy to leave a decent job and go off "exploring" as he calls it. I'll have a hard time saying good-bye to him, that's for sure; I'm really risking something there. Oh, Ben, I'm sorry, but I simply have to move on or I feel I may shrivel up and die.

The ring of a phone stopped her musings here. She didn't rush to answer it; she'd let the machine do that. But she did finish bathing, and dressed quickly. She was anxious to get to the computer to write the formal letter of inquiry that would be sent to English departments at four Chinese universities. To ensure the correct amount of postage, she'd take them to the post office herself.

One of three replies came to Hannah on a crisp day in March. This was the one she knew would be her first choice. After she had examined the invitation from a foreign language university in a southern Chinese city, she knew what her reply would be. Half an hour later when she tried to call Ben, she got his answering tape and left only her name. Hanna still couldn't be sure how he would react to her news. Since she had mailed those letters of inquiry in January, she and Ben had talked about this eventuality. However, they had not succeeded in truly resolving the hard feelings on Ben's side.

When Hanna first brought up the subject of her attempt to find a teaching position in a foreign country, Ben had been stunned by the news. "How could you go off and leave me? What am I supposed to do, sit around and wait?" He sulked for days. This was the one element in Hanna's decision that was irksome and conflicting to her. She and Ben had been a couple for nearly three years. They chose not to live together for practical reasons of space and renter's lease requirements. But outside of work, they did everything together. Ben was the dearest person in Hanna's life. When she tried to answer Ben's questions about her plan, she kept harping back to that nagging need in her to get out there and do something before it was too late. He simply could not understand it. And of course she couldn't ask Ben to wait for her. She could only hope that he would.

When Ben called back, Hanna told him that the acceptance of her application had come through. Ben was polite but distant in his reply. Hanna, too, spoke in a subdued voice understanding too well that the thought of the long separation would not be welcome news to Ben. It was only early March; Hanna wouldn't be leaving until the end of July. She reasoned to herself that there was time left to help Ben arrive at a position of acceptance about what she was doing. By and large, Ben was a happy-go-lucky guy who loved baseball if the Giants were playing, who loved good Italian food, the kind that his mama continued to cook, and who got along with just about everyone. Hanna shared his love of the Giants, his parents' home-cooked meals, and was fascinated by his job. Ben had completed two years of Community College. After that, he entered the world of work. His uncle ran a construction company, at that time building small, affordable single-family homes that dotted the hills in Colma just south of the city. Ben went to work for this uncle, learning the construction trade. It turned out that he was good at working with his hands. He picked up quite a few skills. He also picked up a good friend, Louis, with whom he worked side by side for several months. They went to games together at Candlestick Park or watched them at their favorite sports bar. After a while, Louis moved on to work elsewhere and Ben didn't see him as often. One Sunday, several months later, Louis called Ben to say he had two tickets to the game at the Stick the coming Tuesday. They went together, drank a few beers, froze in their skimpy windbreakers in that cold, drafty stadium, and generally had a fine time. All the while, Louis was telling Ben something, but Ben wasn't paying close attention to any of it.

Finally, in exasperation, Louis said, "Well, do you want it?"

"Want what?" asked Ben, somewhat mystified.

"Haven't you been listening? I said they've made me a team leader at my job and I happen to know that next month they'll be hiring a few new hands. It's demanding work, but it's year-round and indoors and does not depend on any weather or market conditions."

"What are you talking about?" asked his puzzled companion.

"I'm talking about signing on as a stagehand at the opera house. We've a good bunch of guys there. It requires real teamwork. I believe you'd fit right in."

That was the work that Ben was doing when Hanna met him. He had fit right in. And he loved the work. Of course his Italian parents were full of gleeful pride that their son was working behind the scenes at the opera house. They pestered him on a regular basis to tell them any juicy gossip or merely to describe what he saw while at work. He could tell them who showed up on time for rehearsals, what the stars wore as casual clothing, who stumbled on the stairs, and who talked back to the director. Ben's stories spread throughout his large family, sister and cousins, aunts and uncles thoroughly entertained by any little morsel that he dropped. Hanna and Ben dined at the family restaurant every Monday evening for this weekly storytelling. This was part of the shared life that Hanna was prepared to bring to a jarring halt.

"God, do I dare?"

She reread phrases of the letter from China.

> "We are happy to offer you a position in our English Department for the year beginning Aug, 1992. Please attend to the medical exam as soon as possible and return the form to the address shown below. A letter outlining the courses you will be assigned to teach follows shortly. We are pleased that you have chosen to come to us."

In a few short months, could Hanna convince Ben to be pleased that she was taking this step? She hoped so with all of her heart.

CHAPTER 3

"I never knew the campus would be so beautiful!" one of the girls exclaimed. Ning heard her and smiled; she might very well have said that herself. A small group of students were walking together toward the English building on this muggy, overcast morning near the end of August. Overhead, tall, shaggy eucalyptus trees stood guard along the main walkway. Elsewhere, pines that were bare of branches for more than the first half of their height grew straight as poles. It was as if they had never been molded by the clawing hands of wind. Besides a proliferation of trees, there was also evidence of careful grooming of a number of plants and shrubs. A small, formal garden of decorative tropical plants leant color and focus to the lawn area immediately in front of the five-story English building.

As Ning walked along, she was thinking about the upcoming class in Oral English. The thought of meeting her first-ever native English speaker filled her with excitement and doubt at the same time. She wasn't sure she would be able to understand everything that the teacher would say. And she wasn't sure she could make herself understood to the teacher. Until today, all of her English teachers had been Chinese. Since Ning had arrived on campus a week ago, she'd found that many of the older students listened to the news on the BBC every evening at six p.m. She would see students wandering around by themselves along campus walkways or down along the canal with small transistor radios held to their ears. Yesterday evening, Ning accepted the offer of a listener to hear the broadcaster, but his words were accompanied by a buzzing hum that disconcerted her. She was disappointed to discover that she understood very little of what was being said.

So Ning was going to the classroom with mixed feelings. To make matters worse, one of her shoes was pinching her. Ning stopped and leaned over to run an index finger around the edge of the heel. There, that was better. In a few strides, she caught up to the group of students heading into the building.

The assigned seating found Ning in the last row of the classroom on the far right. She glanced around. Most of the faces were already familiar to her. These were her fellow students in a section of the incoming class who would take all of their classes together for the next four years. There was no one from her home village, but there were a couple of boys from the same province who had traveled on the same trains to come to this university. Ning nodded to each of them when she caught their eye. Students were talking in rapid but low-volume bursts as they waited for the arrival of the teacher.

And here she was. Ning saw her the second she entered. The teacher took quick strides to the platform at the front of the room, turning her back to the students as she wrote on the blackboard: Miss Hanna Hobbs, Oral English, Room 209, Sec 92.2.

Aloud, in slow, measured tones, she said "Miss Hobbs. That is my name. Miss Hobbs."

Having turned to face the students, she cast a long, slow glance that moved to connect with every face in the room. Ning saw a woman taller than she, slim yet exuding a sense of physical strength, a pretty face that made you want to keep looking. It was topped by bouncy light-brown hair that was a mass of curls. These curls bobbled every time Miss Hobbs moved her head. They would become an object of constant merriment for her students.

"Okay," they heard Miss Hobbs say, "my name is written on the board. "You know my name, now I want to know yours. As you may already know, it is the custom in Oral English classes for each student to choose an English name for use during class-time. Some of you may have already chosen a name. Others may need a few days to decide. Today, I'll go around and take names of the students who have an English name for themselves, and next week, I'll ask the rest of you for your names. Anyone who wants help choosing a name can speak to me during the break. I've brought lists of the current fifty most popular names for girls and the fifty most popular names for boys. These may help you to choose."

This announcement caused a stir of response from the twenty-four students gathered here. About half had heard from older students that this was the custom: they were prepared. The others, who were learning for the first time that they'd be using an English name for study in this class, were rather thrilled at the prospect. What would they choose, Arnold? Nicole?

Ning was one of the students who had known in advance of this custom. A girl in her dorm had told her about it. She was prepared to give her name, but since it was a bit unusual, she couldn't be certain that Miss Hobbs would find it to be acceptable. As the teacher went around the room collecting names, Ning had time to reach down and run her finger around the inside heel of that shoe, again. Ah … that really relieved the pinching.

Miss Hobbs was speaking to a student seated in the back row two desks away from Ning's. When the girl next to her was asked, she said she'd give an answer next week. Miss Hobbs looked directly at Ning.

"Have you chosen an English name for yourself?" she inquired in a gentle tone.

"Yes, I have," answered Ning. "It is Silent."

"Silent?" said Ms Hobbs, but she didn't expand the question.

"Yes," said Ning. "Silent." And she held her breath.

"All right," said Miss Hobbs.

Ning watched closely to see if she could detect any further reaction from Miss Hobbs, but all the teacher did was write in the little exercise book she was carrying and turn back to stand in the middle of the platform. So, it must be okay, thought Ning. I'm going to be able to use this name. It is a token of great luck to me. This is an auspicious sign.

By the fourth week students had settled into a daily routine. It began at six a.m. with rousing music on high volume broadcast from strategically placed loud-speakers. It was difficult for even the weariest of morning risers to be able to sleep through this racket, not that anyone could afford to sleep late. The music was in no way offensive to the students: they had heard exactly the same music over town and village loudspeakers when they lived at home. This was nothing new. In both the girls' and boys' dormitories lines began to form in front of toilets and sinks in the bathrooms down the hall. Getting dressed was a rush job because there was very little time before they would assemble on the grounds outside their buildings to begin a half hour of group calisthenics. There would be time to dress more carefully in the free time before breakfast. Classes began at eight o'clock.

In the seconds after the noise awakened her, Ning turned over on her side. It was time to open her eyes. When she did so, she caught sight of her friend, Cai, setting her feet down on the floor and standing to collect into her arms the voluminous column of mosquito netting that hung, suspended, over her bed. Cai tied the column into a large, loose knot and pushed it to one side. The nets were needed only during the warmer months of the year. In winter, they wouldn't have to bother with them.

"Good morning, Cindy," Silent said using English words to remind Cai of the English name she had chosen for herself.

"Good Morning, yourself," came a hasty reply. "Now we better get going." Silent, fully awake, stepped into her rubber flip-flops and trailed after Cindy down the hall.

Once outside, Silent and Cindy stood side by side in the formations on the exercise field. When the routines had all been completed, students broke rank in a chaotic rush to get back to their rooms to get ready for the school day. Most had to change their clothing to be presentable for the classroom. One of the more difficult adjustments for Silent had been getting used to the practice of sharing clothes with her six roommates. Since so many lived in one room and the school provided beds for each, there wasn't room for other furniture. The girls picked a corner of the room in which they all placed their clothes in a pile. They all dressed from this pile. At first, they tried to pull out only the items they had put there, but as the weeks went by and the pile became more disorderly, it became impossible to find just the shirt you were looking for so you took the one that came to hand. Making allowances for fit and personal preference, one's wardrobe possibilities did increase enormously. Mix and match, that's what was happening. Everyone benefited. Silent, too, enjoyed the newfound diversity in dress. Her initial discomfort came from knowing how carefully her mother had worked at providing her with some new pants and shirts. It wasn't that her clothes were necessarily better in some way that the factory-produced garments in the pile. It was just that Silent cherished the thought of what had gone into their creation. Some of the others had held back certain items of clothing they were unwilling to share. When Silent saw this, she decided to keep aside one special white blouse on which her mother had hand-embroidered a single peony on each collar point.

CHAPTER 4

At the Foreign Teachers' Residence, Hanna was in her apartment, book bag over shoulder and keys in hand when she heard her neighbor's door shut with a slam. She hurried out of her own door, shut and locked it, and headed for the stairs. She wanted to catch him so that they could walk to campus together. Most of the teachers rode bicycles to work, but Hanna and Milo both preferred to walk. She liked the exercise; he couldn't be bothered to go to the trouble of obtaining a bike, getting it licensed, and looking after it. He'd just as soon walk as go through unnecessary ordeals with officialdom.

Milo was back in China for his fourth year. When Hanna met him at the meeting of the English department, she learned that his first three years had been spent at a foreign language university in Beijing, a sister school to the one here in Guangzhou. Like Hanna, this was his first year at this particular campus. Milo taught English although it was not his mother tongue. He was from Poland and fluent in three European languages, but it was English that he had studied with the idea of becoming a teacher. Thirty-two years later, he was still hard at work.

She caught up to him in the lobby of their residence building.

"Hey, Milo, wait up for me."

He turned and greeted her with a half smile. "Come along, then. We don't want to be late."

Today was the only day on which their schedules coincided; they had walked together to the English building on the same day the previous week. Once outside the building, the two of them set off at a good clip to take the fifteen-minute walk to the part of the campus that housed the classroom buildings. As they strode along, Hanna let her curiosity get the better of her. She decided to ask Milo a few questions about himself.

She began, "Milo … I've never known anybody by that name. Is it a Polish name?"

After a significant pause, Milo reluctantly replied, "It is. It is the shortened form of Milosz." Then he went on to offer, "When I went to graduate school in the States, my fellow students started calling me that."

Hanna's curiosity jumped up a notch. "So you went to school in the States? Where was that, exactly?"

"University of Chicago. Enough of your questions. Let's clear our minds and be ready for our work."

Hanna was not put off in the least by Milo's dour ways. She found him to be one of her greatest resources for getting to the bottom of how life was supposed to be lived around here. He was an experienced teacher; she was not. He knew Chinese ways to a degree that she envied, although he didn't care to speak to her on matters beyond the scope of campus life, the teacher's role, and current trends in the teaching of English as a Foreign Language. Hanna had tried eliciting comments from Milo on such topics as Chinese politics or film-making, both of which interested her enormously. He was quite unresponsive. The troubles that culminated in the student occupation of Tiananmen Square had taken place during his first year in China. All he would say about it was that his government had put him on a plane and he'd been out of the country at crisis-time, so he had nothing to tell. And no opinion to express.

In the ensuing silence, Hanna decided to hazard one more question, her very last, she promised herself. "Did you get your keys?" she asked.

"Yes I did," he answered. "I found them in my box yesterday."

"I guess Brad will be feeling victorious," she continued.

"Umm," he mumbled, apparently unwilling to say more.

Hanna knew she would lose any chance at friendship if she persisted on a conversational course of interest only to herself, so she tried to honor the cues she was becoming able to discern. The keys she asked about were keys recently issued to all the residents of the teachers' building. One unlocked the front door. The other unlocked the padlock on the gate at the end of the compound road. The Foreign Affairs Office which was the agency that took care of all the foreigners living at the university had convened a meeting during the first week of school. At the meeting, the Foreign Affairs Office, commonly called the *Waiban*, had discussed the various regulations regarding life on campus and in the residential area. The director had patiently explained that for reasons of security, doors and gates would be locked at night. All buildings elsewhere on campus were likewise locked from the outside at eleven o'clock. Everyone should be back in the building by eleven because after that hour, there was no way in: the door and gate at the Teachers' Residence were locked from the outside by the building superintendent who then went off to spend the night elsewhere. One of the teachers, an Australian named Brad, objected strongly to the idea of being locked in or out at night after hours. He asked if he and the rest of the teachers might be issued keys so that they could freely enter and depart at their own bidding. A week later, word came back from the Waiban that such keys would be issued, and yesterday, they appeared.

On the way back from that earlier meeting, Hanna had said to Milo, "So what do you think about this locked-door regulation?"

When Hanna had first heard of it she was surprised only by hearing that teachers were treated the same way as students were. As for keeping doors locked at night, that felt fine to Hanna, a city girl. Milo's answer was to be expected.

"I really don't think much of it either way. After all, where could you go around here late at night?"

This morning, as they walked to their classrooms, Hanna glanced up at the sky. It was an old habit of hers, a way in which she expected to be able to get an idea of what the day's weather might be. But here in this suburb of Guangzhou, the sky was almost daily hung with a thin gray curtain that concealed any blue or any cloud movement that might exist just beyond. It was the gray of sooty industrial pollution created in the nearby city. It was one of the conditions of living here that most bothered Hanna. Not to see blue sky and not to walk in a world streaked by occasional sunshine was a worse deprivation than not having the ability to communicate freely at the market or in town. She worried for the effects to her lungs and body. She felt concern for the effects to the bodies of everyone gathered on this campus. Her compassion spread to embrace the whole of this populous nation.

"Hanna," she told herself, "you must remember not to look up at the sky anymore."

CHAPTER 5

"Dear Ma," she began.

Ning was sitting propped up on her bed. Her knees were bent so as to support the notebook of plain paper she would be using to write her letters home. This afternoon her classes were finished for the day. She had a couple of hours before she'd go with her room-mates to the student cafeteria for an early supper. Settling back against the pillow stuffed against the wall behind her, she went on.

"It's been a whole month since our classes began. I can hardly believe it. I'm sorry not to have written sooner. Anyway, today, there is plenty of time to try to tell you some things about the life of your college-student daughter. First of all, I have six classes a week; four classes are to read, write, and speak English and two classes in Chinese are teaching origins of the Republic and practical economics. All my teachers are Chinese except one: for English conversation we have an American young lady, Miss Hobbs. She has bouncy, brown, curly hair and smiles much of the time. We all like her a lot. My only really difficult teacher is Mr. Zhu. He teaches English Intonation and Pronunciation. He is so strict that you don't dare move an inch if he is looking in your direction. They say he is a hard marker; we'll see at mid-term, when we receive our first grades from him. I plan to do as well as I possibly can.

So, Ma, how are you getting along? Do you have as much work as you would like? I hope you aren't too lonely, now that you have our rooms to yourself. At least living in the family compound means there is always someone nearby if you need to ask for something. Please give my best regards to all the relatives.

As for me, I'll never be lonely here. I'm in a room in a dormitory that is shared with six others. The Seven Little Sisters, we call ourselves. And I'm becoming good friends with one of them. Her name is Cai Huang, she's from Chengdu. We go to meals together, go to class together, and walk on the mountain together. Right near he campus there are great hiking trails that go all the way to the top of White Cloud Mountain. Walking there is a way of getting away from the constant activity on campus. The climb is quite steep, so I'm getting my exercise whenever I go. For the girls who have found a boyfriend, the trails are their way to spend time together and get some privacy. No, Ma, I haven't found a boy I like, but if I do, you'll hear all about it.

Take care of yourself. I know it's a long ways until Spring Festival, but we do have that to look forward to. You can write to me at the address shown below,

I hope you will.

Your Loving Daughter, Ning"

Across campus Hanna was preparing to do some letter-writing herself. She would have dearly loved to have had access to that computer of hers that waited in storage with the rest of her things. But she did bring an ample supply of airmail- weight paper with her, so she'd just have to get on with it and revert to the old method of handwriting letters. She was sitting at her desk, chewing on the end of her pen, trying to think of what to say to her father.

Hanna and her dad had a close relationship stemming from the years in Hanna's early adolescence when her mother sickened with the lung cancer that eventually ended her life. It was only a matter of two short years from diagnosis to the time of her passing. Hanna and her brothers did the best they could to be a comfort to their father and to each other. By the time Hanna's mother had died, her brothers had both gone off to college. Their return visits at semester breaks and holidays were joyously received in the small household they'd left behind. Yet it was Hanna who spent the most time with their dad during his lengthy period of mourning. She was grieving as well, but her promise to her brothers to do the best she could to put some life into the home was a mission that helped her with her own sadness.

At their farewell dinner together at her dad's favorite restaurant on Pier 39, he had once again told her how firmly opposed he was to her going to China. Only this time, she had gotten a better sense of what it was that truly bothered him.

"You've got to know, as we all do, Hanna, that China is ruled by a Communist dictatorship. When I was just out of college and working in the financial district, we were glued to our TV sets following the McCarthy Hearings. I tell you, that man was a hero! He understood the insidious nature of that economic system; if it ever took over in the U.S. of A. we'd all be doomed. So he tried his best to root it out before it got started here. He made mistakes, he made some poor choices of people to assist him, so he never had a chance to finish what he started. But you mark my words. You could get yourself into serious trouble living in a communist-run country."

"But dad," Hanna had replied meekly, "foreigners are invited there to teach all the time. In fact, I met a woman my age just the other day who just got back after spending a year there. Shall I tell you what I learned from her?"

"I don't want to hear it. She has her story; you'll have yours. I just hope it doesn't have a tragic ending."

"Honestly, Dad," she had responded, and reached out to touch the hand that lay on the tabletop, "You have nothing to worry about. You just wait and see."

They'd left it at that.

Recalling this conversation, Hanna realized that whatever she decided to say to her father, it had better be fairly upbeat. No point in giving him him any fuel for doubt.

> "Dear Dad," she began. "I just want you to know that your daughter has been treated like royalty ever since she stepped foot in China. I had received an airline ticket for my flight to Shanghai, as you may recall. The trouble was there were no instructions about how to proceed upon arrival. Not to worry. They had it all

planned out for me. A representative from the university was at the airport arrivals holding up a sign with the name 'Hobbs' on it. I went right up to him and he took me politely in tow. It was already nighttime, so we left the airport and stayed in rooms at a sister university nearby, had breakfast there the next morning, and went back to the airport to fly to Guangzhou. Not bad, huh? Personally escorted on the last leg of my journey. It's a good thing, too. I had a chance to glance around in the airport and I didn't see any signs written in English.

The work is going well. I teach five classes, one in every grade level but two to first-year students. The students are great, so polite, so well-mannered. I am one of twenty-five foreign teachers, seven of whom are Americans. We are housed together in the same building, and, this may give you a laugh, every apartment is furnished with exactly the same items, so when you go to visit your neighbor, you feel right at home; you see the same brown-cloth-covered foam rubber couch and matching chair. We're all on equal footing here. Actually, we are not. This may please your fancy: those of us with graduate degrees are given the title "foreign expert". Those with the standard four-year degree are called "foreign teachers". So, how about that, Dad? Did you ever dream your little girl would grow up to become a 'foreign expert?' Come on, I want to see that smile.

Well, that about does it for now. I'll note the address below to which you can write when you find the time. I'd sure like to hear what you're up to these days.

Lots of Love from Hanna"

CHAPTER 6

Hanna glanced at her watch. Six-thirty already. She put her pen down, pushed her chair back from the desk, and stretched her arms up over her head. That relieved the stiffness incurred from writing such a long letter sitting on this hard, straight chair. She'd finish the letter to Ben later. Now it was time to join the others for dinner.

The campus had half a dozen cafeteria-style dining rooms spread throughout its campus. No one served a better meal than another. All served the same low- quality fare, but the one near the foreign teachers' residence had signs hand-written in English that listed the main ingredients of any dish being ordered. So Hanna preferred to go to that dining hall. Besides, it was where most of the foreign teachers chose to take their meals. Thus, Hanna had a chance to meet and talk with her fellow teachers.

Tonight as she stood in line waiting her turn to order, Hanna noticed that there was one empty seat at the table where Milo sat. She hoped no one would take it before she got there. He was chatting with his friend, Jack, an American whom Hanna had met only in passing. She wanted to know more about him and here was her chance.

The dish of pork and greens was Hanna's choice tonight, with a side dish of cooked lettuce and a bowl of white rice. The idea of searing lettuce had seemed quite novel to Hanna at first, but she decided she had liked it. Better than eating it raw, she concluded. Having filled up her tray, Hanna now moved to grab a teacup and a pair of chopsticks. In this cafeteria, the chopsticks lay bunched together in a large container, rewashed and ready for reuse. At first that idea appalled Hanna, who was accustomed to the western way of serving individual sticks in pairs wrapped in paper. But, as someone here had pointed out, it was not much different from using forks and spoons over and over again.

Hanna seated herself next to Milo, who turned to her and said,

"So, what has our little debutant been up to?"

This was the nickname they'd nailed Hanna with, in recognition of this assignment being her first teaching job. Hanna didn't like being known for that. But having grown up with two older brothers, she could give as good as she got.

"Been writing letters home, old-timer. What about you?"

"Oh, nothing so useful as that. Jack and I were just speculating on what to expect next from that madman in North Korea. It seems rather disturbing that he's lobbing missiles into the Sea of Japan. What do you know about it?"

"Not a thing," Hanna was quick to reply. "You two carry on."

And with that, she picked up her chopsticks and dug into the rather unappealing dishes in front of her.

As Hanna ate her meal in silence, she was thinking about what she had just finished writing to Ben. She missed him so much! Of course, she'd told him that. But what she wanted to get across to him was the mixed reaction she was having to being in this place and doing this work. Hanna had quickly grasped what was expected of her in her classroom work, and the students were a joy; there was no problem there. It was just that some of the ways of living were mildly irritating, so that Hanna had a difficult time staying on an even keel. Yet when she put her little complaints to paper they looked so petty. So she held herself back. If only she could have a long conversation with Ben, she felt she could make a better case. Before coming to China, she hadn't known quite what to expect in great detail. It seemed surprising to her to walk into her furnished rooms and find a television and phone in the living room, an air conditioner in the bedroom, and a washing machine, of sorts, in the bathroom. The only trouble was that the air conditioner worked for the first two weeks and never again after the entry into humid August days and nights. And the washing machine required manual filling through hose connectors to the bathtub spigot. It took a labor-intensive hour to complete one load. The television received two English language stations, both controlled by Rupert Murdock's Asian Television Service. They played all the bargain basement programs that his company could find.

"'Thank God for radio with its Voice of America and the BBC," Hanna had written to Ben. But, still, she felt wrong doing too much complaining because, after all, this had been her choice, hadn't it?

Like it or lump it, she told herself. The biggest disappointment was the phone. It was only to be used, as it were, "in house" — only for campus calls going out and coming in. She did tell Ben about the phone so he would know that the long conversation she so vitally yearned for was going to be a happening for another day.

"Hey, Hanna. Talk to us." This from Jack when he and Milo had come to a lull in their conversation.

"Okay," Hanna replied. "Why don't you tell me a bit about yourself? For starters, have you been teaching long and is this your first year here?"

"Nope and nope," said Jack. "I teach when I need the money but mostly I prefer to travel. This is my third year here. I stay because I've found a bit of life on the outside with a former student."

"Oh, ho," smiled Hanna. "The traveler got stopped in his tracks."

"Never mind any of your lip, missy," she heard back. "Now what was all that letter-writing about?"

So Hanna told Jack and Milo a little bit about Ben. When she was finished she remarked that it certainly was convenient having a mailbox to send mail from right here on campus. She saw Milo glance at Jack.

"Shall we tell her?" she heard Milo say.

"Look here," answered Jack, "Don't I see you take the van ride to town once in awhile? It might be better if you held off mailing your letters until you got to the hotel where the van drops us off. That hotel has a regular little post office. You can mail letters and packages and buy your stamps or aerograms there."

"You see," added Milo, "if you mail your letters in town there's a greater chance that no one will read them until they reach the address on the envelope."

Hanna looked up sharply. "Whadya mean? No one will read them. Who would do that?"

"Figure it out, little debutant," Milo finished, but in the kindest voice Hanna had yet heard him use.

CHAPTER 7

Hanna arrived in the classroom a few minutes before the bell would ring to mark the hour. She had time to start writing on the blackboard some of the phrases she'd be teaching in one of this morning's lesson. These were her first-year students. They would be practicing the giving and receiving of invitations.

"I'd like to ask you...

Would you be free to come...

Could you come to..."

She wrote in neat lettering in one column. In another column alongside, she wrote

"Yes, I'd love to come...

Thank you, that sounds nice...

No, I am not free that day...

No, sorry, I cannot come."

Hanna had been very happily surprised by the level of spoken English she had found so far in the students she was teaching. In training, she had worked with real beginners. These students at the university had studied English for six years, on average, before reaching university. Their beginning days were far behind. They were actually at that delicate point in foreign language acquisition where they would be able to put to use in speech and writing the vocabularies and word usage understanding already acquired, a time when this increased language production would, in turn, lead to increased language assimilation. It was an exciting time for teacher and student alike: the teacher felt challenged to create the stimulating work that would dig out the words freely; the students often surprised themselves by what they were able to say and do with their burgeoning language skills.

Today Hanna would have the students work in groups of four. In the first of four activities, they would be inventing and issuing invitations to each other, using the phrases on the board. Their practice would include giving responses. Hanna would oversee, not imposing herself into any particular dialogue unless a student looked to her for help or affirmation.

During the last ten minutes of their scheduled two hours together, Hanna stood before her class for a few minutes before the bell was due to sound. She was preparing to issue her own invitation. It was a custom here for students to be invited to come to their foreign teachers' apartments for tea. Not every teacher complied. But senior Chinese teachers and administrators encouraged the custom, knowing the students would benefit from this additional opportunity to practice their English, French, Spanish, Japanese, or whichever language they were studying. Hanna had immediately liked the idea.

Teachers she had spoken to about it found no unwanted consequences from this mild form of socialization. Most seemed to find these out-of-classroom meetings beneficial to all concerned.

Hanna spoke in her gentle, cadenced way, saying,

"Since we have been learning how to give and respond to invitations today, here is an invitation from real life. I would like to invite all of you to come to my apartment for tea. My place is not very big, so I shall ask that you come in small groups of four or five at a time. The days will either be Tuesday or Thursday of this week and the following weeks. We can meet from seven to nine in the evening. I'll write my phone number on the board. Please call me the day before to say how many there will be. We'll drink tea together and talk and I'll show you my rooms. I look forward to seeing you there."

She turned to pick up a piece of chalk to put the numbers on the board: Phone 744, Apartment: 308.

Out in the hallway, Silent grabbed Cindy's arm. "Let's go tomorrow night. Do you want to?"

"Sure," Cindy agreed. "Hey, Joey," she called out to a boy just a few strides ahead of them, "do you and Nick want to go Tuesday night?"

"Yeah, sure," he answered, "but I don't want to make the phone call."

"Oh, I'll do that," Cindy replied. Then she added in a louder voice, "Okay, everyone. Tuesday night is taken."

"Great," said a smiling girl who came alongside Silent. "You can go first and tell us what it was like."

As she clattered down the stairway, Silent was deciding that Tuesday evening would be the perfect occasion to wear that peony blouse she'd been saving. She wanted to feel special for the visit to Miss Hobbs.

The four students met promptly at six forty-five the following evening to take the walk across campus to the Foreign Teachers' Building. They chatted excitedly, learning that not one of them had yet been inside that particular building, wondering aloud what Miss Hobbs's rooms would be like. Joey and Nick expressed hope that there would be a chance to see TV; Cindy wondered what kind of music, if any, Miss Hobbs liked to listen to. Silent didn't say much except that she wondered if Miss Hobbs had any English novels among her books. The walk took them a full fifteen minutes.

In the lobby, the Chinese building superintendent sat behind a counter next to a row of mailboxes. He rose to his feet as the students paused in the middle of the lobby conferring with each other about where they thought they should go next. It wasn't clear because two staircases were in evidence, one to the left down a short hallway, and the other over to the right. The super, whose name was Wang Cha, called them to his counter with a beckoning hand.

"Who are you coming to see?" he asked when they stood silently in front of him.

"Miss Hobbs," they answered in unison.

"Okay," Wang Cha said, "first you must show me your student cards, then I will tell you how to get to her rooms."

Silent's face fell in reaction to this request. She hadn't brought her card with her tonight. Joey And Nick and Cindy produced theirs promptly. Wang Cha looked at each card carefully, moving his gaze from the photo on the card to the face in front of him. He took his time. He was enjoying himself.

"This is not a good picture of you," he snapped, as he stabbed his right index finger at Cindy's photo. "You weren't supposed to smile. And what about you?" he asked, twisting his upper body slightly so he faced in the direction of a frowning Silent.

Silent answered by giving her Chinese name and confessing that she hadn't brought her card, she hadn't known it would be required. The others joined in to vouch for Silent, assuring their interrogator that she was their classmate, well-known to each one of them, and should be allowed to visit their teacher as arranged.

Wang Cha's raised voice rang out, "Didn't they tell you to carry your card at all times?" But he let her go with the others on the condition that she bring her card to show him if she came here again. Then he waved an impatient hand in the general direction of the staircase on the left.

CHAPTER 8

"Dear Ma," Silent wrote as she began her weekly letter home. It was Friday, of the week of the Tuesday tea party at Miss Hobbs's. Silent liked to stay late in the classroom on Fridays so as to sit at a desk to do her writing. It was quieter here than it would be in the dorm room and she'd discovered that no one came by to ask her to leave until much later in the afternoon. Plenty of time to be undisturbed writing to her mother.

"Last Tuesday evening, four of us went to have tea with Miss Hobbs in her apartment. We were invited to do so by the teacher herself. Ma, it was really unusual. I guess I've never been in the home of a foreigner before. Not hat this is her home. But it was different in her rooms from anyplace I've ever been."

The words were flying out of the end of her fine-point pen, the one designed exclusively to write the characters of Chinese calligraphy. The pen was clutched securely in Silent's fingers. She continued,

"First of all, Miss Hobbs must be a very good housekeeper. Everything was so clean and neat. The furniture was empty of any cast-aside clothing or leftover dishes. All in good order. Then, the place was made to look nice because there were pictures on the wall. Miss Hobbs had brought poster art with her in her suitcase, all rolled up in a cardboard tube. She showed that to us. This was to keep the paper from getting crushed. The posters were stuck to the walls with a kind of sticky stuff that Miss Hobbs also brought with her. Two pictures were Japanese, one a wave that was as tall as a building. Miss Hobbs pointed out that there was a boatful of men rowing into the wave: one can only wonder how they will survive. The other was of a peaceful bridge scene with hanging flowers and a few people walking across. It was very beautiful to look at.

We stayed for two hours, talking the whole time in English. Can you believe it? To my great surprise, it was easy. I felt perfectly able to speak up from time to time. We drank some rather poor tea. I'm afraid Miss Hobbs doesn't know much about Chinese teas. She admitted as much, so two of us have offered to take her shopping in town on a weekend if she wants to learn more about what to buy and where to buy it. One of the boys who was there that evening knows a lot about teas. He helped with the preparation and chose from Miss Hobbs's collection of "experimental teas." That's what she named them. We also were served plates of several kinds of something she called "cookies." They are a small, round, sweet, flat biscuit, very delicious.

This university seems to treat the teachers very well. Miss Hobbs has her own telephone right in the room and her own television to watch whenever she likes. The bathroom is so well-equipped. There is a geyser on the wall that makes hot water run in the tub or shower if you turn it on ahead of time. And there is a washing machine for clothes so you don't have to do the scrubbing yourself. Miss Hobbs hangs her laundry to dry from wires suspended above her balcony, just like everyone here. She pointed them out to us when she was showing us the view from that balcony. It overlooks a big pond in front of the building.

On the way back to our dorms, we all remarked that this school must be very rich to provide their foreign teachers with such nice living quarters. I've already told you about our dormitories, where we stand in line to get a place in the bathroom and where we are housed seven to a room with only beds as furniture. But, really, we are none of us used to much more and, perhaps, these foreigners are.

While we talked, Miss Hobbs got out some photos of her family. She has two brothers, both older than she is, both in business, married, and living far from the father. Miss Hobbs lives the closest to him, so she sees him often. She told us her mother was no longer living. Even so, I thought it odd that she didn't show a photo of her from an earlier time. We also saw a photo of Ben, her boyfriend. Ben was a nice looking man in blue jeans standing close to Miss Hobbs in the photo, with a glimpse of ocean in the background. She told us she writes to him every week. Sound familiar?

That's all for now, Ma. I think of you every day and wish the day when we can be together will come very soon. Take good care.

Your Loving daughter, Ning"

CHAPTER 9

Hanna had to hurry. When the bell rang, ending her class at eleven-fifty, she quickly erased the writing on the blackboard, stowed the chalk and erasers, and stuffed papers into her book bag before zipping it closed. Today, Thursday, was the day on which she preferred to take the teacher's van into town. The van went on Mondays, too, but to different locations. Hanna's chores in town were better accomplished on the Thursday route. Now that she'd been in Guangzhou a couple of months, she was learning these simple things that made life run more smoothly. Departure time was one-thirty from the front of the building where teachers were housed. Just time enough to complete the long walk from the English building to Hanna's rooms, then grab a sandwich lunch and board the van for the trip to town.

Town wasn't very far, only eight or ten kilometers. But the trip lasted almost an hour because part of the road had been under repair since before the school term had begun in August. There was a point along the way where four or five roads converged and the traffic funneled down to allow vehicles to pass through in single file.

When Hanna first watched this traffic jam from the confines of the stalled van in which she rode, she was upset to see that among the collection of autos and vans and trucks of all sizes there were throngs of bicycle riders and crowds of pedestrians all competing to find a way through the maze. How could they breathe? And the noise was astonishing: shouts, bells, constant honking of horns all accompanied by the revving of engines and the release of gray clouds of exhaust fumes from engines that burned leaded petrol. In the van, the passengers were somewhat protected from noise and pollution by a functioning air-conditioning system and its background purr.

On this particular Thursday, Hanna had been happy to see that the woman named Claire was aboard, with her two daughters occupying the seats in front of their mother. Hanna smiled as she took the empty seat beside Claire.

"Mind if I join you?" she asked.

"Please do," came the reply.

Claire was at the university to accompany her husband, Brian. She was not a teacher herself. Brian was here from a university in Edinburgh, on special assignment in the English department, something about a survey that Hanna had not completely understood. But Hanna had been very pleased to meet this lovely, quiet woman who was about her same age. Claire was a breath of fresh air in that her conversation was not all about students and teaching but ranged over many interests. From Claire, Hanna had learned that the campus housed several populations besides those with whom Hanna was familiar. Retired elderly lived here, either administrators or teachers. Because of the size of the campus population, a police force manned by what looked like army personnel existed at their post in the center of the campus. Teachers passed by it every day on their walks to the classroom buildings. No one paid much attention, it was just there. Also on campus was a school for the children of campus personnel and a few local children. This was where Claire's girls went to class. There were half a dozen cafeterias, a dry goods store, and a barbershop where women barbers cut the hair of both men and women. Down a road that ran by an open field, there was a small outdoor market. It sold produce that was grown locally as well as fresh fish, live poultry, and raw meat that had yet to see the inside of a refrigerator. When Claire had taken Hanna on a walk to this market, she had advised her against buying anything except fruit and vegetables. That suited Hanna just fine. She would get most of her groceries in town, anyway. It was one of her chief reasons for going each week.

"So, what's new?" Claire asked after Hanna was settled in her seat.

"Oh, not much. I have some letters to mail at the Dong Fang. Then, while I'm there, I like to pick up a copy of the *Herald Tribune* if they have any left."

"And will we see you at McDonald's later on?"

"McDonald's! Are we going to McDonald's?" the girls asked in chorus as their heads shot up over the seats in front of Claire.

"Yes, we are and so is Hanna," Claire added as she glimpsed Hanna nodding her head. "Now please turn around and stay in your seats."

Thursday's van route took the occupants to a location that was within a reachable walking distance of McDonald's. For the first time in her life, Hanna actually looked forward to a meal at a McDonald's. It made such a change from the daily campus fare. Many of the teachers congregated there in the hour before the van departed for campus. They all gulped down milkshakes after devouring their Big Macs and french fries. A young man named Beng who had recently been promoted to manager had been a student six years ago at their university. He made a point of visiting their table on Thursdays, to see to it that his customers were satisfied.

CHAPTER 10

Milo and Jack had taken to saving a seat for Hanna since they usually arrived at the cafeteria in the evening before she did. Hanna hadn't asked them to do this. But she did prefer their company to that of some of the others here, especially since English was her only language. So she appreciated being able to relax during the evening meal with these two friends. And they enjoyed her company and playing the role they seemed to have adopted of big brother guardians.

"So, how's it going, kiddo?" Jack asked as Hanna seated herself with her food-laden plate.

"Oh, pretty well. But today I had a strange experience in one of my classes."

As she picked up her chopsticks and dug into the pork and greens in front of her, Hanna told the guys about her English conversation class with second-year students.

"It's one of the only classes I teach that issues a textbook. We all know how scarce textbooks are around here. Well, the book obviously is a recopy of a text published in a country outside of China. The chapter today dealt with superstitions. It was only meant to be a way of generating some conversation, but what I got back was a wall of silence. By now, the flow of words in this class has been pretty active, so I didn't quite know what to do. I was completely taken by surprise. What I ended up doing was telling them a few superstitions that I'm familiar with: a black cat crossing your path, the number thirteen, walking under a ladder. Nothing. I got nothing back, so I skipped ahead to the next chapter, which I'd been planning to do next week. Thank God I had looked ahead. What do you think that was all about?"

"I can hazard a guess." Milo spoke up forcefully, and since Hanna had such a high regard for his opinions and insights, she tuned in to his every word.

"Look to the present ruling system. It includes not only rule of law governing behavior, but rule of law governing thought processes. Of course no one has ever been too successful for long in telling others what to think, but the rulers here are giving it a try so as to maintain order and control. Superstitions as a subject; that would probably be classified as a milder form of religion, and if any are remembered, they would be associated with the past and therefore outlawed. No, you won't get students around here to talk about anything so potentially subversive. Of course, the culture is riddled with superstitious practices, but don't say that out loud. Besides, we know the monitor would be taking careful mental notes if any student had spoken up."

"The monitor? Who's he?"

When Milo and Jack heard Hanna ask this question, they looked at each other in disbelief. No one had told her about the system of classroom monitoring.

Jack said, "I'll take this one. You see, Hanna, we are living in a country not much like our own that does things in ways quite differently from what we know."

"Please, Jack. I appreciate the instruction, but not the patronizing tone," Hanna could not keep from interjecting.

"Okay," Jack continued, "I'll give it to you straight. In every classroom on campus, whether headed by a foreign or a domestic teacher, one student serves as classroom monitor. No, he doesn't erase the boards or straighten the chairs. His sole function is to report back to his superiors the subjects and activities in the classroom that day."

"And who are these superiors?" Hanna asked with interest.

"They would be your party officials stationed here on campus. The monitor would be a youth who has already joined the Party or who is being groomed for membership."

Milo took over from Jack. "You do know that only a small portion of the Chinese population are actual members of the Communist Party, don't you?"

"I've never given it much thought. How small?" Hanna asked with interest.

"About six percent the last time I looked it up," came the reply.

"I never would have guessed." Hanna had been somewhat disquieted to know that such a close watch was kept on classroom activities. She knew she had nothing to hide, but, still, it gave her pause. A queasy feeling in the pit of her stomach made itself felt, the same minor disturbance she'd felt when she'd received warnings about letters mailed on campus and phone calls from her room being potential subjects of scrutiny.

She finished her tea in silence. Meanwhile, Milo and Jack had gone on to discuss plans for the long holiday coming up in January. At that time, the campus would be closed. The entire population would have to remove themselves for a period of four weeks. It was a festive time for the students: a celebration of the New Year with their families, the first trip home for many since the term had begun in August.

For the foreign teachers, it was a chance to visit places of interest to them in neighboring Asian countries. But for some, it would be more than that. Hanna harbored the thought that for her and Ben it could be a time of reunion.

CHAPTER 11

The rainy season was a little late in coming that year. But when it did arrive, it brought a succession of days of steady downpour, the kind that would raise the levels in reservoirs, making everyone happy whether city dweller or agribusinessman. In San Francisco on that rainy night in November, Ben was driving to his parents' restaurant for the regular Monday night family gathering. He whistled a few bars of "That's Amore" in time to the beat of the windshield wipers. Ben was a guy who had music flowing in his bloodstream. The job backstage at the opera house was giving him new melodies to absorb, many with Italian lyrics, the language of his parents and theirs. But tonight he was in a Dean Martin mood.

Ben was happy. He carried the weekly letter from Hanna in his pocket. He often shared bits and pieces of what Hanna had to say with his family. In this way, they could all stay current on Hanna and her new life; she could be more alive to him if he could speak of her freely with others. He had felt her absence more keenly in these recent weeks. Perhaps that was because what is commonly known as "the holidays" was creeping up on them.

Ben drove across Columbus Ave. Having reached the heart of the North Beach area, it was time to start looking for a place to park. There! Just through the light in the middle of the next block, a red taillight signaling to turn into traffic from space alongside the curb. Now, if I can only get to it first, Ben thought. And, sure enough, here he was, backing in expert fashion into a parking place just a few steps from the restaurant. "*Grazie,*" Ben exclaimed aloud to no one in particular.

If his appetite hadn't quite kicked in as yet, it did the very moment he opened the back door and was enveloped in a cloud of scrumptious aromas. Mama was cooking chicken cacciatore, his absolute favorite. As he gave her a fierce hug, he peeked into the open pot on the stove to see artichokes bubbling away just the way Mama liked to cook them with whole peppercorns and a few spoonfuls of olive oil in the water.

"Go on," Ben heard her say. "It's almost time. You can help Papa open the wine. The others will be here any minute."

"Sure, Mama." he answered, obediently, and went on through swinging doors into the corner of the dining room, where his father was standing beside the round family table. A small collection of bottles stood in a cluster on a sideboard, mostly Italian reds. Ben picked up one of the corkscrews lying there and went to work.

"So, how's life treating you, Pops?" he asked in his jovial way.

"Never mind that," came the answer, "just finish what you're doing. I hear the others here already."

"Okay, Papa, here's one ready to pour," Ben acknowledged as the popping of a cork made his statement redundant.

The dinner was delicious, of course. Ben's younger sister, Rose, had shown up tonight, coming way across town from her room on the campus of San Francisco State University. Often her schedule prevented her from getting away. When he'd first started going with Hanna, his sister had teased him about his finally showing some good taste for a change. She'd taken to Hanna right from the start. As for his brother, older than he and thus inclined never to give Ben credit for any choice or decision, Ben got nothing but taunts, but because it was this particular family, they were given with the greatest of good humor and genuine support.

At the end of the meal, the dinner dishes had been pushed to the side. Wine remained in glasses that would not be empty until the sink took the last of their contents. As spumoni was being spooned into waiting mouths, sister Rose put her hand on Ben's and said, "What news of Hanna?"

"I have her latest here, just a second," replied Ben as he fumbled for the letter secured in the inside pocket of his jacket.

"Here we are. As usual, I'll only read the bits Hanna would want me to share." Loud groans and hooting from the siblings who had heard this preamble before.

"She writes,

> Not so long ago, I was visited in my rooms by
> the students from the first-year English Conversation

class. They came for tea, four or five of them at a time. You'd be surprised to know how well they already speak English. I made the tea with the help of a boy whose English classroom name is Nick. He knows a lot about teas, I was told. He let me know that I have much to learn, only not in so many words, of course. Still, it is something I'll try to improve on. While they were in my apartment, I showed them photos of dad, my brothers, and you and me taken down on the Carmel beach when we visited there, remember? These students are so eager to learn. But it is hard to get them to speak much about themselves in a personal way. Perhaps it's because I'm a foreigner and they are, by nature, reserved. I don't know; we'll see as we go along.

Ben — there is so much to tell you, but not in a letter. Have you thought over my idea of our spending my long holiday together late in January? Please, pretty please with loads of brown sugar on it."

"That's all from Hanna, but I want to add that I learned only two nights ago that it just might be possible for me to get time off by the third week in January. Talked to Louis and he will put in a plug for me. He says by then the opera season is ending and the madhouse of the Nutcracker performances a thing of the past. Ballet season begins later in February, but Louis says the work for stagehands is considerably less. Looks good from the work end, and I have a couple of thousand put aside for travel expenses. What do you think?"

"Go for it!" came the answer, everyone speaking at once.

"You mean it? Okay, I'll need to start soon with the planning. I hear a visitor's visa is required and a bunch of shots. One of the guys was telling me if I go as far as Hong Kong, why don't we go on to Thailand? It's supposed to be a great place for vacationing. Any ideas?"

"Ask Hanna what she thinks of that idea," Mama wisely suggested.

"That's just what I'll do." And with that Ben stood up, walked to his mother and gave her a loud kiss on the cheek. "Thanks, Mama."

CHAPTER 12

Every Saturday morning, the students of each classroom level were required to spend three hours of instruction on the political history and current affairs of the People's Republic. These patriotism classes covered every aspect of the Chinese governmental system that Party authorities thought an educated Chinese should know. The classes had been initiated soon after the events in Tiananmen Square in June of 1989. The instructors were Party officials who lived on campus.

On one such Saturday in mid-November, Silent sat in her seat in the auditorium. She crossed one leg over the other, silently waving her foot in the air as she listened to the speaker expound on his subject. Next to her, Cindy shifted in her seat. The clock on the wall showed there were another thirty minutes to go before the bell would ring to release them into the day. Silent's impatience was based not so much on what was being told to them as it was on anticipation for what this day would bring. For today was the day that Silent and Cindy would be taking Miss Hobbs to town on the bus to help her with her errands.

"The first thing we must do is ask Miss Hobbs what *she* wants to do," Cindy was saying to Silent as they hurried along. When they left the morning lecture hall behind, they had a long walk through the main campus grounds, past the English building and out to the main street that ran by the school grounds on the southern edge. Their bus stop was along that route. They had told Miss Hobbs where it was, and, sure enough, there she was as they approached the spot in a flurry of excitement.

"Have you been waiting long?" Silent asked in her polite way.

"Not at all," Miss Hobbs replied. "I came a little early because I wasn't sure I'd reach the right place. But you gave me excellent directions, Silent. Do you mind if I call you that?"

Silent hesitated. "If that is what you choose."

Miss Hobbs continued, "Someday soon I hope to call you by your Chinese names. But today we are using English to speak to each other, so I'd like to use your English names." Miss Hobbs's smile included Cindy as she finished speaking. The three of them cast their attention to the oncoming traffic, awaiting the arrival of the bus to town.

The ride into town brought fewer delays than usual. Cindy, sitting with Miss Hobbs, asked what errands Miss Hobbs had in mind for her time in the city.

"Of course, some decent tea," Miss Hobbs answered. "Also, I've been noticing how much cooler it's been lately. I need a warm jacket. When I packed to come here, I'm afraid I put books and shoes in my suitcase and left no room for a heavy coat. Do you know what I could do about that?"

"Oh, yes," the reply came from Silent who was sitting right across the narrow aisle from them. "There's a boy in our class who comes from Hainan. They don't need coats in that warm place. He has found a store in Guangzhou that sells coats and bedcovers, filled with down. Very nice, very cheap, he told us. I know where it is. We'll go. But first, Cindy and I were thinking we would show you a couple of the sights in Yuexiu Park. Have you ever been there?"

"I don't think so, but I can't be quite sure. When I come in on the teachers' van, we always go to the same places. I have no idea what district of the city we are in. I don't recall seeing any park." Miss Hobbs was pleased that these two friends had made a plan to include some sightseeing. "How do we get around? Does this bus take us there?"

Windows guarded the front. The roof sloped up to a point in the center as if the hall were wearing a conical hat. The corners of roof edges tilted upwards, a common feature of Chinese architecture. The colors were attractive grays for the three stories of roofs and strong earthy reds for the supporting columns, blended with a pale shade of clay for other surfaces. Miss Hobbs was enchanted by the sight. Cindy and Silent took Miss Hobbs right onto the lawns and the three of them strolled close to the imposing building. They decided not to take the time to enter, but, instead, walked a complete circle around the memorial to view it from every angle.

"Do you know something about Dr. Sun Yat-sen?" Silent asked Miss Hobbs. "As he is considered to be the Father of our Republic, he is quite a hero to us."

"Yes, I know," Miss Hobbs answered. "And I believe that Guangzhou was his home. Is that correct?"

"Yes, it is," the girls answered together. "We have one more place to visit before going to lunch," Silent added.

As they walked, Cindy and Silent occasionally skipped along for a few steps, they were so happy to be out together on such a nice day. On their right they passed a tall obelisk monument. "What's that?" Miss Hobbs wanted to know.

"Oh, that's only the monument to Sun Yat-sen. We're not stopping here," Cindy replied.

A little farther on, they came to the sought-for destination. A cluster of statuary loomed above them on their right, and a curious sight it was. A great horned creature made of stone stood on its two hind legs lording it over smaller versions of itself placed in uneven circular fashion around it.

Silent explained. "This is the Sculpture of the Five Rams, the symbol of the city of Guangzhou. May I read something to you?" She pulled a crumpled brochure out of the small backpack she carried over her shoulder. Without waiting for an answer, Silent went on. "The legend says that long ago five celestial beings wearing robes of five colors came to Guangzhou riding through the air on rams. Each carried a stem of rice, which they presented to the people as an auspicious sign from heaven that the area would be free from famine forever."

"Thanks for sharing that with us," Miss Hobbs exclaimed.

"Yeah, that was great," Cindy added. "I guess not every city can trace its beginnings back to a legend. Not like this one." And with that, the three of them turned back in the direction from which they had come, to look for a likely place to have lunch.

As it turned out, there was no need to look around for a place to eat. Cindy and Silent knew exactly where they wanted to go. When they'd talked it over ahead of time they had agreed on the place; neither had been there before, but Cindy's parents had stopped for a meal here when they had once visited Guangzhou. It was a name firmly established in Cindy's memory. The only hesitation the girls were feeling was caused by the little amount of spending money they had at their disposal. These qualms vanished on the way into town when Miss Hobbs told them, "Now, no matter what you say, I insist on being the hostess at lunch. In case you don't quite get the message hidden in what I am saying, that means that when the check comes, it comes solely to me. I insist."

The vegetarian restaurant served them a delicious meal. Cindy and Silent chose four items from the menu. When the dishes arrived, steaming hot, at their table, the girls tried to tell Miss Hobbs what the ingredients were. They soon discovered that their English vocabularies did not include most of these food items. This led to some joking back and forth. Miss Hobbs made wild guesses, trying to name the foods in English; the students tried to get Miss Hobbs to say the names in Mandarin. Because Miss Hobbs had not developed an ear for the intonations so important in the pronunciation of Chinese words, her attempts were met with some good-natured giggles. Miss Hobbs's knowledge of the names of Chinese dishes had not increased much since she'd been in the country. In the cafeteria where she took her evening meals, she stood in line at the counter and pointed to her selections. That worked. Miss Hobbs had decided to follow the example of other teachers and not spend much time trying to learn to speak Mandarin Chinese. All of the foreign English teachers were surrounded by English-speaking Chinese who were glad to help out when a foreigner asked them to do so. In the beginning, Miss Hobbs had arranged for a senior student to come to her room twice a week for language lessons. She had dropped that activity after the second month. Her teaching load was heavy: she needed every spare moment for lesson planning. There didn't seem to be enough time to spend on study of her own. She regretted this.

At lunch, the conversation flowed freely. Miss Hobbs knew so little of a personal nature about these two young women that she welcomed the opportunity to learn more.

She began: "When you came to my rooms for tea, I told you I was from California. As you know, that is on the west coast of our country. It is really as close as you can get from mainland China to mainland America. Cindy, I believe I heard you say your home is in Chengdu. Where is that, if you don't mind my asking?"

"Chengdu is in Sichuan province, which is west of here. It's the last province before Tibet. There are many Tibetans living in Sichuan. But mostly we are Han."

"And what is it like there? Are there mountains? Are there rice fields? Are there beaches?"

Cindy grinned. "If we had beaches, that would really be paradise. No, no beaches but plenty of rivers, and mountains in the north and west, and rice fields in the south and east. I've been all over Sichuan. My father is an inspector for the schools. Our home is in a big apartment building in the city. It is quite nice."

"It sounds nice," Miss Hobbs responded. "How about you, Silent? Where is your home?"

"It is in the north of Hunan Province, in a town on the Yangtse River. It is called Yueyang. I live just outside of town with my mother. It is farm country there. You see rice fields and bean fields all around. Our rooms are part of a group of buildings that are home to five different families. We feel as if we are all one big family. We feel proud to say that Hunan is the place where Mao Zedong was born. His village is called Shaoshan."

"Oh, yes," Cindy piped up. "I forgot to say that Deng Xiaoping was born in Sichuan. We're pretty proud of that."

Privately, Miss Hobbs wondered why there had been no mention of a father from Silent. Cindy had referred to "her parents," but Silent spoke only of her mother. If an opportunity ever arose to do so, Miss Hobbs would inquire about the missing parent. On this day she held back. It was only their first real sharing of personal information. Miss Hobbs wanted the students to offer freely whatever it was they chose to share.

She began her next point of inquiry by saying, "You know, when I was a freshman in college, I had no idea of what I wanted to do as work later on. Do either of you have any career in mind? You're both studying English. There will be a lot you can do with that. What would you choose right now, if your wish could be granted?"

Silent looked at Cindy with a slight frown on her face. Of course, these two friends had already spoken to each other about this very thing. Silent simply felt somewhat hesitant about speaking up in front of Miss Hobbs. Apparently, Cindy did not share her apprehension.

"I'll go," Cindy spoke right up. "What I'd really like to do is go on television as a newscaster on one of the big channels. I hear you need at least one foreign language for that work. Of course, I'd have to take some courses in broadcast arts. Fortunately, they offer them at our school. So when I'm a third-year student, I can sign up. That's what I want to do."

Silent took her time. "I guess I don't have such a clear idea as Cindy does," she started. "If I get to be good enough at English, one thing I might do is be a translator for groups of English-speaking tourists. That way I could move around in the country, see some of the big cities, and come to know China a lot better. Yes, I can imagine doing that."

"Both sound like very fine ideas to me," Miss Hobbs began. But she did not have a chance to comment further. The server was arriving with the check. It was time to pay up and go look for those shops.

The bus ride out of town in the late afternoon was a noisy, crowded affair. Cindy clutched tightly at the bulky parcel she was holding for Miss Hobbs. As people jostled about in the aisle, they tended to bump into the seated passenger alongside them. Next to her, Silent held the smaller of two packages on top of her lap. In her window seat, no one disturbed her.

After the bus had stopped to let them off at the campus entrance, Miss Hobbs reached out to retrieve her packages.

"No, no," Silent said. "We'll carry them for you back to your building, won't we, Cindy?"

"Oh, sure," Cindy agreed. "We had planned to do that all along."

"You really don't have to. It's way out of your way." But Miss Hobbs lost the argument. The students walked to the entrance of her building with her before they turned over the packages.

"Thank you so much for lunch," Cindy spoke with enthusiasm.

"And I thank you so much for showing me a little of Guangzhou, and for taking me shopping. You were a great help."

"I'm so glad we were," Silent replied, before turning to leave.

In her rooms, Hanna threw the packages down on her bed. The big, bulky one concealed her new winter coat, a pale-green down jacket sprinkled with multi-colored odd little geometric figures. Rather pleasing to the eye, she thought. The smaller package held two boxes of tea. One contained Longjin, a green tea from Hangzhou that Silent had selected for her. The other was an Oolong tea that Cindy recommended. Hanna felt certain that both would be an improvement over her own, earlier, hit-and-miss choices.

That night, Hanna lay in bed and stared at the ceiling as she reviewed the day. She was coming to see that the time spent with these students had exceeded her expectations. "That's it!" she spoke aloud. Conversation flowed today. Could that be because each of them was more relaxed off campus than on? She felt certain that was the reason.

CHAPTER 13

As Hanna reached out to turn off the insistent buzzing of her alarm clock, she came fully awake. The annoying sound did not permit one to ignore it for long. She yawned and sat up, pulling the covers around her. The cooler temperatures of late November put a chill in the air and a chill in her bones. She must ask Milo about the cold, she decided. It clicked into place that today was Wednesday, the day they walked to the English building together. Yes, she could ask him today.

Once outside, they walked along at a steady pace. It was Milo who spoke first. "Isn't that a new jacket you've been wearing lately? Did you get it here?"

"I did, indeed. Went shopping last Saturday with two of my students. Milo, let me ask you something. What do they do around here for heat in the winter? I've looked all over my rooms and I don't see any outlets."

"That's because there aren't any. Since it never gets cold enough to snow, you don't have to worry. You'll be warm enough. Just keep wearing that nice jacket at all times."

"Not good enough, Milo. Do you mean to tell me there won't be any heat in our building? What about the classrooms? Are we all suppose to stay wrapped up?" "You'll see," Milo replied with a frown, wanting to end this particular conversation. "It won't be as bad as you imagine. We'll all survive."

They completed their walk without further conversation.

That evening, Hanna went to the cafeteria earlier than usual. It wasn't crowded at this hour. Hanna took her tray of food to a table that had four or five empty seats. She wanted to leave places for Milo and Jack. She didn't have long to wait. They entered the dining room within a minute of each other, stood in line at the counter, selected their meal and joined Hanna at the table.

Jack commented, "So, Hanna. Milo tells me you went to town with a couple of your students. How did that go?"

"We had a fine time. They took me sightseeing, and shopping. And at lunch I had a chance to get to know more about them by asking a couple of leading questions."

"Really? What sort of questions?" From Jack's tone of voice, Hanna concluded that he was genuinely interested and not merely setting her up for some teasing afterwards. So she answered honestly.

"We talked about where they were from and what they wanted to do after graduation. You know, general stuff like that."

"Sounds pretty ordinary to me. But tell me, why the interest on your part?"

"I don't know. Guess I'm just a friendly person. And I'm here in a place that is foreign to me. I want to learn as much as I can about how things are done here."

Jack leaned forward in his chair so he could look directly at Hanna. "You know? I'm curious to know if your students had any ideas about their lives after graduation. And did you say these were first year students?"

"Yes, they were two female students from the First Year English Conversation Class. And each had a clear idea of what she had set as a goal for herself."

"Guess that explains it, eh, Milo? They are first year students. They haven't yet learned how the system works, and neither has our little Miss Debutant."

"Whadya mean?" Hanna exploded. "Now what don't I know?" Hanna set her chopsticks beside her bowl, jammed her fist under her chin and stared hard at Jack. But it was Milo who spoke next.

"Hanna? Do you have any classes with fourth year students? If so, and you ever have a chance to speak of future plans with them, you will hear that students here don't have to worry about such things. Many of their futures are decided for them."

"Oh, sure," Hanna responded sarcastically. "They receive notice in a fortune cookie telling them where to go next."

"Not quite," Milo continued in a mellow tone. He couldn't help but notice that Hanna was upset about what she was hearing. "More likely, they are called in by a school administrator sometime during their last term and told the work-unit to which they will be assigned."

Jack went on from here. "You see, Hanna, every person in China is accounted for by belonging to a work unit. Foreigners, too. You and Milo and I belong to the unit of this university. Every student here belongs to this unit. When students leave, they are sent to do work where the government needs them most. I had a senior who had finished Normal College; he was a qualified teacher before he came here for his degree in English. This was a bright young man. Yet I heard about him later, that he'd been assigned to work in a shoe factory. That was his work-unit, like it or not. Your first-year students may have their dreams, but they will soon learn that the system has plans of its own for them."

Milo added, "Some students have more choice than others. They are the ones who have connections that count. But they are in the minority."

"Hanna, you might consider speaking to other teachers about trying to be friends with your students. Of course, I'm just a sour old Pole," Milo allowed himself a little smile. "Perhaps I'm naturally more reserved than you 'friendly' Americans. For myself, I like to stick closely to the work and have little to no contact outside the classroom unless it is work related. Jack has a slightly different view."

"I do. I'd never thought of myself as a friendly American. I like to listen to my students so I try to make myself available inside and outside the classroom. I actually see that as a way of furthering their English language skills, not as a way of being personally involved in their lives. Teachers need to examine their motives just like anyone else. That's what I do."

"Thanks, guys. I guess I needed to hear this. I'll spend a little time trying to sort it all out. What would I do without you two guiding lights to help steer me through these unknown waters?"

Having taken the last sips of tea from their cups, the three rose to walk back to their rooms. The Residence Building was nearby, a brisk five-minute walk. No one bothered to answer that last question from Hanna.

CHAPTER 14

While Hanna walked back to her building after classes, she prayed that today would be the day when Ben's letter was waiting for her. As she passed through the lobby, Cha Wang beckoned to Hanna from behind his counter. "Good," she thought, "it's here."

"Mail for you today," he informed her and handed over a small stack that included a somewhat damaged catalogue from L.L. Bean that her father insisted on forwarding to her. In his joking manner, he'd told her, "just a bit of home not available to you while you're out there seeking adventure." Actually, it was with pleasure that she thumbed through those pages once every six weeks or so. It reminded Hanna that she had lived a previous life very different from the present one, and that there would be a future life also with its own changes. She hurried up the stairs to her rooms, where she tossed her book bag onto the spongy brown sofa and sat at her desk to read Ben's letter.

When she had taken in the news that Ben could definitely spend two weeks with her near the end of January, Hanna felt the need to express her joy with someone right away. She left her room, letter in hand, and ran up one flight of stairs. Still in a hurry, she charged ahead to a door in the far corner. She knocked loudly. This was the apartment of Brian and Claire, the couple from Scotland; Claire was her frequent traveling companion on the weekly trips to town.

"Is your mother at home?" she asked one of the daughters who had opened the door.

"Who is it?" she heard Claire call out just before appearing from an inner room. "Oh, Hanna. How nice to see you. Please come in. We were just thinking about bath time, but I'm sure the girls won't mind waiting."

"Claire, I'm sorry to burst in on you like this, but I've had some happy news. Ben is coming to spend some time with me during the

January recess. He's heard from friends that Thailand is a fun place to visit. I'd love to see it. All I have to do is give him the dates. I'd like to buy my tickets first, so I can be certain of what those dates will be. Do you or Brian know of a place in Guangzhou where I can buy tickets for international flights?"

Hanna had finished in a rush of words, prompting Claire to say, "Whoa, lassie, slow down. Let me think," and she went to sit down on the ever-present brown sofa. She invited Hanna to join her.

"Let's see," Claire mused. "I'd say you would be better off going to Hong Kong for your tickets and travel plans. You've been, haven't you? You do know how easy it is to get there?"

"Oh, yes, I've been several times. Fortunately, I knew ahead of time that a multi-entrance visa would be the best choice. I went with Enid, the Aussie teacher, a couple of times. Why do you think I'd be better off buying tickets in Hong Kong?"

"Because Guangzhou doesn't cater to international travel the way Hong Kong does. We've done all our travel planning there. I can give you the name of a super agent. Wait a minute." Claire sat forward in her seat. "Better yet, I'll go with you. Brian has promised me a break from my domestic routines. If he has a weekend coming along when he can be here with the girls, you and I can go do our errands in Hong Kong together."

"Oh, Claire, that would be great."

The next ten days passed by in a flash. Hanna was busy with her classes. Outside of the classroom, she spent all available time on lesson planning. She didn't have a backlog of previous lessons that other teachers had, those teachers who were here with years of experience behind them. And four out of five of her classes had no textbooks. It was up to the teacher to map out the complete two hours of lessons herself. Quite early on in her time here, Hanna had realized that being kept busy was really a blessing in itself. She loved the work and she wanted to do it well. The focus on her work kept her from dwelling on any of the drawbacks to her present way of life. Time passes quickly when you're not looking.

The following Friday, Claire and Hanna were bouncing along inside a taxicab on their way to the East Train Station in Guangzhou. The ride to Hong Kong would take less than two hours. The train they had chosen departed at around four in the afternoon. They'd get off in

Kowloon in plenty of time to search out a room in a guesthouse within walking distance of the train station. Hanna was discovering that Hong Kong was one of the easiest cities in the world to navigate by public transport. The metro system was impressive with all signs and public announcements posted in English as well as Chinese. The British were still here in 1992: their departure from the "colony" was only a few years away. Meanwhile, Hong Kong was welcoming to English speakers from any country.

Over lunch the next day, Claire told Hanna that she always loved coming to this city and seeing the contrasts between it and the one where they lived.

"Hanna, have you noticed how the people we see on the streets of Hong Kong are often smiling? Perhaps it has something to do with what they are hearing. I've never seen so many cellphones in the hands of pedestrians. Do you have that in San Francisco?"

"Not so many," Hanna answered. "Everything about Hong Kong makes me feel that these people are a step ahead of others," she continued. "Not only are they cheery, but look how much trouble they take to dress beautifully. Except for Paris, I've never seen anything like it."

Claire sat up straight in her chair. "Just for fun, we should go to one of the five-star hotels at teatime. That's where this city really struts its stuff. Let's do that, if we have time. But first, off to the travel agency. Are you ready?"

Once outside on the sidewalk, Claire led the way. These sidewalks of Kowloon were crowded with people, as crowded as the streets were with vehicles. Claire navigated the pedestrian traffic with experienced ease, turning a shoulder and arm as wedge, occasionally, to make a clear path through yielding on-comers. Hanna followed closely in her wake, keeping a sharp lookout for Claire's sudden spurts of speed. They didn't have far to go, only a couple of blocks. As they went along, Hanna peered into as many shop windows as she could afford to look at without losing her place behind Claire. Some might be worth investigating if there was time to do so later on.

"Here we are," Claire said. She had turned into a narrow doorway in the middle of the block. Claire looked around to be certain that Hanna was close by, before pushing open a wooden door to enter a small lobby where she headed straight for the elevator. "It's on the second floor," she informed Hanna.

Claire spoke the agent's name to the young woman seated at a stylish glass table in the center of a spacious reception area. The receptionist pressed a couple of buttons on a small console on the table, leaned over to speak into it in muted tones, and then sat back and folded her hands, not saying a word. They didn't have long to wait.

"Claire. How nice to see you." A woman of elegant dress appeared out of nowhere. "Come in. Come in. Bring your friend." And she ushered them along in a corridor leading to her office a few doors away.

The windows of her office stood ceiling to floor. They gave a view of the bustling street life below. But Hanna's attention stayed within the room. She turned her head to scan the two walls of travel poster to her right and to her left. The office spoke of a world where one wanted to keep on the move to take in as much as possible. Hanna liked being here.

The agent's name was Mei Ling. Her English was spoken with the brisk, clipped accent heard frequently on BBC broadcasts. Probably the product of the British Public School system, Hanna said privately to herself. After Mei Ling had been introduced to Hanna and heard the general outline of the trip that Hanna was proposing to take, the two of them got down to details.

"You said your friend, Ben, would be joining you for a trip to Thailand. Where in Thailand do you want to go? It will be warm anywhere in the country at the end of January, so you don't need to go to the beaches in the south if the mountains in the north are more to your taste." Mei Ling waited for Hanna's response.

"Ben mentioned a place called Chiang Mai in his letter. Some friends of his had a good time there. What's it like?"

"Chiang Mai, in the north, is very popular among young world travelers. The people in the town are welcoming. Not much English is spoken, but enough for you to enjoy most of its featured activities. From Chiang Mai, you can visit the villages of various tribal peoples settled nearby. You can go for long rides on a rented motorcycle. Or you can visit an elephant camp in the jungles outside of town, where you will see elephants doing some special drills for their trainers. It's quite the show. I have seen it. Does that appeal?"

"Ooh, yes, it really does. But where do we stay? Are there hotels in Chiang Mai?"

"Of course there are. But most people prefer to stay in any one of the many guesthouses spread throughout the town. They are less expensive, not luxurious, but ready to meet all the basic needs in clean, friendly, sometimes beautiful surroundings. I can give you a list of names before you leave here."

"Wonderful. Now, about the dates," Hanna went on. "Ben is coming from San Francisco. I wonder, should I ask him to meet me here first so that we could go on together to Bangkok and Chiang Mai? My work ends on a Friday. We could spend the weekend in Hong Kong, then go on our trip."

"Yes, you could do that," Mei Ling responded, "but I wouldn't recommend it. Perhaps you've not been in this part of the world at the time of Spring Festival. Everybody — and I do mean everybody — travels home at that time. If you have the option, you need to make your plans to be on the move either before or after the main body of traffic has gone its way. The holiday begins on January twenty-third. That will be a Saturday. If I were you, I wouldn't go near a train or bus station in Guangzhou before Monday, earliest. They will be mobbed on the weekend. So will the stations here in Hong Kong, but not as bad as Guangzhou. Suppose you come to Hong Kong on Monday, the twenty-fifth. and travel immediately to Bangkok? Your friend will be better off booking a direct flight from San Francisco to Bangkok. In Bangkok, there is a very comfortable hotel at the airport that you can walk to from any of the concourses. Whoever gets there first can wait in a room we'll reserve for you and then you can fly to Chiang Mai together as soon as convenient. How does that sound?"

Hanna turned to Claire who was sitting in a chair next to her. She'd been following every word of this conversation. "Claire. See what you've done for me? I'd never have known any of this, if you hadn't brought me to the right person."

Hanna then returned her attention to Mei Ling. "I like every suggestion that I've heard from you. Let's order some tickets."

It took another half hour, but when Hanna left the office with Claire, she had all the detailed information she would need to prepare a letter to Ben for Monday's mail.

CHAPTER 15

By noon on Sunday, Hanna was closing the notebook in which she had completed writing some instructions to herself for Monday's classes. Her planning for the immediate future was complete. She stood up and walked into her kitchen. She'd make herself a sandwich before settling down to writing that letter to Ben. Hanna had made the discovery that peanut butter was to be found in Guangzhou, good old American Skippy peanut butter. Since bread and jam were readily available, Hanna felt her life was more manageable now that she could feed herself easily at home, and not have to be running to the cafeteria all the time.

Before seating herself on the brown couch, Hanna went to the desk to collect one of the pale blue aerograms that she now used to write all of her letters. She would still have to buy additional postage at the postal service desk at the hotel in town where she mailed her letters. That was fine with Hanna. She preferred the aerograms because she reasoned to herself that if anyone was going to open and read the letter before it was delivered, they would have a hell of a time with such flimsy paper. Hanna still simmered at the thought of mail being read by someone other than the intended. She was much more cautious these days with what she wrote, ever since Milo and Jack had warned her.

"My Love," Hanna began as she often did when writing to Ben "I've been to the summit and the wise man was home."

This was something that Hanna and Ben liked to say to each other. In their coded language it simply meant that everything was better than okay.

"Claire came with me to Hong Kong last weekend and I'm all set with tickets and dates for our journey to Thailand. I'm so excited. It sounds just great," and Hanna went on to tell Ben what the travel agent had told her about Chiang Mai.

"It seems it will be best for us both to travel separately to Bangkok. I will be going there from Hong Kong on Monday, January twenty-fifth. We can rendez-vous at the airport hotel where we have reservations for a night or two before flying to Chiang Mai together. I have round-trip tickets for us for the Bangkok-Chiang Mai leg. We don't have reservations in Chiang Mai, but we don't need them. I was given a list of seven guest-houses to choose from when we get there. The return date is left open on the Chiang Mai to Bangkok return. That's because I don't know when you have to get back. I have more time than you do, a total of four weeks. It'll be fine with me to get back to school early.

You and I could spend a couple of days in Hong Kong on your way back. What do you think? You need to book your ticket to get to me in Bangkok, and get yourself home afterwards, via Hong Kong or not. You'll find me in the Amari Airport Hotel, Don Muang International, Bangkok, Thailand. I'll be the one you stood next to in that photo on the Carmel beach. Remember?"

Having reached the bottom of the page, Hanna had to stop. But because the letter had put her into a certain mood, she went into the bathroom, reached for a lipstick kept in a drawer there, applied a goodly amount to upper and lower lip, and back in the living room, blotted it on the middle of the written page. There! Let everyone have something to look at.

Hanna was not the only one writing letters that day. On this chilly afternoon in December, Silent and two of her room-mates stayed in their room to do some letter writing of their own. Now that the temperatures were cool and the windows kept closed, mosquito nets were no longer needed. They had been folded and put away for those days in March when spring weather would begin raising the temperatures again. For now, the room appeared to have more space without all that netting hanging down.

Each girl sat on her bed with a pad of paper leaning against elevated knees as she wrote. There was much to say to the families back home. Silent and her room-mates were first-year students. They were especially excited at the thought of four weeks at home since not one of them had ever been away from home for this long in all of their young lives. Their departure for university last August seemed to have been much more than five months ago. Before the school-break, finals would be given in all their classes. The first term was ending. It would be their first marking period: the thought brought with it a certain amount of anxiety.

Silent wrote,

> "Dear Ma. It is only five more weeks before I will be standing with you in our room, sitting with you at our table. The thought makes me happy. When next I see you, the first term will have ended. I have done my best and am confident of high marks. There will be much to tell you and much to ask you about when we are together. Here the food is not so good. I will help you make some delicious meals while I'm home. I found out that there are only two buses per day from Guangzhou to Yueyang. The holiday begins Saturday, January twenty-third. If the bus station is too crowded, I may have difficulty boarding. If so, I'll wait and take the next bus. Please don't go to the station to look for me. I can't be certain of when I'll arrive. It takes fourteen hours. If it's night-time, I'll wait at Yueyang Station and walk out to you the next morning. Wait for me at home or at the market. I'll find you. Don't worry. Anyway, I'll write again next week. Good-bye for now. Ning."

PART II

Spring Festival
1993

CHAPTER 16

Ben had dozed off. He jolted awake as the plane hit a patch of rough air that abruptly changed its altitude. He stretched his legs and feet out in front of him as far as the space would allow, not far in a window seat of the tourist section. The departure of the flight from San Francisco had been delayed by an early morning fog that did not allow for sufficient visibility for take-off. The fog took several hours to lift. As they droned on across the Pacific, all Ben could think of was that Hanna would be beside herself with worry and impatience when he failed to show up at the expected time. She had his flight number: he'd been certain to include it in his most recent letter to her. The trouble was, she would be in the hotel room and might not find a way from there to check on his flight information. With these concerns in mind, he was only able to doze in fitful bursts of rest and angst.

Ben raised the window shade a crack, long enough to see that it was pitch dark outside. Still a few hours to go before the connection at Narita in Japan. By then some sunlight would be visible. This trip to Bangkok involved the longest air travel hours that Ben had ever flown. His body, cramped and fatigued from so little movement, was complaining in every limb and joint. His mind, dull and bored, could not lead him out of his dejected mood. He sighed, pulled the window shade down, and closed his eyes.

Next thing he knew, the captain was announcing that they'd be landing in fifteen minutes. Not landing at Narita, but landing at Don Muang in Bangkok. Ben, startled by this news, told himself he must have sleep-walked in Japan through the entire deplaning, showing of documents, and boarding of the next flight. Quite suddenly, he was fully awake, totally conscious of where he was and eager to get to the end of this seemingly endless trip. He got his wish. Baggage arrived promptly for passengers to claim. The line through customs, though long, moved briskly. He easily found his way to the connecting pedestrian crossing to the hotel, and here he was, at the counter, asking the cheerful clerk to please ring the room of Hanna Hobbs.

Today was Tuesday in Bangkok. Ben had left on his flight Sunday morning. Because of crossing the international dateline, Ben had lost a day. He was en route on Monday: he had reached Bangkok sometime after dawn Tuesday morning. In her case, Hanna had departed from Guangzhou by train to Hong Kong, before midday on Monday, then flown to Bangkok from Hong Kong in the afternoon. She was in the hotel room only eight hours after exiting her own rooms at the university.

When Hanna was ushered into the hotel room, she had almost squealed with delight. The contrast in elegance contained in this moment and only eight hours earlier was almost too much to bear. She saw sheets on the bed as white as if they were just out of the box, the bed as wide as a four-lane highway. Highly polished teak furniture, of straight lines and simple design dotted the room. A gold-framed mirror took up most of the space above a dresser opposite the bed; a bas-relief of three Thai dancers hung over the bed. Unobtrusive brass light fixtures gave the room a bright aura. Hanna was charmed by the freshness of this space. She placed her bag on a low luggage rack beside the dresser. She zipped open the long encircling zipper and spread the bag open. Before she went down to a solitary dinner, she wanted to have the satisfaction of seeing that special purchase she'd chosen in Hong Kong when she went shopping with Claire. After securing her travel tickets, she and Claire had retraced their footsteps to stand gazing in the window of a shop that looked like a Hong Kong version of Victoria's Secret. They looked at each other, giggled out loud, then entered to take time selecting their separate purchases. In this room at the hotel by the Bangkok airport Hanna looked down at the item exposed by the opening of this side of her bag. There was a lace-trimmed teddy made of the softest silk in a flattering tone of peachy pink. She tingled with anticipation of the right moment coming to present herself to Ben in this little beauty. As she gazed around this hotel room she told herself that at least this would be the right place.

Feeling extremely pleased with life, Hanna left the room to seek out one of the hotel restaurants. She found a lounge that featured a piano player performing classic tunes by Cole Porter and Jerome Kern. She stopped in to hear the music and enjoy a cool drink before going to the nearby grill room for a meal. As she sipped her nonalcoholic fruit punch, Hanna closed her eyes for a few seconds. She breathed deeply three times appreciating the clean, cool air. She compared the sound of "I Get a Kick Out of You" coming from the eighty-eight keys with the clatter of bins of dirty dishes heard nightly at her local cafeteria. She anticipated the arrival of foods that would have a different taste from the servings of nondescript meats and unknown greens that had been the usual fare for the past five months.

"Hanna, you're on vacation. Bet you've never enjoyed one like you'll be enjoying this one," she said to herself. "If Ben feels up to it, we'll have drinks here before dinner tomorrow night. Maybe they would play 'Why Do I LoveYou?'. I'll request it for Ben."

And tomorrow night there would be something other than fruit punch in her glass, Hanna promised herself.

On her way through the lobby, Hanna stopped at the reception desk to make an inquiry. She was directed to the concierge, who was able to obtain the information she was seeking. The flight Ben was on had made a delayed departure from San Francisco. The connection in Japan would be missed, but there were other flights to which the airlines would assign their connecting passengers. Hanna took the elevator up to her room trying to talk herself into the idea of getting to sleep as quickly as possible. Ben would be here to wake her up at an early hour.

CHAPTER 17

The phone on the night table near Hanna's ear let out a buzz. The only response in the room was a slight stirring under the covers. It buzzed a second time. Hanna, in a delirium of sleepy uncertainty gave in to an automatic reaction and picked up the phone.

"Hi," a baritone voice calmly spoke. "Is this the girl from Ipanima who once walked on the Carmel Beach with the handsome guy from North Beach?"

Hanna let out a *whoop*! "You're here. You're really here." Then she checked herself and lowered her voice an octave. "Would you like to come up and see me sometime?" she asked in a husky voice.

The question hung in mid-air for a moment. Then, "Just tell me the way. Wild horses couldn't keep me from you, but I need to know where you are."

"Seven twenty-two," came the gravely reply. "Got that? I said seven twenty-two," and Hanna set the phone back in its cradle.

As it turned out, Hanna and Ben did not travel to Chiang Mai that day. In answer to Hanna's question not asked until Ben had been in the room for at least ten minutes, the reply from a weary Ben was that he would do almost anything not to have to get back on a plane in just a few hours. Hanna said she'd see what she could do. Quickly dressing herself in the skirt and blouse that lay draped over a nearby chair, she hurried out of the room clutching her small briefcase. She wanted to speak to the concierge in person, to see if he could change their reservations on Thai Airways to a flight sometime the following day. As it turned out, it was easily arranged. Hanna left their tickets to be exchanged for new ones. She returned to the room. The rest of the day was spent behind closed doors.

In the evening, a refreshed Ben and a glowing Hanna made their way to the piano bar. There they sipped from tall frosted glasses of fresh

64

fruit punch that had some dark rum tossed in to add to its appeal. The crowded restaurant just down the hall would inform them when they could be seated in the dining room.

Ben started to tell Hanna all the details of his flight.

"When I woke up that morning and saw the fog, I didn't think anything of it. We've seen plenty of flights take off in fog before. But Saturday, out at the airport, it was right down on the ground. They wouldn't let us leave. Great way to begin, wouldn't you say? The wise man was definitely not at home."

Hanna reached out to put her hand atop Ben's.

"Poor Ben," she soothed. "And so many flying hours ahead of you."

"Yes, Hanna, now that you mention it, why is it that you are living so far away? Couldn't you have an adventure a little closer to home?" Ben asked what was a serious question, but he did so with a sparkle in his eye, showing that his good humor was still intact.

"Ben, I've asked myself that very question over and over, especially during my worst bouts of homesickness. You can't believe how eagerly I long to get back to the life I had. In spite of everything, though — the discomforts, the isolation, the cold, the rules — I would still go ahead and sign the contract tomorrow, the one that keeps me there for a year. I can't explain it. Maybe during this next week or two I'll find a way."

"Hey, girl, I don't need an explanation. I just need to understand a bit better what it is that keeps us apart." Ben uttered these words in a thoughtful way. Afterwards, he ran his fingertips down Hanna's cheek and looked deeply into her eyes. Neither spoke another word. The warmth of the rum in their bellies began to bring a soothing effect to each.

"So, Hanna, did you do much studying up on the Kingdom of Thailand before coming here? Come on, give. What do you know?" Ben was brilliant at setting conversational moods. And Hanna was a perfect foil for his methods.

"I know that the set of English language encyclopedias that I read are fifteen years old. I know that I barely had time to spend with them. I know we are in a kingdom where the king has been on the throne for a long, long time. I know that Thailand has never been a European colony. I know that Thailand is a tourist attraction for honeymooners and celebrities who seek the beach life and viewing the unusual rock formations in the sea off Phuket. I know from Claire, my friend, and not from the encyclopedias, that Thailand is one of the leading destinations for sex tourism. I know that Asian elephants live here, but not many in the wild, mostly in training camps. We may decide to visit one when we're in Chiang Mai. That's about it."

"And I know that these people like to smile a lot. In fact, here comes someone, now, to tell us it's time to go in to dinner. Just look at that face." Ben met the attendant with a warm smile of his own. The attendant picked up their drinks to bring them along as he escorted the couple into the dining room.

Hanna and Ben had chosen the dining room over the noisier bar and grill. Seated here, with a large, elaborate menu in her hand, Hanna looked around. She was pleased with their choice. The room was dominated by a wall-length display of shoulder-high living plants. Seated as they were not far from this display, one could easily imagine that this was a greenhouse, not a public restaurant across from a busy airport. Hanna was charmed. She glanced at Ben. He was deeply engrossed in the reading of the menu, so she went back to her own. She'd already decided she wanted Thai food, something with seafood. When the waiter came back, she'd ask about today's specials.

As usual, Ben started the conversational ball rolling. "So, dear girl, I want to tell you briefly about my life before we get into the subject of you and us. That way, the decks will be somewhat cleared and you won't need to be polite and say, 'Now it's your turn,' as you often do. Just want you to know that I love my work. I feel that one of the luckiest days of my life was the day Louis took me to that ball game and started talking about coming to work with him."

Ben paused to pick up his drink and take a long, slow sip.

He continued, "Being a stagehand at the opera house is not at all what I would have imagined. You can't just show up: you must demonstrate a sincere interest. When I first met you I was just getting started. I had to wait to be called to work. Then, because I almost always said 'yes', I got more and more calls, more and more work. Last year I became an apprentice; this year, only two months ago, I got my union card. You're looking at a card-carrying member of Local 16 of the I.A.T.S.E., the union of all the helping hands that make a stage production possible. It's a pretty great bunch of guys, and of course Louis keeps his eye on me. Am I holding your interest? Do you want me to stop blabbing?"

Ben looked across at Hanna, then took another sip of his drink while waiting for a signal from her.

Hanna hedged. "I see a waiter headed our way. After we've ordered, I'm going to grill you for some answers to questions you haven't yet covered. You know your work is one of the reasons I was attracted to you."

"Hanna, you cut me to the quick," a grinning Ben replied. "I thought it was my bubbling personality."

The arrival of the waiter suspended their conversation for the time that it took to place their orders. When he was retreating, notepad in hand, Hanna leaned across towards Ben with a smile on her face. She told him that on her list of his assets, his smiling face came first, his good singing voice second, his choice of work third, and his personality traits a distant fourth.

"So tell me, Big Ben, is it a long work day? As I recall, you were free on most evenings during the week. Has that changed?"

"Oh, yes. It has changed a lot. When you were still in town, I wasn't getting called to work nearly as often as I am now. We start at eight in the morning and on performance nights might not be finished before midnight. The great thing is, we get paid overtime after five p.m. By finding more work coming my way, I'm putting more money in the bank. This means I can afford to go chasing after the girl of my dreams when she goes bounding off to some faraway country."

"I'll ignore that last crack, thank you very much. But before our dinner gets here, one more question. What work is there after the opera season is over? Do you get to goof off all during the spring?"

"For the dedicated, mature guy such as myself," Ben countered," there is work after opera. Again, you have to earn your way into it. Remember the weeks of Nutcracker ballets around Christmastime?" Hanna nodded her head. Ben rushed on. "You show up to change the scenery and lay the floor for the dancers for as many nights as you can manage, and after a couple of years, the ballet company may hire you for their entire season. February to May. A few scheduled operas in June and on to August for opera rehearsals. Year-round work, good pay, good guys. When I get back, I'll be starting my first complete ballet season. How about that!"

"Ben, I can see that you aren't missing me at all, with all that work to keep you busy. Am I permitted one last question? Do you get to watch the performances on stage?"

Ben looked at her and grinned. "No, Hanna, we don't stand around and take up space after the sets are in place. That's the time for the singers and chorus members to be on tap. What the stage hands do is descend to a room in the basement where in-house TV projects the performance. We can watch, if we want. But most of us sit around a big table and resume the poker game that was started on whatever day you joined the crew. It's ongoing; no one walks away with much, but it's a great way to kill time till we're needed next."

Hanna reached out her hand to give Ben's arm a squeeze. "Oh, Ben, I'm so happy for you. It will warm me on those cold nights to come. It really will. You deserve to have found your way like that. After all, you haven't always felt like singing a happy tune. You've paid your dues."

Each understood in tacit agreement that Hanna was referring to the bitter end of Ben's marriage.

Hanna and Ben had met through a mutual friend a few years after the divorce that had ended Ben's marriage to his high school sweetheart. The marriage lasted seven years and they were as happy as a young couple could be. But when they had remained childless, Ben's wife, still in her twenties, was not willing to stay in the marriage. She wanted both husband and children. Ben could not blame her, but he'd hoped all along that they could find some other solution. None appeared. He allowed her to see to the legalities, and Ben, had become, once again, a single man at the age of thirty. Single and depressed.

Hanna had entered Ben's life as he was coming out of a long period of mourning, mourning the sad end to a marriage that had held so much promise. Hanna and Ben had gravitated toward each other. Each thought to be seeking a kind of casual, fun, dating relationship with sexual monogamy an agreed-upon part, but no serious long-term commitment implied. They saw each other on weekends, and they had dinner with Ben's family at the family restaurant on Monday nights. They each had their own apartment in separate parts of the city. Hanna worked in the admissions department at City College; Ben worked at various construction jobs as they came along, before Louis lured him to the opera house. They went roller- skating on Sundays in Golden Gate Park, and they sat together on their blanket at Crissey Field to watch the fireworks on the Fourth of July. On Chinese New Year, they were in the crowds lining the sidewalks to see the Lion Dance pass by, stirring excitement as it went. On Christmas Eve they attended midnight mass at Mission Dolores deeply appreciative of the scene, the feel of thick, old stucco walls, the reverence of the worshippers, the drama of the Mass. And on warm autumn days, they went for long walks on the beach out at the Great Highway. Or, they got in Hanna's old Volvo and drove over to Marin County to hike in the redwoods at John Muir Woods. They were good company for each other. The affection between them had grown steadily. This trip to Thailand to be with Hanna was the biggest endorsement that Ben could give to Hanna of his continued love and support. Hanna was starting to realize that it might be signaling entry into a new phase of their relationship. When she came to Thailand to meet Ben, she thought of their time together strictly in terms of vacation fun. Now that he was here, and trying to be so patient with her, Hanna felt she needed to be especially attentive to Ben, to what he was communicating to her, and to more closely examine her own feelings.

"Dear Ben, he is like a second half of me," Hanna mused to herself. "Perhaps a better half. With him, I am more completely myself. This I know. Let's see what this next weeks brings." Hanna just had time to complete this thought before it was time to dig into the steaming dish of shrimp pad khing that had been placed before her.

CHAPTER 18

Soon after the small passenger jet departed for Chiang Mai, Hanna reached down into the bag at Ben's feet to retrieve a book. "Mind if I spend a few minutes with this?" she asked glancing sideways at Ben in his seat next to her.

"Be my guest," Ben mumbled as he tried to stifle a yawn. He was still catching up on the loss of sleep only a couple of days ago.

The book Hanna now held in her lap was a *Lonely Planet Guide to Thailand*. Ben's sister had given it to him as a last minute gesture the morning she'd driven him to the airport.

Hanna looked through the table of contents. She noticed a long beginning section on the entire history of the kingdom. She'd get back to that some other time. Right now, she only wanted to read about Chiang Mai. Good. Thirty pages were devoted to this popular small city in the north. Hanna leafed through the pages, looking at the photos and allowing her eye to be caught by some key words. She simply wanted to familiarize herself with some of the main attractions. She thought it best if she and Ben made their decisions about what they wanted to do after they were on the ground and actually seeing and hearing the city scene.

"See anything interesting?" Ben inquired. "Oh, a few things. For the moment I'm just looking. One thing I want to do right away is call my dad. I haven't talked to him since leaving San Francisco. I see that they have international calling centers in Chiang Mai which would make it easy to place a call. I'm going to do that. They also have money changing booths everywhere. That might be one of the first things we should do."

"Yep. It always helps to deal in the local currency if you want to get things done. I'm pretty set on cash for the moment; I exchanged a hundred dollars at the airport hotel, when you weren't looking."

"Great!" Hanna shot back. "You can pay for the taxi that takes us around on our search for a guesthouse."

"Deal," Ben agreed and took the book out of Hanna's hands.

The scene outside the airport at Chiang Mai was one that had not been anticipated by either of them. Two things happened, simultaneously, when they pushed open the double glass doors. They were hit by a blast of hot air and their ears were assailed by a cacophony of sound. It was composed of drivers shouting to attract passengers, plus *tuk-tuks* (the Thai term for motorcycle rickshaws), arriving and noisily departing, auto and truck traffic passing on the nearby thoroughfare, and motorcycles from mopeds to four-cylinder monsters at all stages of coming and going. Hanna put her bag down and placed her hands over her ears. It did little good, so she resumed her stance. Ben was talking to three drivers at once, already starting the dealing process to settle on a price for their transport. It took Hanna a few moments to regain her composure: this was her first time in open air in Thailand, a warm country in all seasons, and her first time on the streets. In Bangkok, she had walked from the air-conditioned airport into an air-conditioned hotel across a pedestrian walkway two stories above the street. These sounds and sights, this warm air, were a new experience. Before picking up her bag, Hanna gave herself a little hug. She loved the feeling of this warmth after the past months of damp cold in Guangzhou.

When Hanna and Ben were seated in a tuk-tuk with their few bags around them, the driver slipped his vehicle quickly into the stream of traffic. Hanna sat forward to take in the sights. Ben leaned back into the cushions behind his back. He could see just as well from there.

"Hanna, what a break that the travel agent thought to give you those guesthouse cards. It will make our search a lot easier. The driver recognized all the addresses." Ben hadn't felt the need to add that this was because they were written out in Thai script as well as in English alphabet. Hanna would know that's what he meant.

The first guesthouse did not appeal. It was built right at the sidewalk. Hanna got out of the taxi to go inside and have a look, but Ben soon saw her exiting the house shaking her head from side to side in negative fashion, bouncing those brown curls of hers that gave her students such smiles and warmed the insides of Ben's heart.

"Too noisy in there," she explained.

The second guest house looked to be in a fine setting. They both went into this one. It looked clean and cool in the lobby, but when Hanna asked to see a room, they found only overhead fans to cool the air, no air-conditioning. Hanna insisted upon air-conditioning. She had learned from her first few weeks in her rooms in Guangzhou when the air conditioning had worked, that A.C. performed the additional function of keeping down insect life. After it had conked out never to work again, the cockroaches and mosquitos entered the territory undisturbed. So Hanna and Ben went on to the next address on the list. They had to drive a longer way to reach it. This guesthouse looked brand new; its tiled roof tilted up at the corners in Chinese style and the reception counter boasted elegantly glazed tile. Before asking to see a room, Ben took the precaution of asking to see a price list. A double bedroom here would cost twice what they had anticipated paying, so Hanna and Ben decided to withdraw as politely as possible and continue their search. At least in all the driving around, they were seeing something of Chiang Mai.

The fourth place was a hit. A large sign over the front porch declared "Pha Thai House." The house was set about fifty feet back from the sidewalk, away from street noises. Lawn graced both sides of the sidewalk leading into the main entrance. Flowering vines spread across the upper porch railing and cascaded down at the two extreme edges of the house, giving it a lovely, alive frame. A young woman receptionist informed them that a double room with air-conditioning was available for the Thai equivalent of twelve U.S. dollars a night. They asked to see the room. They followed her to the back of the house where she opened a door and they stepped into a room with white linen on the bed and fresh flowers set in small containers in conspicuous spots. Through the windows they could see into an enclosed garden. A peak in the bathroom revealed a western toilet, a handheld shower-head, and spotless white, fluffy towels. Ben and Hanna were delighted. Ben excused himself to go pay their taxi driver while Hanna began the formalities of signing in.

In their first few days in Chiang Mai, Hanna and Ben discovered they were in a great town for walking. The small city had once been an imperial city ruled by its own king, not yet a part of Siam. This explained why the town center was a perfect square that had previously been surrounded by a moat and defensive walls. The walls were all down, but the moat had been reconstructed. It helped newcomers to get their bearings. Ben and Hanna had no difficulty in finding their way around. What was an adjustment were the warmer temperatures, both day and night. Ben came here from the cool fifties and sixties of the Bay Area. Hanna came from temperatures colder than those in wintertime Guangzhou. They quickly learned to plan excursions in the morning, leaving their city walks and restaurant visits to the evenings. In midday, they sheltered in their air-conditioned room for a couple of hours to rest from the brunt of the heat.

The warmer climate brought on the need for cooler clothing. On their second morning in the guesthouse, Hanna presented herself to the man at the reception desk with her question,

"Where can I go to buy some clothes?"

"What is it that you are looking for?" he asked her in response."

"Oh, some shirts, or t-shirts, even, and some sandals."

"Ah," came the reply, "you could try the shops along by the East Gate. If you are out in the evening, there is the night bazaar. It sells just about everything, but it doesn't open until after eight o'clock."

Hanna and Ben had picked up a map of the city written in both English and Thai. She pulled it out of her bag and spread it before the clerk. "Would you be able to point out the best way to get to the East Gate, and the place where they hold the night market?" The clerk bent his head to study the map. It was already marked with a big ink dot showing the location of this guest house. The clerk did as Hanna had requested, pointing and speaking the names of the streets. Hanna understood the pointing. The names of the streets were not easily retained.

Back in the room, Hanna found Ben sitting at the writing table munching on various bits of the snack foods they had been accumulating. No food was served at the guest house, so they were picking up bags of chips and dried fruits and bottles of water to keep in the room. Ben looked up as Hanna opened the door.

"So, girl, what's on the agenda for today? Got some ideas?"

"I do, I do. The place to go find t-shirts for us both is not very far from here. We can walk to it. But first, I'm going to cash a traveller's check at the nearest money exchange. We'll find a place to have a meal along the way, I should think. Anyway, I like exploring, don't you?"

"As much as the next guy." Standing and reaching for one of the room keys, Ben added, "When you're ready, I'll meet you in the lobby."

When Hanna came out to the lobby, she found Ben deep in conversation with the reception clerk. Upon seeing Hanna, the clerk broke away and gave her a polite *wai*. Hanna returned the gesture. She and Ben were picking up the custom of placing palms together in the middle of their chests as a token of greeting or of leave-taking. This gesture, the wai, had been explained in Ben's guidebook. Ben and Hanna had used it only in response to someone who was greeting them in this manner. It was beginning to feel natural to do so.

Within a block and a half of Pha Thai House, Hanna saw the first sign of a small office calling itself a money exchange. She went inside. It was a short visit. After asking if they gave Thai Baht in exchange for American Express Traveller's checks, and being assured they did, she then asked what today's rate was. She made a note of it on a pad in her purse and left the shop. Ben had waited outside. She had told him she wanted to get at least two quotes, maybe more, before any transaction occurred. The next exchange booth was quoting a slightly higher rate, not one that would make a lot of difference. Hanna saw no point in pursuing a search for a better rate. She drew out her folder of checks and changed a hundred dollars. She asked for the Thai money in small denominations. She ended up with a handful of bills, in different pastel colors, all bearing a likeness of the bespectacled king.

"Now I'm in business," Hanna thought as she went out to join Ben.

As they made their way to the section of town known as East Gate, Hanna and Ben began to take notice of the numerous *wats* that they passed or that were distinct on the near horizon. Graceful spires rose above domed buildings to various elevations: often a tall central spire was surrounded by four or more shorter ones above square, artfully designed *chedis*, or auxiliary buildings. What was most notable to the first-time visitor were the numbers of buddhist monks as well as local residents and foreign tourists in and around these wats. They appeared to serve as places of modern-day worship: they had not become mere museums housing relics of the past.

Hanna had read about a certain one in the guide book. As they walked along, she said to Ben, "Would you be up for a visit to Wat Prasingh later today?"

"Sure, I'm kind of curious. I've never been inside a Buddhist temple, have you?"

"Nope, me neither," Hanna answered.

It wasn't long before they came to Tapae Road and the beginning of shops that sold everything from clothing to lacquerware, each shop with its own specialty. Hanna loaded up on short-sleeved cotton shirts, t-shirts, and one long cotton skirt of northern Thai-style weaving that was worn rather like a sarong. She found flip-flops for her feet, but no leather sandals. Ben bought some flip-flops as well, and a couple of t-shirts. One of the shirts had a blazing red-and-gold dragon on it: the other posed a monster of Thai origin. The t-shirts had Thai script on them. Ben had no idea what they said, but he'd make up something for the guys in his work crew before wearing them on the job.

They found a place to have lunch that catered to Western tastes; sandwiches, hot dogs, fruit salad, fresh lemonade. It was crowded with young tourists, many from America, in all manner of hot weather dress, most of it inappropriate for conservative Thailand. These were the WTs that Milo had told Hanna about before she left Guangzhou. Milo had been to Thailand several times. When Hanna mentioned Chiang Mai, he'd said, "Oh, yeah, a great place to visit, beautiful mountains visible from town, but loaded with WTs."

"What are WTs?" Hanna was forced to ask when no explanation was forthcoming.

"Those are world travelers, mostly young people out of college or still in, looking for excitement, looking to sow their wild oats on very limited budgets. They go and consume and clutter up the places where they flock. You'll see." And Hanna was seeing.

While they stood in line waiting for space at a table to become free, Ben got into conversation with the person standing behind him. It turned out this man was from Seattle and not a tourist but a past employee at the local USIS center. The United States Information Service had closed this branch a year earlier. David — that was his name — was back in Chiang Mai to show the place to his recent bride, Ellie, who was standing right behind him. Ben had been asking about restaurants to be tried while they were here, and David was offering some suggestions. When four people got up to exit their table in this small diner, Hanna made a dash for the table, followed by Ben with David and Ellie in tow.

Once seated, Ben gave introductions all around. Looking at Hanna, he said "Get out your pad and pencil, Hanna. This guy has some valuable local information to share with us."

After the four of them had placed their orders — hot dogs all around and glasses of delicious Thai iced tea — they got down to the serious business of playing "getting to know you" by way of asking the usual questions.

"What are you doing here?"

"Where are you coming from?"

"Where are you staying?"

"What have you seen so far?"

"How do you like it?"

After the preliminary round of questions, it was clearly established among them that David was their expert on knowledge of Chiang Mai attractions. Hanna and Ben were pleased to meet someone who knew the area, and Ellie was happy to not be the only one expressing first-time outbursts of amazement or dismay.

"Have you been on the roads on the city outskirts? Have you seen how they drive, passing into oncoming traffic as if there were no right-side left-side division on the road?"

David reached out and put his arm around Ellie's shoulders. "It's pretty scary at first, but you do get used to it. Until that happens, maybe it's best not to look."

Hanna jumped in. "We haven't been out of Chiang Mai; we arrived only two days ago. There seems to be plenty to do right here in town."

Ben added, "Although we have been thinking of getting out to that elephant camp we've heard about. I guess the elephants put on some kind of a show. We'd love to see that."

Ellie's face lit up. "Me, too. I'm dying to see the elephants."

"And see them, you shall," David assured her, "I hadn't mentioned it yet, but I've contacted my old driver, and he will arrange a day to take us out there."

David looked at Ben and Hanna. "Say, would you like to come along when we go? If I ask the driver, I'm sure he can arrange for a small van big enough to carry four passengers. It isn't that far, less than an hour's drive. Come with us. It'll be fun."

"Sure, we'd love to," Hanna and Ben answered almost in unison.

"Good, then we'll do it. The camp is called Mae Sa. We'll leave early enough to see the bathing, which comes first. My idea is to watch the bathing but skip the show. Instead, we may be able to drive to an area in the forest nearby where camp elephants are sometimes used to clear land. If you agree, I'd much rather see them at work than see them doing their tricks for a bigger audience."

"Sounds wonderful!" Hanna clapped her hands. "Ben, give David the phone number at our guest house so he can call us."

Ben drew out a fistful of paper items from his shirt pocket. He thumbed through them quickly and separated out the card. Removing a pen from the same pocket, he wrote on the back, Ben Rinaldi and Hanna Hobbs. Handing the card to David, he said, "Here, keep the card. Plenty more where that came from."

"I'll call as soon as I know," David had just time enough to say before their hot dogs were set down in front of them.

"So, Hanna. I guess you don't see too many of these things where you're coming from," Ellie joked.

"Nope. First one I've seen in months. Here goes." Hanna poured some mustard along the edge of the dog and took a big bite. "Hmmm. Now I see what I've been missing."

"I wonder if she's missed me as much." Ben directed his gaze towards the ceiling as he said this.

"Oh, Ben, I've missed you more than a dozen hot dogs' worth." They all got a good laugh out of that.

CHAPTER 19

After lunch, and after the departure of David and Ellie, Ben and Hanna decided to take a taxi back to the guesthouse. The heat of the day was approaching its height; each had an armful of plastic bags to carry, full of the bounty from the morning's shopping expedition. Ben transferred what he was carrying and stepped to the edge of the curb. Using one free arm he waved with gusto at all oncoming traffic. The vehicle that stopped for him was a two passenger motorcycle taxi. There was some fumbling of papers in his pockets before Ben realized he'd given away the guesthouse card at lunch, the card that told taxis where to take them. Hanna saw what was happening. In her clearly precise, English, she spoke to the driver, slowly repeating, "Pha Thai House, Pha Thai House," until the expression on the face of the young driver lit up. He revved up the engine by a twist of his hand on the handlebar, and they sped into the flow of traffic.

Along the way, Hanna brought up the matter of calling her dad. Ben's reply informed Hanna that he had not forgotten her wish. He had spoken to the receptionist that morning and learned that the call could be put through from the guesthouse by personnel there, so that Hanna could call from the room. The cost would be the same as if the call were made from a telephone exchange. The price would be a fixed rate per minute plus a small service charge.

Ben told her, "Now all you have to do is figure out what to do about the time difference and decide when it would be best to try the call."

"Do you know the difference?" Hanna asked.

"I'm pretty sure it's nine hours between here and the West Coast. We can check when we get to the guesthouse."

Their air-conditioned room offered the cool comfort they were seeking after the warm ride back. The driver got an extra tip for being so clever as to bring them directly to the proper address. Later that afternoon, after a good hour of deep sleep, Hanna went to the desk in the lobby.

"I'd like to arrange a call to a party in San Francisco," she told the clerk. "Can you tell me what the time difference is?"

"Certainly madam. Let me just get out the time map and we'll look it up."

Ben had been correct. During standard time, the difference was nine hours. Hanna gave the receptionist her father's phone number, and asked him to try the call that evening at eight p.m. in Chiang Mai. She hoped to find her father in his office at eleven in the morning, that seemed about right. And it meant that she and Ben could have an early dinner somewhere and be back in time.

"Dad. Hi. This is Hanna. How are you?" Hanna's voice, with its rising inflection, revealed the excitement she was feeling when she heard her father's voice answering the phone.

"I'm great. Where are you? Why haven't you called before?"

"We're in Chiang Mai. Remember? I wrote you about this trip. Ben came to Bangkok as planned and here we are up in the north of Thailand seeing the sights and staying in a great little hotel."

"Ben's with you? Why that old fox. You've got him gallivanting around the globe with you, too. Is that it?"

"Dad, I'm not gallivanting around the globe. I'm working, working hard."

"Pretty hard work there in Thailand, is it? Seen any elephants or tigers?"

"Now, dad, get serious. I told you the school year in China allowed for a four week break in January. You know all about the Chinese New Year."

"Sure. I've seen it right out of the office window when the dragon goes by on its way to the parade. But that's only one day. Never mind. Tell me, daughter, how're you doing out there?"

Hanna heard the change of tone in her father's voice and appreciated that the banter was being put to rest. She matched her tone to his.

"Doing fine, doing just fine, Dad. The work is the focus of my life. As a first-time teacher, I have a lot of lesson planning to do, and I'm pretty good at it even if I do say so myself. The students are exceptional, so bright and eager. And so polite. I teach five classes in all to students who are first year through fourth. I'm getting terrific experience."

"Glad to hear it, Hanna. Just wish you had tried to find that work a little closer to home. What is your apartment like?"

"It's all right. Nothing to brag about. Guess you could say all my needs are met except one, and that is heat. Since November, I've been awfully cold most of the time. So is everyone else. There was a rumor in my building before I left that maybe some electric heaters would be issued to us when we get back."

"Why so cold, dearie? Can't you turn up the heat?"

"There is no heat. I told you that. Honestly, Dad, I'm beginning to think you're not reading my letters."

"Oh, I read your letters all right. And you never answered my first question about why you haven't called before this."

Hanna had decided ahead of time that she would try not to say anything to worry her dad. Really, there was nothing to worry about. It was just not possible in a short time to explain that things were done differently in China. To this last question from her dad it was easy to answer that her phone was only for calls on campus and to leave it at that. Her father changed the subject.

"So, how's Ben doing, anyway? Is he still your man?"

At this change in subject, Hanna decided to get up from her position at bedside, and take a few steps, as far as the phone cord would allow.

"You know he is," she answered. "The work behind scenes at the opera house turned out to be a good fit for him. He loves it."

"And do you love him?"

"Of course I do. You know that."

"Then why don't you marry him and get it over with?" Hanna's eyebrows shot up upon hearing this question, but she retained a composed manner.

"Now, Dad, none of that. Remember I told you that the subject is out of bounds. It's a private matter between Ben and me. Dad, I've got to go now. If possible, I'll call once more before returning to Guangzhou. We've not made our plans for next week as yet."

"Next week," her father burst in. "Say, isn't there an important date in my daughter's life along about then?"

"Yep. My birthday on Tuesday."

"What can I send you? Anything special you're craving?"

"No, Dad. Don't send me anything. We'll have a special celebration next June when I'm back."

"Call me on Tuesday if you possibly can. I'd love to hear from you."

"Okay, Dad, I will. And love to the boys in the East. Tell those brothers of mine I'm doing great."

"Will do. So good to hear your voice. Give my regards to Ben. Ask him to give me a call when he gets back from Thailand. I'd like to hear what he has to say."

"I'll do that, Dad. Take care of yourself, now. I'll call again in a few days. Love you. Bye-bye."

"You're my girl. Never forget that. Bye for now."

Hanna and Ben explored the town for two more days before they heard from David. On the second day, they found a message waiting for them when they returned from their afternoon outing. The message told them that David had arranged with his driver to go to the elephant camp the following day. He and Ellie would come by Pha Thai Guest House at eight a.m. The message added, "Wear walking shoes and cool clothing."

"No flip-flops tomorrow," Hanna remarked to Ben as they read the message.

That night they had dinner at a small restaurant that served vegetarian curries with all the trimmings. After using a forkful of rice to sop up the final drops of sauce from his plate, Ben remarked to Hanna that they were nearing the end of the first week of his time away from work. He wondered out loud if they had better start thinking about where to spend the remainder of their time.

"Here, let's look on the calendar," she suggested, pulling a pocket datebook out of the bag.

They examined the dates. By the time they exited the restaurant, Hanna and Ben had decided to stay in Chiang Mai into the middle of the following week. On Wednesday, they would fly to Bangkok, spend one night, and fly to Hong Kong the next day. They would celebrate Hanna's birthday in Chiang Mai on Tuesday. Both wanted to invite David and Ellie to spend the evening with them, and, perhaps, ask them to recommend a special place for dinner.

A little white van pulled up under the portico of the guesthouse promptly at 8:00 a.m. the next morning. Hanna and Ben stood waiting just inside the front door. David jumped out to usher the waiting passengers into the van. There sat Ellie in the back. Hanna climbed back to join her, while Ben and David seated themselves on the seats just the row in front. The driver turned his head to smile at his two new passengers. The words, "*sawahdeeka, sawahdeekrahp,*" were spoken all around in polite greeting. Then the driver, having been given his instructions earlier that morning, drove away towards their destination sixty kilometers to the north.

As the van left the city behind and began its climb into the hills, Ben turned his head to David and said, "It's really good of you to take us along with you today. This was going to be one of the sights that Hanna and I did not want to miss."

"Hope it will live up to your expectations," David replied. "Ellie and I had it near the top of our list as well. It will be a pleasure for me to go out here with friends. I've been half a dozen times before but always as the escort of some visiting dignitary from the States come to see our little set-up at USIS. This time I'll only be wearing one hat, and that's to keep the sun out of my eyes."

"Does the sun always shine in Chiang Mai?" Hanna's question came out of the appreciation she felt after one entire week of seeing blue skies and sunshine.

"About three quarters of the year," David replied, "during those months when the monsoon is not upon us. During these winter months you'll see nothing but sunshine."

Ellie turned to Hanna. "David's been telling me a bit about Thai elephants. Apparently, they once lived in great numbers in the wild throughout these Asian countries, thousands and thousands of them. The Thais learned to domesticate them centuries ago. They used to ride them into battle against enemies also mounted on elephants. Nowadays, they are used mostly by lumber companies and developers to clear land. We get to see them doing that kind of work today, isn't that right, David?"

"That's right, if all goes as expected. First lets get to Mae Sa and see what we can arrange."

CHAPTER 20

They approached the elephant camp along a lightly paved road. After turning off the main road, the farther they drove, the less pavement covered the surface, until they were riding on a dirt road that kicked up a cloud of dust in their wake. They had climbed into the foothills since leaving Chiang Mai. As they got closer to the camp, the road flattened out. The land here was tree covered, with several varieties of palm mixed with taller hardwood trees, perhaps teak. They were driving parallel to a river. Across the river, in land that was partially cleared, they glimpsed their first elephants of the day. Half a dozen or so stood calmly at peace under the shade trees spread sparsely throughout the clearing, each elephant near a tree. At first, the visitors thought each elephant had chosen a tree for himself. But once the van crossed the river on a railless bridge, and dispatched its occupants into the clearing, David pointed out that a length of chain worn around one ankle tethered the elephant to a tree. The animals dozed and flicked at flies with their tails and with their trunks, flapping their big ears from time to time to rid their eyes and face of the pesky creatures. They seemed not the least disturbed or even interested in the four people who walked among them snapping photos with cameras at the ready, and making remarks in soft voices.

David disappeared into one of the two cabins that stood in this clearing. He was checking on today's schedule at the office inside. Ellie, Hanna and Ben gathered around him when he emerged.

"The elephants are on their way to the river for their morning bathing. We can walk there if you like; it's not very far. After that, some of them will return here to the camp for the performance for today's visitors. Other elephants will go to the work area of a local lumber company. We have our choice as to which group we want to follow. I've already told you my preference. How about all of you?"

"Oh, the work scene, by all means. That's my first choice." This, from Hanna.

Ellie agreed.

Ben added with a grin, "I do some pretty heavy lifting and pushing in my line of work. Maybe I could pick up a few pointers."

It was unanimous. Off they went to follow along on a trail at river's edge.

The visitors heard the splashing before they beheld the sights. A few steps farther and there they were, elephants in a river that was wider here, elephants and handlers in the river together. So many elephants! Hanna couldn't count them all. She and Ellie went on ahead to climb up a small grandstand of seats set out for spectators. They found seats in the very top row, making room for the men when they clambered up after them. What a scene spread out in front of them. Some elephants were on their sides, being scrubbed by their *mahout* who used a brush with a very long-handle. Other elephants were on their feet, using the end of their trunks to playfully spank the water sending streams in all directions. A few elephants drank in a sip or two and then spat it out in a fountain of their own creation. Others took water in through their trunks and gave themselves a shower by spraying it out over their own backs. Some were content to merely stand in water up past their bellies, eyes downcast in sleepy appreciation. Any observer soon became convinced that these animals were having fun. There was a sense of joy coming from them as they used a variety of methods to play in the water.

"I could watch them all day," someone said.

That was not to be. At some unobserved signal, the mahouts each moved to the elephant in his keeping and mounted onto the animal's neck, just behind the ears. The next grand sight was that of seeing more than two dozen elephants come into formation, some rising majestically from a kneeling position in the water, to stand together on all four legs with a blue shirted mahout astride, and step, with grace, out of the water. At water's edge the large group immediately split in two. The larger group walked with swinging gait back toward the camp. The smaller contingent of about eight elephants took the trail in the opposite direction, along the river to the north. Spectators did not vacate the grandstand until the last elephant was out of sight. Then everyone streamed back to camp buzzing with comments about what they had just seen.

Hanna joined Ben on the walk back. "Don't you just love them? If I lived anywhere near here I'd have to come see them at least once a week."

"Hold on there, Hanna. Don't get any ideas. We want you back at home where I can keep an eye on you."

"Oh. Ben, of course. I was just imagining."

"Okay. But when you imagine, how about keeping me in the picture?"

"Sure, sweetie. I'll always do that from now on."

The white van had been parked in the shade at the far edge of the camp clearing. As its passengers approached, they could see that the driver had opened all the doors to give it plenty of air. He himself was sprawled under a tree nearby, keeping an attentive eye on everything. He jumped to his feet as his passengers approached. David spoke to him in Thai. The conversation took a few minutes. It seemed this driver had made good use of his time. He had spoken to a tour bus driver who was familiar with the area and learned how to get to their next destination. He had also stocked the van with bottles of cold water and packages of banana chips obtained at the tourist shop in a cabin separate from the office. He told David that the elephants they'd seen standing around when they first arrived were elephants who were being given the day off, due to either old age or illness. The driver went on to point out a place where public restrooms could be found for use before they set off.. David thanked him and told the others what had been suggested. Ten minutes later they were in the van ready to move on.

The day was warming up. There was cool air in the van, but back on the stands, the spectators had been seen fanning themselves with all manner of pamphlets or anything they could get their hands on.

David remarked, "It'll be hot pretty soon. We won't want to spend too much time where we're going. None of us has had the time to become acclimatized. When you live here, you build up some sort of tolerance so the heat is not such a bother. We'd better drink some of this water, then carry some with us at this next place."

Sounds of agreement came from the others. Ben reached out and grabbed two water bottles from the plastic cooler. He screwed off the tops and handed them back to the women.

"You first. We'll share." Hanna took three long pulls on the bottle and handed it back to Ben. "Your turn," she said.

"Hanna, what do you do for drinking water in China?"

David's question came unexpectedly, but all were curious to hear Hanna's answer now that it had been raised. David refined his question further.

"Do they sell water in bottles?" He listened carefully to Hanna's reply.

"They may, in some places, but not where I live. In our building, which houses about thirty-five people, there is a boiler in the basement that is like a huge urn. In it water is kept at a low simmer. We are issued thermos jugs. I use two at a time. I go down there every other day, fill my thermoses with water, carry them into my apartment and allow the water to cool on the counter. Then I store it in the refrigerator. I have to be pretty consistent in keeping up the supply. None of us would think of swallowing tap water. Nor have I seen bottles of water for sale at the campus store."

Ellie remarked, "You know? Those of us who haven't travelled that much never think of details like that. David, good for you for thinking to ask," and she took a final sip from her bottle of water before passing it along to David.

Ten minutes' ride on a bumpy dirt road brought the white van to the work site they were seeking. The elephants stood quietly together in the care of one or two blue-shirted mahouts while the other elephant trainers clustered around a tall man in khaki shirt and trousers who sported a whitish pith helmut that set him off distinctly as the boss. David told the others to wait, he'd get out to see what was happening. They saw him approach the group of men and stand quietly to the side, awaiting his turn to speak to the boss. When his turn came, the conversation didn't last long. David came back to tell the others they were welcome to stay, they'd just have to stand well back from the work area and park the van in a spot that David pointed out to the driver.

"Wear your hats," David added.

Each dutifully reached into bags or pockets and placed caps from hometown baseball teams on their respective heads.

"Right. I'll carry the water. Ready?"

Hanna stayed close to Ben as they stationed themselves among the trees. The elephants were out in the open, in the middle of the clearing.

Each was approached by his mahout and ordered to bend a knee to lower its front end so the rider could climb aboard. Six elephants went to a shady area at the edge of the clearing, on the far side from where the visitors had stationed themselves. Two elephants went as a pair to a forest section to the right. One of these was ridden straight up to a tree until the flat of her head rested against it; the tree was twice her height. The mahout used voice and body as well as a long, thin, flexible stick held first in one hand, then the other to tap the elephant on shoulder or flank. In this manner he commanded his elephant to push, push hard against the tree. The elephant obeyed, then stepped back one pace. The mahout allowed it a brief pause, then rode it hard against the tree again. It didn't take more than five or six major assaults on the tree for it to make a sound like a creaking door and go crashing to earth. Although tall, the trees that were being removed had small girths. They were easy for an elephant to push over. When the tree was down, the pusher elephant stepped back and deftly turned aside. Its partner elephant stepped forward to command center stage. This elephant was ridden straight into the forest and positioned to stand and face the fallen tree in its approximate center. Its rider then commanded the elephant to wrap its trunk around the the fallen tree and lift it. The lifter elephant tugged hard to raise the felled tree. There was some adjustment to be made to get the balance right, so the lifter elephant was allowed to put the tree down and pick it up a second time, having moved a little toward the heavy root end. Satisfied, the elephant could now be ridden to a designated area to deposit the tree. Here the other elephants went to work stripping the tree of foliage and small branches before a couple of men with saws came out to complete the work.

Hanna and Ben, Ellie and David watched the work in quiet appreciation. The elephants moved slowly and carefully. The mahouts used words of command that seemed to beget a specific action. None needed to raise his voice. An elephant might seem slow to respond, but in the end he always did what was asked of him. The visitors were amazed. Seeing man and beast work cooperatively like this was a real privilege.

As the hour went by, the stripped logs piled up. The work would go on for a total of only three or four hours to preserve the health of the animals and of the men as well. The elephants would work in pairs of pushers and lifters, so no single animal would be overworked. It was hard work, that was plain to see. But it seemed to be undertaken with due consideration of the workers and the conditions.

The visitors had exhausted their water supply after the first hour. Noon heat was upon them, yet they lingered a little longer, not wanting to end witnessing a spectacle they would not be seeing again anytime soon. Finally, Hanna looked over to where Ellie was standing and indicated with a swipe of her brow that the heat was getting to her. Ellie put her arm through David's.

"Time to go," she told him.

"Okay. I'll have a word with the boss before we leave."

David waited to make a move until one more elephant carrying its felled tree had deposited it in the area where it would be stripped. After that, he waked over to express his thanks to the headman.

In the van on the way back to Chiang Mai, everyone had something to say. The words tumbled out in their excitement to make comment. David told them what he'd learned from the boss.

"I asked him if the elephants did any other tasks besides the ones we saw. They do. When it's time to move the stripped trees to barges on the river, they use the elephants as carriers. First, a path through the forest must be cleared, one wide enough to accommodate an elephant carrying several twelve-foot trees in its trunk. Boy, that's a sight I'd like to see. But I guess we can all pretty well imagine what it would look like."

Ben went next. "You know, what I can't get over is the way they get the elephants to work in teams. It's very good for getting the job done, but how do they know which animal is good at what and which animals get along with each other? Really incredible, when you think about it."

Then Hanna had told them, "I watched the riders closely. They use aids to command their elephant just the way a rider does on a horse — this leg signal for that move, this positioning of the body for that direction. I saw the mahout using his bare toes behind the elephant's ear to tell the elephant what he wanted him to do. Must have taken months of training, if not years."

Ellie added, "I looked up this camp in a guidebook at our hotel. One thing it said was that each mahout has been with the same elephant since the day the animal was tamed. Same mahout, same elephant. That helps to explain how close and complex the communication between the two can be. That, and the fact that elephants seem to be so gentle."

Before the van dropped them off at their guesthouse, Hanna and Ben told their companions that they hoped to see them again.

"We're leaving next Wednesday," Ben informed them. "Any chance we could all have dinner together on Tuesday night? It'll be Hanna's birthday. We'd love to take you out to dinner."

"Oh, yes," Ellie said quickly. "Let's celebrate together."

"By all means," David agreed. "Do you have any place in mind?"

"I was going to ask you, David, if you have any suggestions."

"You know, I just might. There's a hotel here that serves a nice meal and it also features a show twice an evening of classical Siamese dance. I went once a couple of years ago, and I think you'd like it. But the place is pricey, so let's say we go as your friends not as your guests."

"No, I insist. Hanna and I really want to treat you after all you've done for us to make this a great vacation."

"Well, we'll see about that. But the feeling is mutual, isn't it, Ellie? You've made our time here more fun by being such good company."

"Cut it out, you guys," Hanna butted in. "Enough of this mutual admiration. David, do we need reservations for Tuesday's dinner?"

"Yes, and I'll make them. Early show or late?"

"Early," Hanna replied.

"I'll call with the time and place" David said before the van pulled up to the guesthouse at the conclusion of their memorable outing.

CHAPTER 21

Tuesday evening a few minutes before six o'clock, Hanna and Ben stood ready and waiting just inside the front entrance of their guesthouse. Hanna had taken special care in dressing for the birthday dinner. Her long Lanna skirt was topped by a dark magenta silk blouse made for her on two days' notice by a tailor she'd been told about by the receptionist one morning. The color of the silk matched a thin stripe in the woven fabric of her skirt. The tailor spoke a little English. It was he who told Hanna that the weaving in the skirt was unique to this northern Thai city, that Lanna was an ancient name for this district. The same tailor whipped up a shirt for Ben, a short-sleeved shirt with collar and buttons down the front, made of a heavy linen, deep blue in color, shot through with streaks of lighter blue and turquoise threads. When Hanna saw Ben in this shirt for the first time, she shook her head and asked, "Hey, when did you get to be so handsome?"

"Just trying to keep up with my girl," he answered.

As they stood by the door, Ben reached into his pocket and came out with a small package in rumpled tissue paper.

"Hanna. Here's something to remember us by" he said as he handed it to her. "It won't take up much room."

Hanna took the small package from his hand; the paper came off in no time. On the palm of her hand stood an elephant of carved, dull silver metal.

"I love it, it's adorable. Where did you find it?"

"Never mind that. Just know that this elephant never forgets. Nor will I."

"Forget what?" Hanna smiled a knowing half-smile as she asked her question.

"You. Our time here. Us."

Hanna was silenced by the sincerity in Ben's voice. She pushed her gift, paper and all, into a deep recess of her purse and stood close to Ben.

"Thank you," she whispered.

As they watched, a car pulled up to the front door and David stepped out of the front passenger seat to come and collect Hanna and Ben. They had recognized him immediately and were already on the way to taking seats with Ellie in the back. Once everyone was safely settled and the doors closed, David instructed the driver to take them to the Rincome Hotel.

"The hotel is a bit out of the way, but it won't take long to reach it" he informed his fellow passengers. "It's near the old Chiang Mai Cultural Center where you see the different type houses — huts, really — of the hill tribe peoples. Did you get a chance to go there?"

"No," Hanna answered from the back seat. "I wish we had. My recent find was the locally made Thai celadon. Thank God Ben was along to slow me down or I think I would have sent some to everyone I know. The pale-green color and the quality of the pottery really impressed me. But Ben persuaded me to go back several times before making my decisions. I found a lovely bowl with an intricate design carved on it. That I'm having sent to my father. A round platter is going to Ben's parents. I hope they can use it at their restaurant. And I couldn't resist sending a pair of lotus flowers to Ben to brighten up his place. But I credit him with stopping me there. Or I would be headed for the poorhouse."

This last was heard as the car slowed to make a turn into the hotel driveway.

While the four of them stood inside waiting to be shown to a table, David looked at Hanna.

"Perhaps I should have mentioned that the seating here is on the floor at low tables. I thought to tell Ellie so she could wear something easy to move in. Hanna, in that skirt you may have to sit sideways, Thai style."

"Don't worry about me." Hanna replied quickly. "I'm pretty flexible. I'll figure something out."

Shoes were left inside the entrance. Barefooted, the diners followed a slender Thai waitress to their table. She walked so gracefully, Hanna wondered if she also doubled as a dancer. The floor was a highly polished dark hardwood, as smooth as walking on silk. This restaurant had a comfortable old-Thai ambiance. Once settled around the table, the service of a fixed menu of southeastern curries began. Dishes of fish, prawns, pork, chicken and all manner of vegetables were set down from which they helped themselves. Accompanying the curries were the fixings, the condiments: raisins, shredded coconut, sweet or hot chutney, chopped peanuts, pineapple pieces — a rich selection. The food had been set down in silver bowls of small or medium size. Last to appear, placed in the very center of the table, was a large silver bowl filled with something David was calling sticky rice. This was a dish of the North, they were told. It was exactly what its name implied, a glutinous rice that was so sticky you ate it with your fingers. David demonstrated. Reaching into the bowl, he broke off a small glob of rice and began rolling it around in his fingers until it had formed a ball. This he bit into, reserving the remainder for the next bite. They all took some rice and began rolling.

"Mmm. They don't have anything like this in Guangzhou," Hanna remarked. "It's really good."

"Wait 'till I tell my parents about this," Ben exclaimed. "Do you suppose I can get any in San Francisco?"

"Maybe if you ask someone at a Thai restaurant," David suggested.

The dinner was excellent. They took their time with it, trying a taste from each dish on the table. In between bites, the women sipped from frosted glasses of iced coffee, while the men drank from tall glasses of Singha beer. Conversation lagged until the dishes were all but empty. David told them it was good manners in Thailand to leave something in the bowls. When the dishes were cleared away, plates of fresh fruit were set before them. Cool slices of papaya lay beside lumpy green orbs that David told them were custard apples. Large chunks of coconut meat rested beside mangoes split open and ready to be spooned up by appreciative diners. They could help themselves to rings of pineapple or slices of tangerine. The platter was attractively arranged to show off the offerings.

"David, you certainly have chosen well for us tonight. Thank you. This birthday could not be a happier one," a smiling Hanna told him.

"Let's not forget that Hanna has given us a reason to make a special night of this" Ellie added. "Hanna, how many years is it this year, if you don't mind my asking?"

"I don't mind in the least. Today I turn thirty-six."

"Happy birthday, Hanna," she said and they all chimed in.

The waitress returned to begin removing unwanted dishes from the table. The dance presentation would begin soon. Ellie chose this moment to dig a small box out from the deep interior of her vintage evening bag and deposit it in front of Hanna. Before opening the box, Hanna took the time to switch the position of her legs from one side to the other. David had been right: she needed to sit sideways on this bare floor.

Ellie told Hanna, "David and I wanted to order you a birthday cake, but we were told they don't do that sort of thing here, so we got you this little gift, instead. Happy birthday, Hanna. Hope you like it."

"Ellie, that is too kind. Thanks a lot" Hanna responded. "Now, lets see, what do we have here ..."

She quickly removed the lid of the box to see, hiding inside, a miniature silver elephant of the same dull metal she'd seen before; in fact, an identical twin to the one Ben had given her.

"Oh, I love it. Thank you, Ellie. Thank you David." Hanna placed the elephant in front of her on the table.

"What is it about these elephants?" she asked. "I seem to be attracting a whole herd of them." And Hanna went on to tell Ellie and David about Ben's gift, actually bringing it out of her handbag to let it stand beside its partner.

"Well, we did see them working in pairs at Mae Sa," Ben pointed out. "Maybe they do better in pairs."

Hanna made a mental note: Ben is being a sweetheart about having someone duplicate his choice of gift. She gave him a radiant smile, then turned to ask David, "Is there anything I should know about these elephants? I assume they are made in Thailand."

"Not exactly," David replied. "Actually, they were almost certainly made in Burma. They served as weights in the opium trade there. They are antique. Refugees who fled to Thailand carried them here to use as barter for foodstuffs and such. I'm not sure how pure the silver is, but their value also lies in their age and design."

Hanna picked up her two elephants, one in each hand. Each was the size of a large hen's egg; she could easily close her fist around one. She tested the weightiness of them, then passed them around the table so that everyone could get a sense of their heft. She told herself they would always be permanently housed with her, never more to roam and never more to serve such a dubious purpose.

"They are a pair, like Ben and me. Thanks ever so much. What a wonderful gift."

Ben, still glowing from Hanna's last remark, regained his equanimity in order to ask David a question.

"You know, I've noticed as we go about in this town that there is a picture of the king in every shop and restaurant, or hotel of any size. You can't go out in public without coming across his picture. Do all Thai people love and admire their king? Or is some of this public display merely for show?"

"No, no, not merely for show" David was quick to reply. "Although there is a rule on the books that mandates the posting of the king's photo in public places, the Thais truly love their king. On that they can all agree. Just think of it. He has been king since 1947. Most people in this country have not known another. He comes forward at times of crisis and speaks publicly to his people. Every day he is seen on television or in person, fulfilling some civic duty or other. He is a real part of daily life here. You'd be hard-pressed to find a single word spoken against him."

The lights over the dining area were dimming, leaving a space at the end of the room still brightly lit. Two musicians had arrived to sit on the floor at the side of this cleared space. One held a large wooden box in the shape of a trapezoid. It was a *khim*, or a Thai version of a hammered dulcimer. Strung with seven or eight strings tightly wound across two bridges, its music was produced by the player striking strings with two soft hammers, one held in each hand. As the lights dimmed and conversation came to an end, the lovely soft tones of this instrument could be heard. It rested on a low stand in front of the young man who sat cross-legged behind it. The other musician, also a young man, sat with a small keg of a drum in his lap held in such a way that he could beat one end or the other with one of his hands. After a short period of tuning, the two started right in on the music that would bring on two dancers, one male, one female. In elaborate costumes, they made a striking sight. Both were barefooted and both had extensions on their fingertips to exaggerate their hand movements. Both wore fanciful headdresses. They wore tight-fitting costumes of heavy silk that gave the impression of metallic fabric, silver in hue, sinuous in motion.

Each dancer wore pantaloons loosely fitted to allow for freedom of movement. Each had panels of cloth that hung down from their waists; these panels were trimmed with narrow bands of brocade around the edges; the panels moved in accord with the steps of the dancers. Their faces remained expressionless, but their movements, which always were performed full-face to the audience, told a simple Thai story that was easy to follow. A hunter goes into the woods to shoot a deer with his bow and arrow. The deer, the female dancer, wears a set of antlers on her head. She takes evasive action, but when cornered, pleads for her life with such irresistible expression that the hunter relents and frees her. The head-dress, by clever slight of hand, is changed from antlers to crown, and the prince and princess dance in joyful unison at the end.

The dancers performed well, the music was rhythmic and engaging. The performance took only fifteen minutes. It was received with polite applause, but when the lights came on, diners went right back to their conversations. Hanna and Ben felt a little disappointed that there was not more. David echoed their thoughts.

"They used to put on a longer and more elaborate show than that. I feel rather let down by such a short performance."

Ben countered this remark by saying, "David, we've had a really good dinner, we've seen a bit of Thai dance, and we've been in great company. I'm sure Hanna won't soon forget this birthday, and neither will I. Before we go our separate ways, how about exchanging addresses and phone numbers? Could we find a way to get together when we're back in the States?"

There were nods all around from Ben's suggestion, and quick searching for pen and paper in handbags and pockets.

Ben added, "And give me your e-mail addresses if you don't mind. I'm quite liking this new way of making contact."

"Me too," Ellie joined in.

"Any chance you can get to use a computer where you are?" she asked Hanna.

"Not a chance. I got my first computer about a year ago. It's in storage along with the rest of my things. When I get back, I'll get your e-mail addresses from Ben. For the time being, it'll be post cards and letters from me. And not too many of those, I'm afraid. There's little time to spare once classes begin. The Chinese pay all our expenses, but they do extract their pound of flesh."

"I know what," Ben spoke again. "Lets try to meet once a year either in Seattle or San Francisco, maybe on a weekend. Think we could manage that?"

David and Ellie were certain that they could, and Hanna applauded the idea.

"We'll do it. We'll definitely do it."

She looked around her. Many of the tables now stood empty. They were being cleared and reset for the next groups who would be arriving shortly.

"I get the idea that it's time to go," Hanna observed. "Looks like they need to make way for the new."

On the way back in their hired car, Hanna told the others,"You know, I haven't heard much of the news making the headlines at home these days. How about filling me in?"

David answered. "I guess it would be the new president, Bill Clinton. He's at the top of the news. His election in November was no surprise — after all, the country was in a bit of a recession under his predecessor. No one in Washington seems to know the new man very well, and everyone's kind of sitting back taking a 'let's wait and see' attitude. Did you read about the election?"

"I did," Hanna replied. "And my father wrote me about it, too. He's pretty much on the fence about bringing a guy from a southern state into the White House to make things better. I doubt that he voted for him."

"What else is new? Am I missing any good films?"

Ellie was the one to answer this time. "Did you get to see *Howard's End* before you left, or Clint Eastwood's *Unforgiven*?"

"Yes, Ellie, I saw *Howard's End* but stayed away from *Unforgiven*. Did I miss something?"

"Not in my opinion, but David liked it. What's your favorite TV show?"

"I love *Northern Exposure*. And Ben likes it too."

"Yep. And it's still going strong," Ben interjected. "You'll probably get to see it in reruns for years after you get back. Hanna, tell them about your movie going in Guangzhou."

"Oh, sure. I've gone a few times to films shown on campus. The first one I went to last August was shown outdoors in a courtyard. It was projected against a concrete wall. The movie was a Chinese film, but the story was not that difficult to follow. The trouble was, I had to carry my own chair from my rooms down two flights of stairs and for quite a long way outside in order to get to the site of the show. Only a few of the other teachers bothered to go. They told me that later we would be seeing films in an auditorium with proper seating. They were right. I've gone twice since. It's really a kick. The US or UK films are all new. They are mostly projections of pirated DVDs. In the theatre at the beginning, when the FBI warning appears on the screen, the students whoop and holler and have a raucous old time until it finishes giving its warning. Sorry, but I am as amused as they are."

"Whoops!" Hanna interrupted herself. "Looks like we're here. Guess it's time to start saying good-bye. David and Ellie, it's been a treat to meet you both. Thanks so much for all you've done."

Ben reached forward from his seat in the back to shake David's hand. Ellie and Hanna gave each other a quick hug on their side of the back seat. The evening came to an end with assurances by each and every one that they would meet again without fail. Ben and Hanna stood waving as the car drove away.

CHAPTER 22

On the morning of their departure from Chiang Mai, Hanna and Ben went out for a quick breakfast before returning to their room to get ready for the flight to Bangkok.

Once in their rooms, the packing began in earnest. On her side of the bed,

Hanna was placing an item out flat, then carefully rolling it into a slim cylinder. Her older brother had taught her this method, the one who had served in the navy. She was amused to see Ben out of the corner of her eye over on the other side of the bed spread a shirt out as flat as he could get it, fold back first one side, then the other, and fold again from stem to stern to form a lumpy bundle.

"Ben," she exclaimed, "where'd you learn to pack like that?"

"Don't you like it?" Ben asked back. "I saw it in the movies. I'm pretty good at it, don't you think?"

But Hanna did not reply to that. She kept looking out the window as she moved around the room.

"We really lucked out finding this garden room, didn't we? I love the beauty and peace of our little hideaway. I can't tell you how happy I am that you came to Thailand with me."

Hanna raised both arms in the air as if to confirm what she had just finished telling Ben. Ben extended the flat palm of his hand toward her.

"Hanna, stop. We have a few more days. Let's live them as if we'll never have to say good-bye."

"All right, that's what we'll do. But Ben, I was going to ask you to do something, and it's related to the leave-taking that's coming along. Shall I wait?"

"No. Go ahead and ask. You've made me curious."

Hanna went to the top drawer of the dresser and brought out the two silver elephants that she'd received as birthday gifts.

"Here," she said, holding one out to Ben. "I was hoping you would keep one in your home to remember us by. I'll keep the other with me to be a constant reminder of our time together."

"I like it. What a great idea! And when I look at this elephant, I'll also remind myself that one day the four of us might be living under the same roof."

Hanna laughed.

"Tell me, Ben Rinaldi, is that a proposal or a proposition?"

"Take your pick," Ben laughed back as he reached to receive the elephant from Hanna's out-stretched hand. "I'll take good care of it. Hey, are you all set? I've ordered a taxi for noon. We'd better hustle."

They zipped their bags closed, then each did a quick, walk-around scan of the room before proceeding to the front desk. Ben toted their bags, one in each hand, while Hanna took care of her handbag plus the overflow bag they had managed to fill with items from the night bazaar. They had visited this underground mini-mall on several of their evenings in Chiang Mai. It turned out to be a great place to pick up inexpensive gifts. Hanna had items to bring to her friends at the university and Ben had a handful to take to relatives and friends. The checkout was quick. The receptionist who had told Ben about the silver elephants was on duty. They'd been there a week, but from the way he was treating them, you would think they had been long-time residents.

"Good-bye, good-bye, come see us again very soon."

"We will just as soon as we can," Hanna played along.

"Give me a few cards of this place," Ben requested. "I want to tell all my friends about Pha Thai House."

"Certainly, sir, here you are," and the smiling clerk placed a small stack of cards in Ben's hand. "Tell them all to come see us," he added.

Polite wai gestures all around, and Hanna and Ben headed for the door.

At the airport, they learned that the departure of their flight to Bangkok would be delayed. They parked themselves and their bags at the end of a row of seats in the waiting area, and settled down for a wait of uncertain duration. The airport was not large; everything they might want was near at hand. And it was nice and cool. They each settled back into accommodating imitation leather seats; eyes closed, just time for a quick snooze. Fifteen minutes later, the jumbled words of an announcement in Thai blared forth from the loud-speaker system.

Hanna and Ben waited to hear the English translation. Their flight would be ready to board in thirty minutes, it informed them.

"Okay, that's not so bad. Ben, do you see that little dining area over there? Do you suppose they would sell us a couple of iced coffees? I'll wait here with our things while you go and ask."

"Will do," and Ben got up to stroll over to the corner diner and see what he could find out.

The announcement informing awaiting passengers to Bangkok that their flight would start boarding came thirty-five minutes later. On the plane, Hanna read Ben's guide book again. She wanted to look up the sight they would be visiting the next day. Ben leafed through a flight magazine at her side.

In the late afternoon, they were checking into the airport hotel, the same place they had reached by walking across a pedestrian bridge from Don Muang Airport eight days earlier. The room this time was as spacious and bright as the last one had been. Hanna let out a sigh of sheer pleasure.

"You know what?" she stood very close to Ben as she spoke. "I'm not up for getting dressed to go downstairs for dinner. How about ordering room service and having a relaxing evening?"

"I'm all for that," Ben answered as he lightly brushed away a clump of curls that had fallen across a corner of Hanna's forehead. "A very private evening it shall be."

CHAPTER 23

When the phone buzzed at seven the next morning, a sleepy Hanna reached her hand toward the annoying sound without even opening her eyes. She pushed hard on a button on top of the phone. Nothing happened, it just kept buzzing. She would need to open her eyes. She did so, picked up the receiver and heard a much-too-cheerful voice say, "Good morning. It is now seven o'clock."

"Thank you," Hanna muttered in a sleepy voice and replaced the phone in its cradle.

Keeping her eyes open by an act of will, she lay back down, wondering to herself why it mattered that it was seven o'clock. Ben stirred next to her.

"Is it time to go?" he asked, not really having given much thought to what he was saying.

"Get up, Ben," he heard Hanna say as she sat bolt upright in the bed. "We've got to get dressed. We're going into the city today. Remember the plan?"

Ben vaguely remembered that as they had checked in yesterday afternoon, they had questioned the young woman at the reception desk about transportation into the city. She, in turn, had sent them to another employee, the bell captain, dressed in the smart livery of the hotel. He asked Hanna and Ben which section of the city they wished to visit. They didn't know. Hanna answered by saying they wanted to visit the Grand Palace and see the Temple of the Emerald Buddha.

"Ah, then you would be going to Banglampoo. Many of our guests make that trip from here."

"Is it very far?" Ben wanted to know.

"Yes, pretty far. None of the taxis around here would take you there. What others have done is hire a private driver and car to go to the Grand Palace and Wat Phra Kaew."

So Ben had arranged for a car to meet them here at eight a.m. the following morning.

Once fully awake, it hadn't taken long for Hanna and Ben to get ready to face the day. They even had enough time to grab a quick bite at the hotel's generous breakfast buffet. When they had finished, they found the same smiling bell captain awaiting them near the front entrance. He followed them through the swinging doors. Once outside, he approached a small man standing beside a mid-size automobile of unknown origin, perhaps of Japanese or Korean make.

"Here is your driver. His name is Thongchai. He speaks some English." After making this simple introduction, the bell captain wished them a good day and returned to his post inside. The passengers climbed into the back of the car through the door which the driver was holding open for them. When the driver had seated himself behind the wheel, Ben spoke to him.

"So, you'll be taking us to the Grand Palace today," he said using a friendly tone.

"*Bpy Wat Phra Kaew*" came the reply from the front seat.

"I didn't quite catch that," Ben responded in diplomatic fashion.

But the car had already edged a space into the traffic flowing along beside them. The driver stared fiercely ahead, prepared to prevent any car from obstructing his progress. Not another word came back to them from the front seat. Ben sent a quizzical glance to Hanna.

"What do you think?" he whispered. Hanna put her hand over Ben's where it lay resting on the seat between them.

"I'm sure it's all right. I heard him say 'Wat Phra Keow'. We learned yesterday that this is the Thai name for the Temple of the Emerald Buddha. We'll get there."

The traffic was just as heavy as everyone said it would be. Streets on which they drove were wide avenues for long stretches at a time. Traffic signals controlled every intersection, allowing cross-traffic to make its breakthrough. Along with the vehicular traffic, crowds of pedestrians overflowed the crosswalks, further slowing progress. Vehicles of every description were to be seen: autos, buses, trucks, vans, pick up trucks, motorcycles, and the motorcycle rickshaws called tuk-tuks swelled the ranks of road traffic. Clouds of exhaust fumes were sent into the air by poorly maintained buses and trucks using leaded petrol as fuel. Although the car they were riding in had its air-conditioner going full blast, Hanna and Ben both began to sense that they, too, were inhaling those fumes. Neither spoke of it until they were closer to the even more congested center of the city. Here Ben was the first to spot a traffic control policeman wearing white gloves and a white surgical mask, busily gesturing for the on-going traffic to keep moving.

"Guess if you have to spend hours at a time breathing these fumes, you'd want to take some kind of preventative measure."

Hanna squeezed his hand in silent response.

They drove into a round-about that circled an elaborate monument of some sort. Ben remarked, "Wonder what that is."

Hanna broke silence to say she now regretted having left the guidebook at the hotel; it contained a fine map of the city of Bangkok.

"We're going so slowly, I could have read the whole thing by now. Do you realize we've been in this car for an hour? If I knew what that monument was, I could see how far we are from the Grand Palace. Why don't you try to ask the driver how much longer?"

Obligingly, Ben leaned forward in his seat. "How much longer will it take?" he asked.

"Not far," came the cryptic answer. Ben thrust his arm across the back of the seat and pointed to the watch on his wrist.

"When we get there?" he said in a raised voice.

"One hour, one hour," the driver repeated for emphasis.

Ben sat back. He leaned toward Hanna and lowered his voice. "Guess the claim to speaking some English was a bit exaggerated."

They both went back to looking out the windows.

At the end of a nearly two hour drive, the sprawling palace complex loomed into view. Hanna recognized the tell-tale signs from photos she had seen in the guide book. Spires from a variety of buildings pointed their skinny fingers at the sky, rooflines not visible anywhere else in this large city commanded attention. Their driver pulled the car up to the curb in front of a cluster of buildings set behind a wide entrance gate. Wats, *chedis*, the palace, royal reception halls, pavilions, assembly halls, government administration buildings — all were set among gardens and courtyards in a city-within-a-city laid out on over two hundred acres of land. Every king since Rama I had added buildings to the Grand Palace compound. Today's king, King Bhumipol, carried the title of Rama IX. He lived elsewhere in the city. Yet the Grand Palace was a beehive of government business and royal receptions, bursting with life in the twentieth century. And more than half of the structures at the Grand Palace were open to the public. From the car, Hanna and Ben could see processions of tourists entering through the large gate where the driver had stopped the car.

"We'll need to make some arrangement to meet the driver later. Look, Ben, it's almost ten o'clock. The place closes at eleven thirty. I'll bet we won't get to see all we would want to in such a short time. Why don't we make a day of it. Are you game?"

"As game as you are, my sweet. They open again at one o'clock, is that right?"

When Ben saw Hanna nod, he continued.

"Lets see. I'll go ahead and tell the driver to pick us up right here at three o'clock, how does that sound?"

Again Hanna nodded her head, but decided to add, "Good luck getting the message straight."

Ben leaned down to speak to the driver.

"Come back at three o'clock, okay?"

He pointed to the car and then to the pavement below his feet hoping to fix the place as well as the time. Out of the corner of his eye, he saw Hanna furiously scribbling on a scrap of paper she had taken from her handbag.

"Here, show him this."

Hanna had drawn a round clock-face with the big hand pointing straight up and the little hand pointing to three. Ben shoved it through the window for the driver to see. When the driver saw it, he immediately broke into a wide grin. Bobbing his head up and down, he pointed to Hanna's drawing.

"*By sahm mohng, kow jy,*" he said mysteriously.

Ben held up three fingers hoping that this would confirm the understanding that he was trying to develop between them. Again the driver's head bobbed up and down.

"He gets it, Ben, I'm sure. Besides … we haven't paid him yet. He'll be here at three."

But Ben wasn't as convinced as Hanna. A scowl appeared on his face as the car drove off.

"Come, on, Ben. Look what lies ahead of us." Hanna looped her arm through Ben's as she said this, then pulled him along to the gate where they would gain entry after purchasing their tickets.

No one had told Hanna and Ben that there was a strict dress code for visitors to the Grand Palace. They first learned of it right after they had paid their two hundred baht in ticket fare to enter the grounds. A man who had been standing a few paces behind the ticket seller now approached them. He spoke to them in English.

"Do you see the sign on the wall there?" he asked pointing to a picture with two rows of cartoon figures, one for upper body attire, the other for lower body attire. In bold letters at the top of this drawing, they read the words "Prohibited Outfits."

"Yes, we see it," Ben answered for them.

"Right," the official continued, "there is no picture of only feet, but if you will notice all of the figures are wearing shoes." He aimed his gaze at Ben's feet in their flip-flops. "You are not permitted to enter with bare feet. That office over there will rent you proper attire to use during your visit."

He pointed to a small building only steps away along the outside of the palace grounds. Then, turning on his heel, he indicated there was to be no more conversation regarding this matter.

Hanna saw the scowl reappear on Ben's face.

"This is turning out to be quite the excursion. Another delay, another expense. How can he say I have bare feet? What about my flip-flops?"

Hanna cut him off. "We didn't know about the dress code," she purred. "If I'd read the guidebook more carefully, perhaps I could have caught it. Come on. We're not going to let a little thing like this spoil our day. Away to rent you a pair of shoes. I'd love to give it to you as my treat."

Ben couldn't help but smile at the offer. "Then I could tell my friends about the day Hanna saved my soles by renting a pair of shoes for me in Bangkok. I'll take you up on that."

The shoe rental was a simple transaction. Hanna would get a full refund when the shoes were returned. Just because it seemed to make good sense, Ben bought a pair of cheap socks to wear with the shoes. They made for more comfortable walking and eased his mind at the thought of being in shoes previously worn by countless others.

CHAPTER 24

By the time they handed in their tickets at the gate, they had agreed that the first place to visit would be the Temple of the Emerald Buddha. When they asked for directions, the ticket taker pointed them to an information booth just inside the gate. Spread out on tables in front of the booth, Hanna saw a variety of pamphlets that were free for the taking. She helped herself to a map of the Grand Palace grounds, a schedule of the hours, a guide to Wat Phra Kaew, a guide to the main attractions within the complex, a history of the place, and a listing of the important attractions within the grounds. Armed with all the information they would need to get around, Hanna and Ben bent their heads together to study the map for a few minutes, raised their gazes to the sights immediately around them, then walked slowly along. The map indicated that Wat Phra Kaew was in a section of its own off to their left. Meanwhile, they were seeing small buildings of incredible beauty of classic Thai design. Some had entire roofs of reddish-orange tile edged in tile of dark green; some had golden spires rising to thin points high above, some showed columns or spires elaborately carved; another had a roof on which highly polished green tiles predominated. Everywhere there was statuary of exotic mythical characters, a half-man-half-bird, or a fierce guardian figure not to be crossed. Trees shaped in topiary design added allure.

Wat Phra Kaew was a complex of half a dozen buildings, the main one being a golden building topped by a dome also of gold, ending in its pointed spire of unique design. The building was visible from far away, not because of its height — it wasn't particularly tall — but because of the glow of its golden dome. Hanna and Ben saw it after about five minutes of walking and followed the paths that led to it. Their ticket was good for entry here, as it had been for entry to the grounds. They went right in.

Hanna had to blink her eyes several times. It was dark in here. Dark and cool. There didn't seem to be many visitors. As their eyes adjusted to the dimly lit interior, the splendor of the room emerged like a photo in its development medium. In the center of the long wall on their left sat the Emerald Buddha, enshrined on a throne that framed him where he sat. The throne rose in tiers; the throne's topmost section rose in ever diminishing tiers. The effect was stunning: a dark green buddha dressed in gold seated on a golden lotus throne surrounded by framework also of gold. It left them speechless. Hanna and Ben stood side by side in front of the throne. Her shoulder pressed into his arm. They remained motionless for several minutes. When they had their fill, they left the temple without uttering a sound. Back in the sunshine, they headed for a stone bench on which to seat themselves and continue a silent retreat for a while longer.

Finally, Ben gave voice to what was on his mind. "Until this week, I'd never heard of the Emerald Buddha. If it hadn't been for David and his last minute suggestion, I still wouldn't have heard of it."

Hanna agreed. "How lucky we were to have come across David and Ellie. They've added wonders to our time in Thailand. Be sure to write them or call when you get back. They should know how much we loved seeing what we've just seen. You did love it, didn't you?"

"Oh, yeah. I love and am amazed by it. Knowing you, you'll find out more about it. Be sure and tell me, won't you?"

"Of course, my love. Don't I always do that?"

The next thing to break the silence was a whistle alerting the visitors that it was time to vacate the premises for the long lunch interval. Hanna and Ben got to their feet and walked slowly back to the entrance gate.

"Be sure you can find your ticket for when we return."

"Yes, mother," Ben replied with an impish grin.

But he took the time to be certain the item was in the pocket where he remembered putting it.

They had a quick lunch in a small Japanese restaurant on a side street off the large avenue across from the palace gate. There they sat on rickety metal chairs and slurped up bowlfuls of wide noodles swimming in a delicious broth. The place was crowded and filled with noisy conversation. Hanna heard at least three languages being spoken in her immediate vicinity.

They prompted her to say to Ben,

"You know, the university where I teach has teachers from all over teaching classes in English, French, Spanish, German, Russian, and Japanese. Our resident building is like a mini UN. I live next to my friend, Milo on one side and a young woman called Carmen on the other." Ben raised the palm of his hand towards Hanna.

"Stop. I can guess what Carmen teaches."

"Of course you can, silly," Ben heard Hanna say. "I was only telling you because the chatter around here made me think of what I hear in the cafeteria in Guangzhou."

Ben picked up his bowl to drain it of the last swallows of broth. After he put it down, he leaned one arm on the table and gazed intently at Hanna.

"You know, I was thinking … you're more than halfway through your contract time at that school. Doesn't it end in mid-June?"

Hanna nodded, then waited for him to continue.

"Right. So it's already the first week in February, and your classes don't resume until later in the month."

His sentence ended in the rising inflection of a question; again, Hanna nodded.

"Then you'll have less than four months to go. The worst is over for us. The longest part of the separation, that is. Hanna, I want you to think about something for a couple of days."

Hanna, all her senses tingling, was suddenly alert to the plea in Ben's tone. She returned his steady gaze with close attention.

"Have you thought about where you are going to live when you get back? I have an idea. How about I look around for a place we could take together? My place is too small for us and you don't have a place. But I could look ahead of time and have something all lined up by mid-June."

Hanna twisted in her chair; she looked as if she were bursting to say something.

"No, don't say anything," Ben hastily interjected. "I haven't finished. We would be living together for the first time. If we like it, fine; if we don't … well, we'd have to cross that bridge if we come to it. But if we *love* it, we might think of getting married. Ah, ah, ah … I asked you to think about it first. No need to say anything just yet."

Ben had been thinking about this idea for the past few months: he feared anything that smacked of a "no" answer from Hanna. By trying to prolong an impulsive response, he hoped to put off an end to his hopes. But nothing could hold Hanna back.

"Why you old sweetie. Ben, I think it's a great idea."

And she jumped up from the table to stand over him for a public kiss on his surprised mouth.

"We'll talk about this later."

Arm in arm they walked to the counter at the front of the restaurant to pay for their lunches before making their way slowly back to the Grand Palace for the afternoon visiting hours.

Something that had caught their attention during the morning visit was giving them a goal for the early afternoon. White walls surrounded the outer boundary of the grounds of Wat Phra Kaew where they had seen the Emerald Buddha. The inner sides of these walls were painted with murals that told the story from start to finish of the Thai national epic, the *Ramakien*. This legendary tale had been borrowed freely from the Hindu *Ramayana* and rewritten to fit the Thai sensibility. A pamphlet in Hanna's collection told them that there were one hundred and seventy-eight pictures in the long mural rows, which stretched along two kilometers of walls. By the time Hanna and Ben reached the entrance to this display, they were ready for a plunge into the story of the abduction of Sita from her beloved, Rama, and the battles and hardships fought or overcome in order to bring about their eventual reunion. The evildoer, *Ravana*, was something of a magician. Rama was helped in his search for Sita by a monkey god, *Hanamun*, also something of a magician. Hanna and Ben walked the entire length of the display, not quite understanding the characters in some or the action being undertaken, but appreciative of the craft that went into the painting and into the storytelling.

The afternoon passed quickly after their visit to the murals. They walked without thought through parts of the Middle Court section, admiring the buildings and the statuary with its colorful inlays of semi-precious stones. Hanna checked her watch from time to time, conscious of the uncertainty of that last communication with their driver. As it turned out, when she and Ben arrived early at the pick up spot, they were happily surprised to see that the driver had also chosen to show up early. Smiles of acknowledgement all around. Hands together at mid-chest in Thai greeting.

Once seated in the car, Ben said in a loud, firm voice, "Amari Hotel." He felt confident the driver would be returning them to their starting place of the morning, but it didn't hurt to issue this command. After a few minutes he slumped down in his seat trying to rest his head against a backrest. But it was too low for him, so he sat back up. Hanna was looking through the pamphlets now resting in her lap. Ben looked out the window. He was feeling deeply satisfied with himself and with this day. Satisfied with himself because he'd found a way to broach the question of their future together. Satisfied with the day because, together, he and Hanna had seen some amazing sights and added a whole new chapter to their personal history. Thailand, it turned out, had been a remarkably rich choice for a foreign vacation.

"Listen to this." Hanna broke his reverie.

"Tell me," he said.

"The Emerald Buddha is dressed in different clothing according to the season of the year. His three costumes, all made of gold, are kept in a special museum at the Grand Palace. There is a costume for each season. Hot season begins sometime in March, rainy season in July, and cool season in November. The king, in solemn ritual is the one who dresses the Emerald Buddha. No one else is allowed to touch him. The exact dates depend on moon cycles. By the way, the Emerald Buddha is not made of emerald; he is called that because of the color. He is carved from a piece of flawless jade. He measures twenty-six inches from base to crown. The statue was installed at the Wat Phra Kaew in 1784 by the first Rama emperor in the Chakri line. Emperor Rama I is also the author of the written version of the Ramakien that the murals are all about."

"Hanna, that's quite a story. Speaking for myself, I got a ton out of seeing what we did without knowing all that. But having seen it, the three outfits and the king dressing him just seems all the juicier now. What about you?"

"Oh, Ben, you have such a special way of putting things. I agree. I didn't need to know any of this to have enjoyed what we saw. It is more valuable to me to read about it now."

After a short pause, Hanna changed the subject. "Ben, what do you think? By the time we get back to the hotel, it'll almost be time to think about dinner. What if we relax with a tall, cool drink in the piano bar and then have a nice dinner before even going to our room? Those noodles at lunch aren't going to keep the hunger at bay much longer."

"That's my girl. Always one to think of the basic needs. I'm right with you on this one."

CHAPTER 25

Hanna walked alone into the piano bar. She seated herself at a table next to the piano; she wanted to hear the music. Today had been exhilarating but exhausting. Ben would be along shortly. He had gone to the room to change his shoes. When the waiter came by, Hanna ordered two rum punches, the drink that she and Ben had enjoyed on their first evening together here ten days ago. Hanna sat back deep in her chair and lowered her gaze. She just wanted to breathe. It occurred to her that her feelings were in turmoil. She knew that Ben would want to talk some more about the idea of living together. She needed to determine what she would say, but for that, she needed to look closely at how she felt about it. Hanna liked the way they had been up to the time of her departure for Guangzhou. These past few days in Thailand had put her in a completely different place. Her feeling for Ben had grown well past the easy affection of that previous time, but was it now so all-encompassing that they would want to live their lives together into the unknown future? Hanna let out a deep sigh.

"I don't know, I just don't know," she told herself.

The sounds of a Cole Porter tune interrupted her thought process. The piano player had returned from his break and started in on a soulful rendition of "Night and Day." Hanna silently sang some of the words to herself. Her dad collected records of all the great American song writers from the decades of the twenties and thirties. She'd grown up hearing this music. At this particular moment, it brought a serenity to Hanna that she more than welcomed. The drinks had arrived. Hanna didn't wait for Ben before taking her first sip. Ah ... cool and sweet and packing a punch. What heaven! The rum found its way through her bloodstream, numbing the sore spots, loosening the tensions. Inhibition lost its grip. By the time Ben arrived, the glass in front of her was half empty. Hanna was no longer singing the words silently; the lyrics were quite audible.

The current tune, "Begin the Beguine," found Hanna warbling, "It brings back the night of tropical splendors."

Ben slipped into a chair close to Hanna. Not needing any courage from a sip of rum, he joined her at the beginning of the next verse. A warm baritone voice crooned forth, "I'm with you once more under the stars," and he and Hanna finished the song in a duet that had people at the nearby tables applauding in appreciation.

"I see you've started without me," Ben observed. He took a large sip of the drink waiting in front of him. "Won't take me long to catch up," he added.

When the waiter came along to ask if they would be ordering anything else, they both agreed to order another round. When the waiter asked if they wished him to book a table in the dining room, Ben asked if there was another place in the hotel that served dinner. The bar and grill which served hamburgers and french fries sounded right in keeping with the feeling of the moment, so they asked to be seated in there half an hour from now.

The piano player had gone on his break by the time the fresh rum punches arrived. Hanna spoke into the silence.

"Ben, would you do me a favor?" She continued after noting the positive answer in Ben's smile. "All of these great old songs are reminding me of my dad. I promised to call him a second time on my birthday but never quite got around to it. Would you call him when you get back? Tell him I'm doing just fine, he doesn't have to worry. You do think I'm doing just fine, don't you?"

"Not till you've answered a couple of questions to my satisfaction," Ben replied. "But to answer your first question, yes, I'll be glad to call your dad to give him an eyewitness account of his daughter's behavior at the piano bar in Bangkok. And other matters."

"Now, Ben, be fair. Can I help it if I'm completely out of drinking condition? When I think about it, I haven't had any alcohol since I left San Francisco."

"What, no discos in Guangzhou? What d'ya do for fun?"

"We troop around from room to room in the fortress of our residence building trying to drum up some adult conversation, preferably in

English." Hanna picked up the orange slice from her glass and pressed it to her lips, rind side up, signifying a frown.

"Sounds like fun." Ben made a thumbs-up gesture as he said this. "But seriously, Hanna, what would you say is the worst thing about your resident teacher life so far?"

"Hmm, I'd have to think about that," Hanna said. She slowly took another sip from the tall glass in front of her before replying. "The best way to put it is that I miss you and my dad and my friends when it comes time to speak of something that really gets to me. I have no one to confide in."

"Is it really impossible for you to call me once in a while, or for me to call you?" Ben wanted to know.

"I guess it's not impossible, but it has its drawbacks, the biggest being that our call might be heard by others. That spoils it for me. It would ruin everything."

"We could talk about the weather," Ben suggested, but Hanna was not amused.

"Ben. Trust me on this. I sometimes experience terrible moments of homesickness. My best defense so far is to keep my past and future life at bay while I live out the present. End of subject." At that very moment the waiter arrived to escort them to a table in the bar and grill.

Their dinner was a jolly affair. Hanna took several bites from a juicy hamburger topped with all the trimmings and covered in ketchup. She paused to tell Ben about going to the McDonald's in Guangzhou on teachers' afternoons out. It had opened only a few months after the school year began.

"Ben, you can't imagine how good a Big Mac tastes after a week of Chinese chow or peanut butter and jelly sandwiches. Think of me, on most Thursdays, chowing down on french fries and hamburgers."

"And you think of me on Monday evenings dining on my mamma's delicious for-family-only meals in a warm corner of the restaurant. You've come along with me in the past and will again, someday soon." In order not to let the pleasure of this evening lapse into negative territory, Ben changed the subject.

"I forgot to tell you. When I was upstairs, I began thinking about the wall paintings we'd seen today at the palace. Let's call our elephants Rama and Sita. 'You know' I said to myself, 'Hanna and me are like Rama and Sita. Sita was abducted, taken away from Rama, and he did everything he could to find her and bring her back.' You were taken from me by your strong urge for an adventure of your own. I was left, bereft, at home. And here I am in Thailand ready to rescue you. Want to get on the plane with me next Monday?" 136Ben pressed his two hands together in front of his face as he spoke these words.

"Oh, Ben, you are my hero, but you know I can't do that. The adventure isn't over, I'm still a prisoner of my fate. In a way, you have rescued me. I've loved every minute we've spent together over these past ten days. The next months will fly by, carried on the winds of what we've set in motion here. I hope they will pass just as quickly for you."

Ben's answer was to put his arm around her and whisper, "I'll be waiting."

CHAPTER 26

As the plane flew low on its final approach to the airport that served Hong Kong, Hanna leaned across Ben sitting upright in his seat to get a better view out the window next to him. She had never seen Hong Kong from the air. Lots of water, lots of small boats, glimpses of land, then suddenly high rise buildings at eye level just outside the plane: she felt she could reach out and brush them with her hand. The final steep descent brought the plane down hard on its inflated tires.

"Whew, how'd you like to live in one of those buildings on the flight path and have jets go hurtling by all day long?"

"Geez," Ben considered. "I guess if you went deaf it would be a blessing."

As the plane taxied into the gate, Hanna reminded Ben that they were looking for any transportation that would take them into the district of Kowloon. Possibly a hotel van would serve their purpose. Once into the area, the plan was to go to the office of the travel agent who had helped her before. Mei Ling had told Hanna on her previous visit that if she and her friend came to Hong Kong for a night or two, she could get them into a really nice hotel using the discounts of the day, but they'd have to come to her to find out what the best deal was. Ben and Hanna thought it worth their while to make use of Mei Ling's offer.

So it was, that dragging their suitcases behind them, they arrived in the glass-fronted offices of Mei Ling's agency. The receptionist let them know that her boss was busy with a client, but they wouldn't have long to wait. She also suggested that they park their bags beside her table and she would keep an eye on them. After following that suggestion, Hanna and Ben seated themselves on a leather settee, happy to have a few moments of quiet.

When Mei Ling appeared, her face broke out in smiles as she she walked up to Hanna and let out and an exclamation of delight.

"And who is this handsome man?" she wanted to know immediately, not waiting to be introduced. Offering her hand, she said "How do you do? I'm Mei Ling" to which Ben gave a little bow and held the hand for a long moment as he said, "And I'm Ben Rinaldi."

"Come into my office and tell me what I can do for you."

Mei Ling returned to stand behind her desk until her guest had taken their seats. Then she seated herself and leaned forward expectantly.

Hanna began.

"When I came to see you with my friend, Claire, I believe I heard you say that you would like to help recommend a hotel if I ever wanted such information. Ben and I are at the end of his vacation and will be spending the next two nights in Hong Kong. Do you have any ideas about where we should look?"

"Indeed I do, you sweet thing. Just you sit here while I look into this."

Mei Ling now swiveled in her chair to face a desktop computer set up on an adjoining wing of the desk. Her bright red finger-nails sounded clickety-clack as they raced across the keys. Using the mouse, she scrolled down a list of names until she brought it to a halt at a certain point and puzzled intently over the line on which the highlight had come to rest.

Turning back to her guests with a smile, she beamed. "You've come at a great time. One of my favorite places is offering a discount this weekend. If it sounds all right to you, I will make the arrangements in the time that it will take you to get over there. The hotel is called The Royal Pacific. It's in the Tsim Sha Tsui district, an area full of fine hotels and night life and within easy walking distance of Kowloon and all its shops and restaurants. It's also close to a metro station and only a couple of blocks from the Star Ferry, so you can get around to wherever you decide to go."

Again, Mei Ling leaned over to stare at the screen on her desk monitor.

"This weekend you can stay in a double room for two nights for five hundred twenty-one Hong Kong dollars."

Drawing a small calculator from a slim drawer in her desk, she continued. "Let's see. That would be about seventy-five U.S. dollars per night. Is that more than you care to spend? If so, I can keep looking. You would be very comfortable and well looked after at the Royal Pacific."

Hanna looked at Ben. She wished she had told him something before they got here. Soon after she'd first come to Guangzhou and found her way to Hong Kong, she had opened a bank account in Hong Kong at the advice of her father. He had contributed half, and she had matched him. Most of the original five hundred U.S. dollars was still in the account. She could treat them to this hotel stay if Ben would let her. She'd have to explain it to him later. For now, she responded without hesitation to the question that Mei Ling had left hanging in the air.

"Yes, we'll take it. That sounds lovely."

Hanna gave Ben a darting look that was meant to quell any objection he might have been considering.

"Great," Mei Ling again used one of her favorite words. She turned to Ben. "Tell me, how did you like your travels in Thailand? Hanna mentioned that it was you who suggested Chiang Mai."

Ben smiled as he said, "You did us both a great service. Thanks for all your help. We were lucky enough to find a fine little guest house, we ate delicious food, and hooked up with some visiting Americans who knew the place well. My first time in Asia, and I gotta say, I was impressed."

Mei Ling went on. "Now, tell me," she said, turning her gaze to Hanna, "what are you going to take your first-time visitor to see here in Hong Kong?"

"I was just about to ask you for some ideas on that," Hanna replied. "When I come here, it is merely to be away from work and the everyday life. Being teachers, we stay in the inexpensive guest houses here in Kowloon, and do little sight-seeing. It's as if I were a first-timer myself, although I do know how to get around on the Metro."

"Hmmm." Mei Ling muttered. "Different people like different things. Do you want to shop? Do you want to visit Buddhist Temples? Do you like horse racing? Hong Kong people are crazy about it, and the season is on right now."

Ben answered, "I live in San Francisco, a city with cable cars. Someone told me that Hong Kong has a cable car to something called 'The Peak.' Should we look into that?"

"Look, it isn't yet noon. If you go to your hotel and check in, you can have yourselves a meal either there or in any nearby restaurant. Afterwards, check the sky. If it isn't overcast or cloudy, if the sun is out and blue sky shows through, then a trip to The Peak would be a great idea for you to do on your first day. If it's cloudy, wait until tomorrow. The whole pleasure of The Peak, besides the ride up there, is to see the view of Hong Kong harbor and its surroundings. You'll be on Hong Kong Island but you will see all over the New Territories where we are now, and the large islands that lie to the West. Definitely worth a visit. Is there anything else? I'm afraid I must get ready for an appointment in just a few minutes."

Hanna and Ben quickly got to their feet. With thanks and hugs all around, they left Mei Ling carrying a sheet of paper with the hotel's name and address on it and a scribbled signature under the line, "From the Desk Of Mei Ling".

CHAPTER 27

In the afternoon, the day was still fine, the sky clear and bright. A quick walk of only three blocks brought Hanna and Ben to the landing where they could catch the Star Ferry. Hanna squeezed Ben's hand as they started across the bay. Her joy at sharing this ride with him, and the one to come, was tempered by the fresh memories of her trips solo across these very waters. So much more satisfactory to have Ben along as company.

The passenger ferry seemed to be filled to capacity. It was capable of carrying about a hundred passengers. Ben and Hanna would not have known that only a few years ago, in 1988, the Star Ferry had celebrated a centennial; it had been a feature of Hong Kong life since the late 1880's. The modern fleet of nine electric-diesel boats continued to transport thousands of locals on a daily basis even though it competed with a subway system that served the same destinations.

The ride was smooth. Skyscrapers of glass and mirrors, or concrete with steel inserts, dominated the skyline in all directions. Hong Kong was a vertical city. With such crowded land areas, the only room for expansion was up. This was clear to the observant first-time visitor. Ben was such a one.

"You know, San Francisco is built on a peninsula, but I'll bet it has more land mass than this entire metropolitan area. And probably half the population. How about where you live? Is Guangzhou reaching for the stars like this place is?"

"Not like this. What it's doing is spreading out in all directions. Farmlands are being taken over to build more factories. Let's not talk about that place. I just want to enjoy the ride and your good company."

"Oh, okay. I'll just add that I'm glad I don't work construction around these parts. I'd have to get used to heights beyond my personal danger zone."

"I'll remind you not to seek work here."

The rest of the ride passed in conversational silence. Hanna was thinking about their next step; they'd neglected to ask in Kowloon about where, exactly, to catch the tram to The Peak. But their way was made clear as soon as they exited the ferry. Direction signs in the terminal pointed to awaiting buses. The ride lasted five minutes and in no time they were climbing aboard the tram — hardly a cable car as Ben had been mistakenly informed — and were on their way to the top.

The tram ride itself was a unique Hong Kong experience. Instead of climbing up the sides of row after row of steep mountain cliffs, as one would do in a funicular in the Swiss Alps, in Hong Kong they climbed alongside banks of sky-scraping buildings before ascending into lush greenery on both sides of the tracks. Passengers were pinned back against their seats; the angle of ascent was that steep. At the crest, the tram swept into the terminal building. The nearly capacity crowd spread out in all directions once they had disembarked. Hanna and Ben found their way to an information booth where brochures were arrayed for the taking. Ben glanced around as Hanna buried her nose in the pamphlet on the top of her pile. She glanced through it to discover on the back a map indicating the trail walk that circumvented The Peak.

"Want'a go for a nice long walk?" she asked Ben, waving the map in front of his eyes to gain his attention. "There's a trail that goes all the way around the mountain. You get many views along the way. Come on, lets have a look."

Ben and Hanna walked out of the building side by side.

Once outside, Ben asked, "What are we looking for?"

Hanna consulted the pamphlet. "We're looking for a junction in the road called Victoria Gap. It is there that we will pick up Lugard Road to begin the walk that loops The Peak."

As she said this, Ben stopped a man who was approaching the building to ask him if he could point the way to Victoria Gap.

"Right over there," the man said, waving a hand in the general direction of straight in front of them. And off he scurried.

The walk was along the side of a paved road, not a real trail. This was a disappointment to Hanna, who would have preferred to walk on good solid earth. At least the traffic was sparse on this road. After ten minutes or so, Hanna began to appreciate its features. They passed the gates of several large homes, hidden behind luscious landscaping.

These were the homes of wealthy Hong Kong Chinese. At one time, they had been the summer getaway houses of the British governors of Hong Kong and their European colleagues. It was not until 1947 that a Chinese citizen could own property on The Peak. Here they were in 1993, living as next door neighbors to the foreigners who would be turning over the government of Hong Kong to the People's Republic of China in just four short years. Many of these wealthy Chinese were wondering, behind closed doors, what changes the future would bring.

Between properties, there were open spaces where Hanna and Ben would pause to look out at the view. The day remained clear, the sky blue. Hanna remarked on this.

"You know, I've gotten used to seeing blue sky from our days in Thailand and now here. But at the end of the week, I'll be back to the gray skies of Guangzhou. You'd be surprised what a difference it makes to one's disposition."

Ben cleared his throat with elaborate emphasis.

"Hanna, we have blue skies in San Francisco, occasionally. Why don't you come home with me on Monday and leave your gray skies behind for good?"

Too late, Hanna realized her mistake. She never should have given Ben an opening like that. In response, all she could think of to say was that she'd just have to learn to ignore the gray for a few more months.

They walked on. At first, the views had been of the buildings on Hong Kong Island and across the waters to nearby inhabited islands, but after thirty minutes, they were around to another side of The Peak. Here, they looked out at vast stretches of water and smaller islands covered in their original greenery. Large container ships slid back and forth across the horizon; all manner of fishing boats darted around in the waters nearer Hong Kong Island. Sight-seeing sampans, fishing boat trawlers, junks used as houseboats or fishing boats, some with flat roofs, others with an arch; diesel-driven ferries hired for private cruises — all made for a spectacle of activity that kept Ben and Hanna rooted to the spot.

Ben couldn't keep from saying, "You don't see too many of those craft in San Francisco Bay."

Ben and Hanna stood for several minutes absorbed in the seafaring sights. They moved on only when a noisy group of strollers came to take in the scene from this same spot. After another twenty minutes, they were back at the starting point and ready to take a tram back down to the bottom and retrace their footsteps to the comforts of the hotel room.

It was late afternoon by the time they reached their room. They had already decided not to go out again that evening: the day had begun early in Bangkok to allow them to catch their flight; the two mile walk around the mountain had served to energize them, somewhat. The effect rubbed off, however, somewhere among the crowds they encountered on the rides back to the hotel. One more day awaited them. Tonight they would enjoy the service of a meal brought to the room of a couple of weary but very contented people.

CHAPTER 28

Last night before going up to their room, Hanna had spent a few minutes in the hotel lobby talking to a receptionist. She asked about placing a call to California. The time difference confounded her utterly: every time she tried to calculate it herself, she came up with a different time. So she asked for help in getting an accurate answer. The quiet young man to whom she spoke, looked something up on his computer screen, then informed her that if she placed her call at ten o'clock on Sunday morning, she would be calling at six in the evening the day before in California. Hanna had thought she'd have a chance to find her father at home at that hour. She replied in the affirmative that "yes" the hotel could go ahead and place her call Sunday morning at ten. She would take it in the room, the other choice being phone booths in a hallway off the lobby.

It was Ben who woke up first on Sunday. He got out of bed to take a short turn in the bathroom. On the way back to bed, he went to the window at the far end of the room to get a sense of the day. When he peered through a crack in the vertical blinds that allowed him to look out, he saw the same blue water and the same blue sky as the day before. Happy, he got back in bed and snuggled close to Hanna to await her first stirrings of the day. He had an idea. He wanted to go somewhere, but he'd have to suggest it in a tactful way. He wanted Hanna's complete agreement.

A foot crossed his, a pair of knees bumped up against his when Hanna turned over to face him as her awakening began. Ben adjusted his own feet and legs to accommodate her; he knew it would be a few more moments before she was fully awake, so he remained as still as a queen's guardsman. And as poised. More stirrings from Hanna.

"Wake up, sleepy head," came a gentle baritone voice.

"Mmmf, where am I? Is this paradise?"

"It is, and we both know it. Now what are we going to do about it?" The answer came not in words but in arousing gestures that would prolong the entry into the day for a little while longer.

Showered, dressed and combed Hanna and Ben took the elevator down to the lobby to find their way to a restaurant that was described as having an international buffet, beginning with breakfast choices. Seated with trays of steaming food in front of them — scrambled eggs with mushrooms and sautéed onions for Hanna, a plate of roast beef hash with two fried eggs on top and home fries on the side for Ben, hot mugs of coffee for both — they began to talk about the day that lay ahead. Ben reminded Hanna that she had that phone call scheduled for ten o'clock. She hadn't needed reminding.

"I promised dad I'd call on my birthday. That was twelve days ago, and here we are. Hope he's home last night to answer the phone."

"You know this business of you being in a part of the world a day ahead of the rest of us is taking me a bit of time to get used to. Will I ever get the day back that I sacrificed in order to get to you? Or do I chalk up one for Hanna?"

"Shut up, Ben. Get used to it. Yes, you will get the day back on your way home. Just see you put it to good use." And with that, Hanna stabbed at a forkful of eggs. Ben took a long drink from his coffee mug. Then he asked, "So what else do you have in mind for today besides the call? Anything you'd care to share?"

"Not really. Seems you and I have about shopped ourselves out, so no need to think of that anymore. Probably a big meal at one of Hong' Kong's fine restaurants. Have you got any suggestions? Maybe you've thought of something?"

"As a matter of fact, I have." Ben proceeded slowly. "While you were arranging your phone call last night, I was speaking to the folks at the travel desk. Seems the passenger ferry to Macau leaves right from somewhere near this hotel. The trip takes an hour. I was thinking we could go check out the casinos in Macau for a couple of hours, maybe play a little black jack. I'd really like to see the place. How about you?" Hanna had taken note of the enthusiasm in Ben's voice. "Sure. That sounds like fun. Lets do it."

Back in their room after breakfast, the phone rang only once before Hanna had the receiver in her hand. "Hello, dad. Is that you? Did I catch you at home?"

"Hanna, my god, what a surprise! It's great to hear your voice. Is everything all right?"

"Everything is fine, dad. Ben and I are spending a couple of days in a really splendid hotel in Hong Kong before our vacations come to an end. Sorry I couldn't call on my birthday. Things were kind of busy then."

"That's okay. Here you are now. This is only the second time we've spoken since last July. I keep score, believe me. Any chance we could talk more often?"

"I'm afraid not, dad. So, tell me, what's new with you?"

"Well, we're still talking about this new guy, Bill Clinton. Did Ben tell you about the inauguration?"

"He missed it because of his travel plans. What was it like?"

"Just what you might expect. Everyone was all smiles and on their best behavior. One interesting note: he had the poet, Maya Angelou, read a work she had written just for the occasion. Pretty good stuff. It reminded some of us that Jack Kennedy had Robert Frost read at his inauguration. Does Clinton expect to be another Kennedy? Our discussions haven't stopped yet.

"Say, when are you coming home? Is it time to make up the bed? Your room is still your room, you know."

"Hope you keep it that way. No, dad, it isn't quite time to make the bed. I have months more to go. We finish up sometime in mid-June. The schedule for this next term will be ready when I get back the end of the week. I'll let you know."

"Anything I can do?"

"Just keep those cards and letters coming. They are always the bright spot in my day. I love you, and I miss you."

Mr. Hobbs took a few seconds. He lowered his voice. "Take care of yourself, little one."

"I will. I really will. And I'll tell Ben to call you when he gets back. He can give you a full account of our travels. Okay?"

"Yes, Hanna. please be sure and do that. Besides, I'd love to hear from the guy. 'Bye, Hanna."

"'Bye, dad."

After Hanna hung up the phone, she went over to where Ben stood to give him a hug. The call had brought on a sadness that she couldn't explain. Ben assured her that he would be calling her dad; he would give him a glowing report of their time together, the places and people they'd seen and met. And he would tell Hanna's dad that she continued to be dedicated to the work she was doing, that they all could take pride in that. Hanna was somewhat calmed by Ben's words, but part of the sadness remained.

CHAPTER 29

Both Hanna and Ben scooped up their jackets before leaving the room. They were headed for the cashier's office in the lobby downstairs. During a brief conversation each had decided on the amount they would be willing to spend gambling in Macau. They would need Hong Kong dollars to play with. Ben told Hanna that the only way to avoid getting caught in impulsive behavior at the tables or the slots was to set a definite limit before even waging the first bet. Hanna was going to play the slots. She planned to cash a check on her Hong Kong dollar account for the equivalent of fifty U.S. dollars. Ben was going to play black jack up to the limit of one hundred dollars US. The cashier was able to comply with both of their requests. Fifteen minutes later, they were headed for the ferry terminal to catch a ride to Macau.

Hanna had never ridden in a hydrofoil before. Ben had been on one a long time ago, when his parents took the whole family on a trip to Italy to attend the wedding of his uncle in Rapallo. He still had a distant memory of the feeling of speed.

"You see what happens," he told Hanna, "is that the boat gets up on a pair of skis and flies across the water."

"Come on, Ben, I don't feel us flying."

"Just wait. You'll see."

The ferry was plodding its way out of Hong Kong Harbor, through the heavy boat traffic. They passed by a dozen or more small islands before reaching more open sea. Once they were clear of the congestion, passengers began to hear the engines accelerating, and feel the thrust that propelled them forward at a much faster clip.

"Whew. You spoke truly, Ben. We are *flying* across the water. This is quite the ride."

The cabin of the ferry held all the passengers in an enclosed space. It was warm out of the wind and weather. The seats were comfortable and roomy. After the harbor, there wasn't much to see. The route took them along the coast of China, the province of Guangdong, to their right and way out to their left, the South China Sea. After a couple of days in Hong Kong, it was a relief, in a way, to see the open, unoccupied land they were passing. Both Ben and Hanna gave in to the torpor overcoming them, and dozed off into short unexpected naps.

In Macau, they had to clear customs. As they waited in line, Hanna asked Ben, "What's the plan? Do we know where we're headed?"

"Not really. I think we might walk around a little, see the town, and take pot luck on finding a casino. There'll probably be a dozen to choose from."

"Okay," Hanna replied as she inched forward in line. "The town itself should be pretty interesting. More than a century of Portuguese rule, including the Catholic Church, blended with a local Chinese population. Can't wait to see what that looks like."

What it looked like was a small city of contrasting architectures. A short taxi ride carried Hanna and Ben to the center of town, an area where the Portuguese had built their public buildings during their long history of using Macau as a trading port. On the hills above the roofs of these public buildings, the more recently constructed residences of the local population were clearly visible. At the center of town, a large circular plaza known as Senado Square gave one a vantage point to view the surrounding sights: three and four-story buildings with long rows of arches over doors that led to warrens of shops and offices in their twentieth century incarnations. Above the ground floor, two or three storeys of arched windows carried out the same design on block-long buildings. The colors were striking: warm yellows, whites trimmed with dark edgings, creams, saffron. A fountain surrounded by lavish floral planting of reds and yellows with abundant green leaves crowned the center of the square. People hustled about on their way to everyday activities; the place was lively but not nearly as crowded as the last two cities visited by Hanna and Ben. Most enthralling of all to Hanna, was the pavement under her feet. The street was set with curving bands of black and white paving tiles, When she walked on them, at first, Hanna got the strong impression of movement, the kind of slow rolling one might experience on a large boat. "It's a good thing I'm not the seasick kind. This street definitely delivers a slow pitch." But Ben did not feel it: he was wondering if they were in walking distance of any casinos.

As they strolled along, Ben noticed a small group of bicycle rickshaws half-way down a narrow street off to the right.

"Hanna, I'll be right back," he told her, and he quickened his stride to go over and ask his question.

"Say, can you tell me where the casinos are?" His question stirred up a trio of querulous voices all speaking in a language Ben could not understand. In the end, one driver stepped forward. He told Ben, "The casinos are all together along the waterfront. It is far from here. I will take you there."

From previous experience, Ben knew to ask, "How much?"

"Twenty dollars." This brought hoots and hollers from the other two drivers. "I'll take you for fifteen."

"I'll take you for twelve." In the end, Ben agreed to pay ten Hong Kong dollars to driver number two. Hanna had been watching this little drama from the end of the street. Ben signaled to her to come join him, and they climbed into a rather rickety bicycle rickshaw which gave a bumpy ride over pavement no longer smooth.

Their rickshaw driver dropped them off in front of a round squat building ablaze in brightly colored lights, inscribed in Chinese script. He told his passengers, "Here the Casino Lisboa, oldest in Macau. There," and he waved his hand in a wide gesture at the street ahead of them, "many more casinos." Hanna spoke one of her few Chinese phrases, "xie xie" as she slid out of her seat. "Thank you." The driver took no time in pedaling away; they had brought him to a likely neighborhood to find his next fare.

Ben and Hanna entered the casino. They were immediately struck by the quality of the air, thick with cigarette smoke from the many patrons. This would take some getting used to. Together, they strolled around. "What d'ya think?" Ben whispered sotto voce into Hanna's ear.

"I don't think much. Lets see where else we might go." The whispering couple walked back into the street.

"Sorry, Ben. It just felt creepy to me in there."

"That's okay, curly locks, we'll find something more to our liking." Ben ran his hand playfully up the side of Hanna's head to set her bouncy hair in motion. "Come on. You get to pick."

Hanna chose a place much less grand that the first one, yet containing the necessary ingredients. She disappeared along a hallway to the room that held slot machines. After exchanging thirty dollars for chips at the caged window of a cashier, Ben found his way to a table to take up his game of choice. As he took his seat, he glanced at his fellow players. He was seated between two men. One seemed young, but it was hard to tell. The other was a middle-aged man, well-dressed in a suit that had probably been tailor-made for him. To the right of this gentleman, an attractive woman could be seen in profile, closely studying her cards. After a few rounds, Ben had concluded that the two people on his right were a couple. His neighbor had piles of chips in front of him: his lady-friend did not. Ben played for twenty minutes before really getting into a feel for the game. He'd lost most of his original stake by then, so he took a quick break to go buy some more chips. His seat was waiting for him when he returned. Armed with a better supply of chips, he began to win. He won by changing his strategy slightly. Before, he had lost, usually, by calling for too many cards and going over twenty-one. When he geared back and started sticking with some lower numbers, he began to do better. The couple to his right continued to play, but the young man to his left had quit the game. His chair remained empty.

Another half hour went by. The large pile of chips on the table had moved to a spot directly in front of Ben. New players occupied the seats beside Ben. One seat at the end remained empty. While Ben sat out the continuation of the present hand, he considered the situation. He was having fun because he was winning: but it wasn't as much fun because Hanna was not there being a part of it. He glanced around. As he did so, didn't she appear over there walking in a small crowd of people? And here she came. He picked up his cards from the next deal, took a look, and placed his bet. All the while he was waiting for the moment he could lean back to hear what it was that Hanna wanted to whisper in his ear.

"How much longer?" was all that she said. Two more hands, both small losses, and Ben got down off his high chair. Hanna followed him to the cashier's window to stay with him as he cashed in. A smiling Ben pocketed three hundred and forty dollars. He had to take his winnings in Hong Kong dollars. That was not a problem for Ben: he'd soon be exchanging them for the other kind when they got back to their hotel. As they walked towards the elevator, he said, "Come on, I'll take us out to dinner. Tonight it's my turn to treat."

CHAPTER 30

Ben sat back in his chair and let out a sigh of satisfaction. "That has to go down as one of the best meals I've ever eaten."

He and Hanna had found their way to a Chinese restaurant in Macau that featured Beijing Cuisine. They'd dined on a crab with ginger appetizer followed by a dish of glassy noodles accompanied by a dish of snow peas and water chestnuts cooked together in a mild sauce. The main course was the dark, succulent Peking Duck which they were tasting for the first time. A bottle of Vinho Verde wine exported from Portugal complimented the selections. With her first sip of wine, Hanna had raised her glass towards Ben to salute him:

"Here's to the best travel companion a person could ever hope to find." They clicked glasses and sipped. Then it was Ben's turn.

"And here's to the best tour guide a person could ever dream of."

Ben had been happy, almost exuberant throughout the meal. Hanna and he were at the end of a vacation that had been a total success. They had met some new friends in Chiangmai, found unexpected royal sights and stories in Bangkok, had a good long walk at The Peak in Hong Kong, and won at the tables in Macau. They'd stayed in a simple guest house and luxurious hotels. Each was going home with a silver elephant as souvenir: each was going on with memories that would last a lifetime.

Another ride in a bicycle rickshaw took them to the terminal where they caught a fleet hydrofoil back to Hong Kong. It was an hour after sunset as the hydrofoil came down off its lifts to proceed at slower speeds through the traffic of Hong Kong Harbor. The sight of so many brightly lighted buildings was another picture to store in memory; a phalanx of lights above the water-line, a gently moving picture of lights reflected in the waters below.

Hanna remarked, "You know, if it hadn't been for you, Ben, I might never have seen the sights in Hong Kong that we've seen together."

"Why is that, Hanna? Besides my charming company, I don't quite see how it is that you spend your time when you come here."

"I know. It's not easy to explain. For one thing, I'm usually alone. For another, I'm pretty careful with what I can spend. My little account here has to last for a few more months. And I come to get away from the smoggy air and the poor food. All I do is walk around in Kowloon, mostly, sometimes go to a movie — Hong Kong people love American films — and read or write letters in my room. No sight-seeing, no excursions to Macau. Nothing like that."

Ben thought to ask, "What will you be doing here for the next few days? Didn't you say you won't go back to your school until later this week?"

"That's right. After you leave in the morning, I'll check out and go find a spot in one of those guest houses in Kowloon. Or I might treat myself to a room at the YWCA if they have one available. It's several degrees nicer than that other choice, but also a little more expensive."

Ben remained thoughtful for several minutes before noting, "Guess our days of sheer pleasure are behind us now. It's back to the real world for Hanna and Ben."

"Seems so. But we really did make good use of our days in paradise, didn't we, Ben?"

"I'd say so, yes, I'd definitely say so."

PART III

Spring Term
1993

CHAPTER 31

Hanna went into her kitchen to prepare a bowl of oatmeal. It was the Friday before classes were to begin. Students and teachers alike were returning to campus from the month long holiday that celebrated the New Year. Hanna had been back for over a week. She had found the building to be nearly deserted. Thank God Brad was around: he was good company. Brad was that adventurous Australian who had been instrumental in obtaining keys for foreign teachers to use after hours. Hanna didn't inquire into his history of use of the keys. But she did come to learn that in his wanderings, Brad had found his way to several eating places within walking distance in the neighborhoods surrounding the campus. They had been to several of these small restaurants during the previous week. There, they had eaten meals that were several degrees better in quality than what was to be found in the campus cafeterias.

She carried her oatmeal and a second cup of tea to the desk in the living room. It did double duty as workspace and dining table. This morning she had been asked to attend a meeting for all foreign teachers in the English Department. Hanna recalled attending just such a meeting three days before the beginning of the Fall term. She hadn't taken note of how many teachers were there — perhaps a dozen at most — but she had been interested to see that English teachers came from five different countries. She hadn't expected that. Today's meeting had been convened by Mr. Zhang, the Chinese Chairman of the English Department. Hanna had a favorable opinion of Mr. Zhang, starting with a strong first impression. It was his name that had appeared at the bottom of her letter of invitation to teach here in Guangzhou.

Since her arrival, Hanna had met with Mr Zhang on several occasions to discuss work-related questions. She had found him to be accessible and responsive. At one time before the fall term began, Hanna had requested a copy of the textbook to be used in her third year writing class. The book appeared in her mail slot the very next day. Mr Zhang knew that this was Hanna'a first real teaching experience. So far, there had been no complaints. She felt she had been up to the task. Her training was serving her well. If the English Department met as a group only twice a year, it was all right with Hanna. Her work was going smoothly.

Hanna locked her door on the way out of her rooms. As she did so, she glanced at the magazine picture taped to the door. It was a photo of nine decorative doors from around the world, each very different from the others. She had clipped it from a *New Yorker* and added it to a collection of post-cards and pictures she used to spruce up her immediate surroundings. The collection traveled easily in a flat file at the bottom of her suitcase. This morning, the photo of the doors brought a smile to her lips. She felt happy she had thought to bring it.

A ninety degree turn to her left, and Hanna stood facing the entrance to her neighbor's door. She knocked. Milo had come by for a minute last night to suggest that they walk to the meeting together this morning. Milo had been his usual brusque self, but she was glad to see him. It meant that the life she had known before the long vacation break was returning to normal.

As they walked along, Hanna took the opportunity to ask Milo about the one question she did have concerning the up-coming term. All the teachers had received copies of their assigned schedules in their mailboxes. When Hanna studied hers, she noticed that one of the classes she would have again for the second term was the senior thesis section. What Hanna wanted to know was why she was being kept on with the same students for that class but being transferred from the course on "American Society" to a class of "Teacher Training"? Milo smiled and glanced sideways at Hanna.

"Sounds like a vote of confidence to me. They wouldn't assign you to assist rural Chinese English teachers with their written and spoken English if they didn't think you would be effective in that role. Anyone can teach American Society: it has a fixed curriculum, as you know. I've heard about that from Jack. He gave the course two years ago in the spring semester. As for the fourth year senior thesis class, I, too will be going on with my section. We've discussed this before. They keep the same teacher for the same students in this class to give the students a sense of consistency. Between you and Brad and me, the students have learned the necessary skills differently. It will work to their benefit to write their papers for the one that taught them how."

"Ugh," was Hanna's reply to this long monologue of Milo's.

"And you'll be saying 'ugh' more than once when, in a few weeks, you sit and plow through several thousand words of what comes your way."

"Thanks a lot, Milo. You sure know how to cheer up an inquiring upstart." But Milo was unperturbed. As often was the case, Hanna received more than she bargained for when asking a question of Milo.

A sharp breeze on this winter's day caused Hanna to pull at the collar of her jacket so that it would be tighter around her neck. It continued to be as cold at the end of February as it had been one month earlier. Hanna knew that she felt the cold more keenly after her weeks of warm temperatures in Thailand and warm indoor heating in Hong Kong.

"Hey, Milo," Hanna spoke out. "When does it start warming up around here?"

"Not until April. You'll see. It happens very suddenly and sets the frogs to croaking."

"What frogs? I've not noticed any frogs around here."

"They lie in waiting in that pond in front of our building and start singing about the first of April. They don't stop until May. At night, they'll be serenading all of us to sleep."

Hanna's scowl registered the disbelief with which she received this news. "I'll believe it when I see it. But back to the cold. Will it really last until April?"

Milo paused before answering. "When I got back yesterday, I found a portable electric heater had been placed in my room. First time I'd seen one of those. I assumed that the university had issued one to every resident of our building. Didn't you get one?"

Hanna nodded. "I did, and I've been using it all week. It does help when I'm sitting right on top of it. Guess I shouldn't complain so about the cold. I was only wondering what to expect. Here we are," she added as they approached the building that housed the English department.

"See you at dinner?"

"Yes," Milo agreed. "See you there."

At the meeting, Mr. Zhang introduced them to a new teacher, an American woman who was coming to the university after spending two years teaching in nearby Shenzhen. Her name was Grace Carmona. When the meeting adjourned, Hanna went over to the new-comer to introduce herself. The two decided to walk to the cafeteria and have lunch together before returning to their rooms. After they had gone a short way, Hanna asked Grace how she liked her rooms at the Teachers Residence.

"By the way, where are your rooms? Mine are on the second floor at the front of the building."

Grace answered, "Mine are at the back on the floor above. I'm thinking of asking for another choice. These old legs won't appreciate climbing all those stairs every day."

Hanna sympathized, "No, I suppose not. Have you spoken to the people at the Waiban?"

"Not yet, but you are the second person who has suggested that they were the ones to ask."

Once the women arrived at the cafeteria and were seated with bowls of steaming food in front of them, they continued their conversation.

"What was it like in Shenzhen?" Hanna wanted to know.

"It was new, everything seemed brand new. The city rose straight up into the sky within a few years after having been declared a Special Economic Zone. Have you heard of that?"

Hanna had not.

Grace continued. "It put Shenzhen into an exclusive fast-track category towards modernization. Before that, it had been a fishing village. It was selected because it is close to Hong Kong but on the mainland. More control for the Central Government. And Shenzhen has an excellent harbor. The university there was more like an office building than a school, being housed entirely in one of the new high-rise buildings. It was kind of weird. I've taught in several parts of East Asia, but never in a place like Shenzhen. The spread-out campus here in Guangzhou is much more to my liking."

"What courses have they assigned to you?"

"I'll be teaching Literature courses to third and fourth-year students, a business writing course to second-years, and a course called American Society which I haven't had a chance to look into, as yet."

Hanna was smiling. "Grace," she said, "I taught that course in the Fall term. It's a straightforward lecture course with a fixed curriculum set by the English Department. Although now that I think about it, maybe the Waiban may have some input into it. You'll see what I mean as you go along."

A curious Grace asked, "Can't you give me a hint right now about why you said that?"

"Not right now. I'd rather you form your own opinions about the selection of subjects and we can talk later in the term." Grace saw that Hanna would say no more so she agreed to postpone any further discussion.

Back in her rooms after lunch, Hanna turned on the heater and prepared to spend the afternoon seated at her desk. She would be working most of the time on lesson plans. Before she set to work, she stared up at the poster on her wall and took a few moments to think about this new teacher, this American woman named Grace. "I'm glad she's here," Hanna told herself. "She's older than me by a couple of decades, but around here that doesn't much matter. She'll be someone to talk to, someone with whom I'll have something in common. I'll try to be here for her. It sounds as if her past two years were a bit lonely. Yes, I'll do my best to be a friend." Satisfied with that thought, Hanna got down to work.

In the late afternoon, the need for more light interrupted Hanna at her work. She got up to go turn on some lights. As she did so, she noticed that it was already after five o'clock. If she wanted to catch Jack and Milo at dinner, she would have to leave soon. They liked to go early.

Hanna had not seen Jack since before vacation; she'd seen Milo for the walk this morning, not a good time to speak of personal matters. So she was pleased to see them seated at a table in the cafeteria, with an empty seat between them. When she had her tray of food, she headed straight for it.

"Is this seat taken?" she jokingly inquired.

"It's reserved for our favorite debutant. Would that be you?" Milo replied. Hanna seated herself without further comment. She noticed that her companions were only just beginning to empty their bowls of the nondescript contents. She wasn't very good at eating and talking at the same time. So the three of them assumed a companionable silence to get on with the important matter of consuming their meal. Each knew there would be plenty of time for conversation over the cups of tea to follow.

Milo began by asking, "Did you make it to Chiang Mai?"

"Yes, and we had a great time there. Met a couple who we palled around with. Stayed in a lovely guest house. Visited the elephant camp.

Celebrated my birthday." Milo interrupted. "Which birthday would that be?"

Hanna hesitated, before answering, but she really had no reason not to answer truthfully that it was number thirty-six. "Go on," Milo said. "Tell us something about the boyfriend. Had your absence made his heart grow fonder?"

"I can't speak for him, but his presence certainly made my heart grow fonder."

"Oh, oh, Jack. Our girl is going to behave like a moon-struck puppy."

Jack let out an explosive couple of laughs, to accompany Hanna's quick retort. "I am no such thing, you two. You asked about Ben. I'm just saying that he and I enjoyed our time together. After remarks like yours," and Hanna turned so she was looking directly at Milo, "I'd say that the subject of Ben is off-limits with you guys."

"Okay, okay, calm down dear girl. I'm sorry if I stepped on your toes. I'll try not to do it again. Lets ask Jack about his vacation travels. Maybe he has a story or two to tell."

Jack had chosen a warm-weather destination for his vacation.

"My girl-friend and I got on our bikes and rode straight down to the bottom of Guangdong Province. There, we took the ferry over to the big island of Hainan known for its balmy breezes, palm trees galore and long sandy beaches. We stayed in a guest house that Xiaoling knew about, and spent the weeks touring the island by bicycle or laying on the beach."

Hanna broke in. "You sound like a guy planning a release for a tourist agency. And may I assume that your companion uses the name Xiaoling?"

"You may assume because that's her name. As for the descriptive phrases, the place lulled me into that way of dreamy thinking. I'll snap out of it after a couple of weeks back on the job." That was as much as they were going to get from Jack. He concluded by saying, "Come on, Milo, now it's your turn to tell us something about your adventures."

"Mine are hardly worth mentioning," Milo began. "I took a flight to Manila. I'd visited the Philippines before, but this time I wanted to look into the legal requirements of being an ex-pat and retiring there. You know, I probably won't be teaching for too many more years. No one will hire a man past seventy no matter what his CV says. And I'm sneaking up on that number. I spent my time in the Belgium Embassy talking to various officers there. I also spent time with a couple of local real estate agents to get a sense of what type of housing is available at what costs. All pretty boring stuff. But necessary. I'll be looking into Thailand as a possibility and also Malaysia. All I can say for sure is that I will end my days somewhere in a place of my own choosing."

"Amen to that. I really hope you do," Jack repeated with feeling.

"Say, Jack, not to change the subject, but while I think of it, do you happen to know what the toll was this year at the train station?" Milo asked.

"I do. It was thirty-eight."

A puzzled Hanna spoke up. "What's this all about? What toll at the train station?"

"Never mind, Hanna," Jack answered. "You wouldn't want to know."

Hanna's voice rose with impatience. "But I do want to know. I use that station every time I go to Hong Kong. Tell me."

"Oh, for Christ's sake, Hanna. I'll tell you. You're living here for the time being. You might as well know what goes on around here." The fierce tone in Milo's voice stayed with him as he continued. "Jack is letting me know that there were thirty-eight deaths at the main train station in Guangzhou during this year's Spring Festival. He has a way of finding out these things, since they are not made public. He knows someone who knows someone who works there. They always get it right."

In a small voice, Hanna asked, "Thirty-eight deaths but how? Why?"

"You see, Hanna," Jack interjected, "The crowds swell beyond the point of being manageable. People fall under the feet of the many rushing to find a place on the crowded trains. The fallen have little chance of survival. It happens every year."

"That's horrible. I'm sorry I asked."

Milo asked her, "Is it better to know, or not to know? Think about that, Hanna."

"I will," came her muted reply.

CHAPTER 32

My dear, dear Ben -

We've completed the first week of classes in the second term; only nineteen more to go. Not much change in my teacher life from term one with two exceptions: I'm teaching a teacher training course. And I miss you terribly. Milo thinks it's a tip of the hat in my direction to be assigned to the training. He's his same old gloomy self, by the way. I think teaching a training class will keep me on my toes. Fortunately, there is a textbook for the course which makes it much easier on the teacher. Did I mention how scarce textbooks are around here? Yes, I probably did.

Ben, the missing you is awful, it is positively painful. Why did you have to be such good company? Why do I wish I could share every day, every thought with you? As it is, I'll probably be writing more often than in the past. Hope you can take it.

What I can't take is coming back to winter cold. Let me describe a scene to you. I wear a down jacket every day all day long. Since the classrooms are the temperature of the great out-of-doors, somewhere in the high forties, the entire school population keeps outer clothing on in the classroom. I stand before my class, wrapped in a pastel green puffy jacket, hat upon head, half-gloves on hands and look out at a sea of jacketed youths, scarves wrapped around heads and faces, dark eyes peering at me over the tops of these wrappings, hands out of sight in pockets or mittens. You know, Ben, I have to say that these Chinese students are a hardy bunch. They live with so few comforts that it makes me want to cry for them. As for myself, I've decided that since we may have a few cold weeks ahead, I'm going to buy another down jacket. That way, I can wash the green one and give it the two days it needs to dry hanging out on my balcony. To do the shopping, I need my guides, so I've asked my two favorite students to go to town with me and help find the store. We go on Saturday.

The silver elephant keeps me company. Rama moves from room to room with me as I go about in my apartment. He's seldom out of my sight. Have you found a place for yours? The thought that someday we may all be living under the same roof has great appeal for me. And it gives me comfort at my loneliest times.

You asked me once if you could send me anything. There is something I might mention. My music tapes, the few I brought with me, are getting pretty stale. I would love to have you buy something new to add to my modest collection. You decide what you want to send. Just about anything would be appreciated. That's all for now.

Having arrived at the bottom of the page, Hanna was forced to end there. Those aerogram forms left little space for compromise. Since they were easy to obtain, Hanna continued to use them.

Somewhere during the past month, Hanna had learned that there were no telephones in the student dormitory buildings. In order to make phone calls, students needed to go to a central telephone exchange on campus. Placing a call could be a lengthy process. For this reason, Hanna would no longer be asking her students to give her a call. Last Tuesday, after class, she had stopped Silent in the hallway to ask if she would go to town with her on Saturday. The student was pleased to be asked. It was a chance to break the monotony of school life, especially on weekends. Silent told Miss Hobbs she was sure that Cindy would want to come with them. It was arranged that they would meet outside the campus gates at the place where public buses made their stops. Silent and Cindy would be free right after the Saturday morning patriotism class had ended. Silent thought that would be a little after eleven o'clock.

They met as planned just outside the main gate to the campus. On the way to town, Hanna asked the girls if either had ever been to a McDonald's restaurant. What Hanna had not realized was that Guangzhou's McDonald's was only one of three in all of China as of this time in early nineteen ninety three.

"I was thinking that if you like, we could go there for lunch today after the shopping."

Silent eagerly agreed. "Oh, I would like that. I've heard a lot about the place. No, I've never been. We don't have one where I live."

"Okay, that's settled then. I treat you to a lunch at McDonald's after you help me to find a warm coat."

The coat shopping did not take long. The girls knew which bus stop was closest to the store, a building on a narrow side-street that was not well-marked. Hanna told herself she never would have found her way back here on her own. Once inside, Hanna pawed through the collection of jackets, not being particularly taken by any of them. She moved on to a selection of full-length down coats. Here she spotted the very thing. It was a coat of a metallic coppery color, very unusual. She asked Silent to hold her jacket while she tried on the coat. It fit perfectly. She was elated. It was soft and warm and would go far in helping her through the next few weeks of cold. It cost little more than a jacket. She would be paying with some of her teacher-earned Renminbi. Having few expenses in Guangzhou, Hanna saved most of her earnings for times like these. A happy customer exited the store wearing her new coat, the green jacket in a bag under her arm.

A short bus ride took teacher and students to their destination in another district of the city. Hanna suggested they find a table and consider the menu possibilities before going to the counter to order.

"Cindy, do you like ice cream?"

When Cindy said that she did, Hanna went on to say that in that case, she might like a milkshake.

"Has anybody heard of french fries?"

"No. What are they?" Cindy wanted to know.

"They are deep-fried spears of potato that you can dip in ketchup, if you like. Most people do. How about a hamburger? Have either of you ever tasted one?" Cindy made a face. "My father told me they were made from cow meat. We don't eat much of that."

"Of course," Hanna remarked.

But Silent had spoken up. "I'd like to try a bite, just to see what it tastes like." Hanna concluded by making a suggestion. "I'll tell you what. I'll place an order for one big Mac, one vanilla milkshake, one chocolate milkshake, two orders of french fries, and two servings of apple pie. We'll get plenty of forks and spoons and cups and share the food among us. That way everyone can get a bite of something, but no one has to eat anything they don't want." Together, Silent and Hanna went to the counter to order leaving Cindy at the table to guard their bags.

The meal was a complete success. The french fries disappeared in a hurry. Bites of hamburger were tried, but Hanna ended up with the biggest share. Apple pie created excited commentary in native language between Silent and Cindy.. At the end, each had a glass of milkshake in front of her, and conversation could take its time. Hanna began. She told the girls that she had travelled to Thailand with her boyfriend, Ben, during Spring Festival. She told them about going to an elephant camp to see the animals at work. She told them about the Royal Palace in Bangkok and the sights there. But Hanna didn't want to spend time talking about herself. What she really wanted was to hear about how the holiday was celebrated by these young women in their homes. She looked at Cindy, then at Silent.

"Tell me, what are some of the things you do for this special holiday."

Cindy went first.

"It is the New Year, so everything is about things being new. My parents got me two new outfits, one a dress for evening parties and such, another a set of everyday clothes to replace some older things. The party dress and a new pair of shoes were left at home. They aren't for school. My dad also gave me a book. It is written by one of China's best news reporters and tells the story of how she trained and got her job. I want to be just like her. My mother gave me this pair of warm mittens, see? They have the face of a puppy on the front." Cindy held up her hands for the others to see.

Hanna looked toward Silent, thinking she might need encouragement. But she didn't have to do a thing. Silent started her remarks on her own.

"Yes, the holiday is all about new things, but it is also about getting ready to receive new things. At my home, I help my mother do a complete house cleaning from wall to wall, from ceiling to floor. We live in only two main rooms, so there is not a lot of space to cover, but we do a thorough job. After our house is clean, we sit down at the table and get to work filling dumplings, the ones we will be serving the next day. On New Years, we leave our door slightly ajar so that our neighbors or friends from the village, can come in When no more visitors seem to be coming along, my mother and I go to visit the people we have not yet seen, to wish them happy new year. The nearest town to us is on a river. This town puts on a great display of fireworks at sunset on the day of the new year. Bonfires are lit for the sake of all who go to watch. We settle down near one of the fires and watch the display in the sky. It is very beautiful."

"It sounds beautiful."

After taking their last sips of milkshake, they gathered up their belongings, and headed for the exit. It was time to pick up the threads of ordinary life which awaited them just outside the door.

CHAPTER 33

On a Thursday afternoon in the middle of March, Hanna walked into the Residents' Building and stopped by the supervisor's counter to pick up her mail. Wang Cha was standing as she approached. Hanna spoke a courteous *"ni hao,"* nodding in his direction. She glanced at her open mail slot and saw that it contained a couple of items. She pointed to them. Wang Cha obliged by reaching in and handing her the contents of her box. Hanna glanced carelessly at the items in her hand. By now, Hanna had grown accustomed to the fact that mail was treated none too privately here at the university. It made little difference, really, as she knew she had nothing to conceal. Besides, others who had been here longer than she had, told her right from the start that the contents of her rooms including the drawers in her desk would be searched from time to time. In the beginning, Hanna doubted the truth of what she was being told. Now, she had reason to know that such was the case. In her mail, she received a monthly statement from the firm in San Francisco where the assets of the Trust left by her mother were kept in a managed account. When Hanna returned from Hong Kong one weekend, she discovered, while filing away the latest financial statement, that the pages of a previous statement were in a mixed order, not following sequential page numbers. Hanna always filed them in order. It was a small matter, but it did confirm that the tales she'd heard from others had more than a grain of truth to them.

Hanna's dad had sent the latest L.L. Bean catalogue. She got pleasure from this gesture of his; it gave them another link of connection that was personal to the two of them. This afternoon, Hanna set it aside for later viewing. Something else was demanding her attention. Hanna moved along to the other end of the counter, away from the watchful gaze of Wang Cha. A flimsy brown envelope with the name, "Miss Hobbs," was begging to be opened. Hanna had not received such an envelope before, so she had no idea of what to expect. Inside, a white rectangle of stiff paper informed her that she was invited to attend a performance of a visiting Beijing dance company on Friday night of the coming week. The invitation had been issued by the Foreign Affairs Office here on campus, the group that everyone called by the more familiar term, "*Waiban,*" A simple form to be filled out was enclosed, in which Hanna was to indicate her decision about attending this special event. The Waiban would provide the ticket as well as transportation to and from the Arts Center.

"I'll say 'yes', of course," she told herself. "A night out on the town? Haven't been out at night since I was in Hong Kong with Ben. That was over a month ago." The instructions were to fill out the form and leave it with Wang Cha at the supervisor's desk. Hanna filled it out right there and then. She dropped her book bag to the floor and filled in the required spaces. Then she went back to stand in front of Wang Cha and hand him the form.

"Thank you," she said to him before going to retrieve her book bag and heading for the stairs.

In the kitchen once Hanna had entered her rooms, she grabbed the thermoses standing there. Time to replenish the water supply. As Hanna walked down the flight of stairs to the basement, she met Grace, the new teacher, on her way up.

Grace stopped Hanna on the stairs to ask, "Did you see the notice about the ballet performance? Are you going?"

"Oh, yes. I've already turned in the reply. How 'bout you?"

Grace nodded her head. "Yep, me too. I had a chance to go to a visiting ballet performance in Shenzhen last year and was pleasantly surprised by the quality of the dancing. Oh, good, I'm glad you're going. Maybe we can sit together in the van."

"Sure. Let's do that," Hanna agreed as she continued down the stairs to get to the water urns.

One night at dinner early in the following week, Hanna spoke of going to the ballet and asked if Milo or Jack had decided to go. All she got for an answer were sour looks and grunts of derision. She was sorry she had asked. But she had heard from her friend, Claire, that their whole family was going, father, mother and the two girls.

"The girls are pretty excited," Claire confided to Hanna. "It will be their first classical dance performance. I hope the program has something pretty with European music in the background, and not one of those patriotic pieces that the Chinese are apt to throw in."

But Claire did not get her wish. From an excellent seat, second row center, Hanna was witness to an evening of dance that could hardly qualify as ballet. The Beijing Central Ballet performed a Chinese full-length work entitled "Women's Red Brigade". The audience sat in rapt attention as the corps de ballet arrived on stage. The young women dressed in khaki uniforms and visored hats carried long barreled firearms as props while they moved quickly in and out of military formation dancing to music that needed only a bugle solo to remind the audience that this was the special branch of the army known as the Red Brigade. It was a youth movement, appropriate that young dancers were portraying its members. Vitality and precision were on display; but the choreography omitted most of the dance steps one expected from a ballet performance. Instead, the marching and formation line-ups and leaping served to show off a certain graceful athleticism. The story told of the rise through the ranks of a country girl, rescued from her dead-end farm life by the Brigade; she turned into one of its most savage leaders. She became a hero to them. Hanna, in a repetitious moment during act two, wondered what Claire and Brian would be saying to their girls when they got home. Perhaps not say much of anything, in a case like this. Or speak to them about what some well-known classical ballets were like.

Grace sat with Hanna on the way back to the campus. They didn't say much. Grace had invited Hanna to come in for a cup of tea when they got back. Both knew a discussion could wait until then. Once the cups and teapot were set out on the coffee table in front of the brown sectional, and the women were seated, Hanna started right up.

"Was that ballet we saw? Or was that some kind of political theater? I may not be very up on my ballet knowledge, but I really don't quite know what that was, Grace. In San Francisco every Christmas season, the SF Ballet puts on two weeks of Nutcracker performances. Everybody goes. I must have been about five or six times, and it was lovely every time. The dancing, the music, the costumes, the story. That's about the sum of my ballet education, so I ask, in all honesty, was that ballet we saw tonight?"

Grace took her time. She had been wondering about that herself, since the end of tonight's first act. "Technically, I don't know how to answer, but aesthetically, it was a travesty. The Chinese ballet company I saw last year was nothing like this one. It did three short numbers, two Russian and one Chinese that was classic in its style. I think what we saw is one that I'd heard a little about, but not witnessed before tonight. Here's the background." Grace picked up her teacup, drained it in two long sips, and settled back into her seat on the couch.

Then she continued, "During the years when Mao Zedong was in power, his last wife, Jiang Qing was one of the members of what was called the "Gang of Four". This small group were the movers behind the ten years of Cultural Revolution, which Mao started in the mid-1960s. It is said that Madame Mao visited every music conservatory, film studio and school of dance to see what needed to be improved. She approved of the hard training going on in the ballet schools but when she saw a recital, she asked aloud, 'Where are the stories of our glorious revolution?' "After that, musicians and choreographers raced to create such numbers as we saw tonight. It will be very interesting to see how history treats these Chinese ballets."

Hanna got to her feet. "Okay," she said, standing and reaching arms overhead to perform a lazy stretch. "Thanks for the tea. And thanks for your remarks. So many around here do not speak of anything the slightest bit political as freely as you just did. I appreciate that. It's a big help. Good-night, Grace."

"Good-night, Hanna. See you soon."

CHAPTER 34

When the phone rang, Hanna was in the kitchen spreading strawberry jam on a slice of bread to be used as the top half of her peanut-butter and jelly sandwich. She was startled by the sound; so few phone calls came her way. She had just returned to her rooms after morning classes and, feeling a bit tired today, she thought she'd feed herself in her room instead of going to the cafeteria. Before the second ring, she had put down the knife and started towards the living room. She picked up the receiver just as the third ring was about to sound.

"Hi, Hanna. This is Grace. Seems I guessed right, that you would be back by now."

"Oh, hi, Grace. Yes you did. Just spreading the jam for a sandwich. Would you like to come over? I've got plenty to go around."

"No thanks, not today. I'm calling about something that has just come up. Thought maybe you might know about it."

Hanna reached out as far as the phone cord would allow, to grab the top of the chair that she used at her desk. She wanted to be seated; this might be a long conversation.

"Yes, Grace, you were saying?"

"Yesterday, after class, a small delegation of students asked me if I would come and bring some friends to entertain them in some fashion at one of their student-teacher evenings. These were students from the American Society class, so I figured they would be familiar to you from last term. What I don't know is what goes on at these student-teacher nights? What passes for entertainment? I'm not exactly a veteran of the vaudeville stage, so I'm in the dark here. Hanna, have you ever participated?"

"No, I haven't. I've been asked but I was always too busy with school work and such to even think of saying 'yes'. I hear it's very low-key. Do you know Brad? He's the Australian." When Grace acknowledged that she had met him, Hanna continued. "He's done it and he told me all about it. What he did was some joke routine where he needed one other person to be his straight man. He chose Jack. He told me the students liked it so much they ended up repeating the whole routine. Grace, you could sing a few songs, if you're musical, or write a short skit. But do you have the time for that?"

"Not really," Grace's replied. "I would like to do something for these students, but not anything that smacks of a lot of preparation. Tell me, Hanna, do you like to sing?"

"Well, sure, but mostly for my own pleasure or to join with friends. But I'd consider doing something with you. I take it you like to sing."

Grace answered with enthusiasm, "I really do. And that sounds easy to me. All we have to do is decide what to sing."

"Grace, lets think about it for a day or two. Are you by any chance going to town tomorrow on the teacher van?"

"No, I hadn't planned to."

"Well, I'm going to go and so is Claire. Have you met her? She's Brian's wife and they're the ones with two daughters."

"Yes, of course I've met Claire. Their rooms are near mine here on the third floor. Why do you ask?"

"I was just thinking that we might invite Claire to sing with us. She's not exactly a teacher, but her husband is. And I know she loves to sing. She has songbooks and she teaches her girls."

"Great idea, Hanna. See what she says. Will you call me tomorrow night after you get back?"

"Will do. Thanks for calling, Grace. 'Bye."

Back in her kitchen, Hanna finished making her sandwich. As she carried it to her desk in the living room, she found herself humming a tune. Was it the sandwich or the thought of singing for students that made her happy? She couldn't decide.

The next day was a rainy one; all manner of rain gear was in evidence when the ten or so passengers began climbing into the van for the ride to town. Hanna took a seat next to Claire, with the two girls directly in front of them. The girls wanted to show their new boots to Hanna. To do so, they stepped into the aisle so that Hanna's view was not obstructed. Two pair of bright green rubber boots with frog faces at the toes came into view. Hanna gave sufficient praise for the girls to be willing to return to their seats just as the driver turned on the ignition. Claire wanted to know what Hanna's plans for the afternoon would be.

"Oh, the usual. Get the paper at the hotel, mail a couple of letters there, do some grocery shopping at the Friendship store when we get there. What about you?"

"Brian asked me to pick up some things for him. And I've found a place to have the girls' hair cut that we'll be trying out. Supposed to be better than the barber shop on campus."

"Anything would be an improvement over that place. Listen, Claire. Grace asked me to speak to you. She wants to get together a small group to take part in the student-teacher entertainment night. She was thinking of something simple like singing a few songs for them. Any chance you would consider joining us?"

"I don't know. I'd have to speak to Brian about putting the wee lassies to bed on that night. If he says 'ay' then I'm all yours. Does Grace have any ideas about the music?"

Hanna shook her head. "Nope. We said we'd be thinking about it. I gather the students perform a lot of karaoke which is very popular with them. The trouble is, someone told me, the machine has a limited list of numbers. By now, in the month of April, the various students have performed all available numbers at least a dozen times. We need to sing a cappella and choose something they know but haven't heard over and over."

"Ay, and, Hanna, wouldn't it be guid if we could do numbers that have lyrics as a chorus that would be easy for the kids to pick up so that they could sing along?" Hanna smiled and asked, "You aren't by any chance thinking of the Beatles, are you? Trust a Brit to come up with that suggestion."

Claire could take the mild dig. "I may be a Brit, but I'm a Scot first. But ask anyone, don't the Beatles have world-wide appeal?" Claire followed her question by a few lusty bars of "All you Need is Love, All You Need Is Love" which both startled and amused her fellow passengers. "And, Hanna. I've got a songbook of theirs. If you trust me to do it, I could choose the songs with the most likely choruses and copy out the lyrics for you and Grace to review."

"Would you really do all that? Oh, thank you Claire. You are the walrus."

Claire's immediate smile expressed her pleasure at hearing that song's reference. Aloud she replied, "Never mind calling me names. We'll have a great time doing this."

The evening worked well, just as Claire had predicted. She and Hanna and Grace had assembled two times in the past week to try out their group sing and get some order into the presentation. They decided to wear blue jeans and T-shirts in keeping with the spirit of the evening. They had three songs to start with and two to encore and conclude with. Since they had no musical accompaniment, there was some concern about how they could all start a song on the same note. Grace had the strongest voice; she offered to hum the first note under her breath for the others to hear and make use of.

The room for the event was a large loft room on the second floor above the student cafeteria. It was crowded with noisy young Chinese when the trio arrived. The air was thick with cigarette smoke; fortunately, it was warm enough to keep some windows opened. Lights were dim, a small raised stage occupied one end of the room, there was no furniture, students and teachers stood or sat on the floor. A couple of students performed numbers with the karaoke machine before a tall, broad-shouldered Chinese M.C. stood up with a corded microphone to announce,

"And now, the feature of the evening. May I present Grace Carmona and her trio, the Three Graces? They're going to give us a tribute to the Beatles."

Raucous applause.

Grace seized the mike and announced, "We hope you'll enjoy the songs of the Beatles sung here tonight. To make it more fun, we ask that you join us for the choruses. I'll give you the key words before each number to help you along. Okay? For the first song, you'll be singing 'I want to hold your hand'. That's all you need to know. 'I want to hold your hand,' got it? Here we go."

After a short hum from Grace, the three women looking closely at each other, launched into their first lines.

"Oh yeah, I'll tell you something

> I think you'll understand
> When I'll say that Something
> I wanna hold your hand"

Grace had given vigorous waves of her hands to indicate when it was time to join in. From the end of the first verse chorus, the response had been loud and uproarious.

Grace, Claire and Hanna performed two verses of "I Wanna Hold your Hand" with chorus. They followed up with two verses of "All You Need Is Love" chosen for the ease of its chorus for any first-time Beatles listener. It seemed there were few of those here tonight. Once again, the response was whole-hearted and full-throated.

The third song followed quickly. The trio sung forth the words

"Little Darling, it's been a long cold lonely winter
Little darling, it feels like years since it's been here"

at which point everyone in the room without the need of Grace's prompting, burst out with

"Here comes the sun, here comes the sun

followed by five lines of

"Sun, sun, sun, here it comes"

By now everyone in the room was on their feet, cheering and clapping. The three women on stage were clapping as hard as they could, hands extended towards their audience. After a few minutes, Grace blew into the mike to get everyone's attention.

"That nearly concludes our Beatles Tribute tonight. Thanks for being such a great audience. Looking at the clock, I see we have time for one more song but you must promise to get back to your dorms in a hurry afterwards. We don't want any lock-outs tonight. Okay, shall we do one more?"

Cheers from the floor.

"You may want to sing part of the verse with us. The words are:

"Hey, Jude, don't make it bad
take a sad song and make it better."

"The Chorus is:

"Nah Nah Nah, Nah-Nah-Nah, Nah-Nah-Nah-Nah,
Hey Jude"

for as long as you feel like singing it. No matter what, we'll be exiting this room when the clock says nine-thirty. Okay?"

Forty answering voices shouted out, "Okaaay."

The trio began.

"Hey Jude, don't make it bad
Take a sad song and make it better."

At the conclusion, still singing the chorus, the trio stepped down from the stage and walked through the door and down the stairs. They kept their silence on their walk home so as to be able to hear the students who were headed in a different direction singing out the words in choral harmony until out of hearing range.

"Nah Nah Nah, Nah-Nah-Nah-Nah, Nah-Nah-Nah-Nah, Hey Jude."

The Beatles lyrics proved once again to have had universal appeal.

On this spring night in April, the trio and the student audience were not the only ones who were raising their voices in song. Just as Milo had predicted to Hanna not so long ago, the frogs in the pond in front of the Residence Building had begun their nightly chorus. Hanna's bedroom window faced the pond. There was a little distance between her room and the frogs in the pond; yet, the space just enhanced the volume of their insistent song. It was warm enough to sleep with an opened window. Hanna welcomed the fresh air after a winter of being shut in at all hours. Spring rains had not only awakened the frogs, they had given life to new hordes of mosquitos as well. While Hanna lay in bed waiting for sleep to come, she counted among her many blessings the appearance of mosquito netting for her bed, recently installed, arriving at just the appropriate moment. She fell asleep secure in the knowledge that no little pests could attack her when she wasn't looking.

CHAPTER 35

Silent stirred in her sleep. She was dreaming. The dream found her in the company of some cousins walking along a path at the edge of a rice paddy when a huge, black bird came shrieking towards them out of the sky, making a horrible cry, acting as if it would dive-bomb them. Silent awoke in a state of paralyzing fright. The first awareness that hit her was that the air was full of acrid smoke and someone was screaming. Her eyes flew open to behold a column of orange and blue flames. They made an ominous swooshing noise, rather like wind blowing through a tunnel. The screaming increased in intensity; there was more than one voice contributing to it. The flames were very close to Silent. She had to stand and leap to the end of her bed in order to avoid them before stepping to the floor. She accomplished this in a split second after awakening. Her roommates did not have to tell her anything about the fire. From a vantage point in the middle of the room, Silent saw that her friend, Cindy, was still on her bed, trapped there by a flaming tent of mosquito netting.

The girls had picked up articles of clothing from the pile in the corner. They were frantically beating at the flames with whatever came to hand. Silent was momentarily stunned by the ghastly sight of smoke and fire. Recovering quickly, she sprang into action along with the others. She found something with which to beat at the flames. She beat with a frenzy. They all did. The room filled with others who found pillows and towels and brooms and shirts and jackets in their hands, all put to use to extinguish the flames. There was no more screaming from the bed. There was only the sound of the thwacking of cloth and fabric against mattress and net.

The flames died down, defeated by the action of the girls. The extinguishing of the flames greatly reduced the light in the room. Only ambient glow from street lights outside permitted the students to detect the details of the gruesome scene. Thin wisps of smoke proceeded to rise from the smoldering mattress. But it was not of immediate concern. What was the most urgent matter was removing the occupant of the bed, getting her to a place where she could rest and breathe, if, indeed, she were capable of drawing breath. It was agreed they all needed to vacate this room with its stench of burning and its smokey air. Silent stood aside while others lifted Cindy as gently as they could and placed her on a seat two girls had formed by grabbing each other's wrists in a criss-cross fashion. Silent stepped forward to help support Cindy's head and shoulders. A short walk took them to the room at the end of the hall closest to the main staircase. The light was dim in the corridor, but someone pointed the way with a beam of flashlight.

It was a long night. Barely a few minutes past midnight as they lowered Cindy to an empty bed to wait with her. No one would come by until six in the morning to unlock the front door, the door that was locked from the outside. Silent and two of her other roommates stayed with Cindy. She was covered with charred skin, black in places, red with blood in others. Here and there a yellowish secretion oozed forth. Her hair and eyebrows were singed, making them appear to be coated in gray ash. She was breathing a shallow, steady breath. Her eyes were closed and her body, still. The color of her face matched the grayish tinge of her eyebrows. There was no place on her body where it was safe to give her a soothing stroke of comfort.

Everyone in the building was awake. The main room downstairs filled with girls in various forms of attire carrying lighted candles or a pocket flashlight. They spoke in subdued tones. The question was: what could they do to summon help? The older girls took charge, telling everyone to keep quiet and speak only if they had a suggestion. Ten minutes later, it had all been decided. Some people would take turns pounding on the door at the front of the building to see if they could call the attention of anyone passing by outside, perhaps a security guard on patrol. Groups of two or three girls would explore ways of getting out of the building from any room on the first floor, only one story above the front entrance. All ground floor windows were barred in every building on campus, so there was no point considering them as an outlet. If some of the girls did manage to escape the building, they would race to the campus medical clinic to see if they could alert someone. Others would go to the upper floor windows to yell out as loudly as they could in the hope that someone would hear their cries. The girls desperately wanted to do something that would be of help. A few agreed to remain near the scene of the fire to keep an eye on the smoldering mattress. Others would wait quietly outside the room where Cindy now lay, in order to be of any possible assistance.

In that room, Silent and her two companions spoke quietly among themselves. "How does she seem to you?" Silent asked no one in particular.

"I don't like her color. It would be better if a doctor could see her right away," one of them answered.

"What about water?" Silent continued. "Do you think it would be good for her to swallow a sip of water? If I held a cup to her lips and let some trickle into her mouth, would that help her?"

The other companion pointed the beam of her flashlight at the figure on the bed. "I don't think so," she replied. "See? She seems to be unconscious to her pain at the moment. She's probably better off that way."

They sat on quietly, each lost in her own thought. No one shared a word out loud. During the hours that followed, Silent had plenty of time to allow her imagination to present the entire scene of the fire to her. At eleven o'clock, there would have been the regular extinguishing of all electric lights. Through closed eyes, the roommates might have noticed the warm glow of a candle, but they would pay it no mind; they'd seen that before. Cindy would have needed only a dim light to finish writing the letter she was anxious to get into the morning mail. Silent imagined that once the letter was finished, perhaps Cindy had decided to read a few pages in the novel she'd recently checked out of the library, only a few pages before falling asleep. Then, perhaps, she had become so engrossed in the book that when she went to shift her position, she had not thought to be especially careful about the candle's location. It would not be far from the flame to the netting. And — whoosh! — the flame would climb.

Silent had no way of knowing if any of her imaginings came close to the truth of the fire. But they satisfied her.

A movement in the room brought Silent back to the present. One of the others had risen to walk over to the bed to look down on Cindy. She was perfectly still. Silent and the other watcher also rose. The flashlight beam focused on Cindy's face. Three girls, all strangers to each other until eight months ago, hovered over the bed of a fourth, a fellow-roommate during this first year of undergraduate life. The sharing had been considerable: meals, clothes, routines, classes, studies, walks, hopes, fears, dreams, opinions — all these were pieces that made up the exchanges among them. To have one of them injured was to injure each of them. To think she might die of her injuries was to imagine ripping a limb from the body of the whole. Silent knelt down to be at face-to-face level with Cindy. She could detect no movement. She was alarmed. She glanced inquiringly at the others. Soon, three heads hung within inches of Cindy's upturned face. One of them dared to reach out and feel for a pulse at the side of the throat. Nothing. She reached towards a foot and searched for a pulse in the ankle. Nothing there. Slowly, the three of them stood up. They walked a few strides from the bed. They stood looking at each other without speaking.

At last, Silent whispered, "I'd better tell the others. I'll just say that it doesn't look as if Cindy is breathing anymore and that's all we know. Do you agree?"

They did.

CHAPTER 36

Hanna was emptying ice cube trays into a bowl, when she heard the knock on the door. That would be her friends, Claire and Grace. The three of them had enjoyed themselves so much at the Beatles Night that they made a pact; let's get together on Saturday nights and have party-time: The Three Graces. Claire could come only on the weekends when her husband wasn't away gambling in Macau. That was occurring less and less frequently as Brian's work was nearing completion, requiring more attention from him now that the end was in sight.

On these partying weekends, the women got into all manner of discussion based mostly on the days of their lives lived outside of Guangzhou, China. It was an escape from the everyday that was as good as a mini vacation. Helped along by rations of gin added to their glasses of orange juice, the evenings maintained a steady stream of good-will and endless topics for conversation. The gin was a new feature of life in the Foreign Residents' building for all three. Although it was not a written rule, any drinking by foreign teachers was usually done off campus. The gin in their glasses would have been carried in from Hong Kong by one of them. In Hong Kong, good British gin was readily available.

Hanna went to open the door to escort her friends into the living room. While they seated themselves, she carried a tray with glasses and ice and placed them on the surface of a sideboard where she proceeded to pour their drinks.

Handing them around, Hanna asked, "Are we all looking forward to the month of June? The end of the school year?"

"I am." Claire answered immediately. "For us, it means our first visit home to the heather in almost two years. I'm more than ready to see my folks and have the girls get to know our families back home."

Hanna wanted to know, "Why is it two years? Doesn't Brian sign a one-year contract like the rest of us?"

"Nae, he doesn't, you see. His work is a two-year project for which there was no leave time until the end. Mind, you, we get annual local leaves but must travel at our own expense. They aren't the same thing as a glimpse of home, now are they?"

Hanna had to agree. "No, I'm sure they are not."

She turned to Grace. "Will you be going back to the States? I'm not sure I've heard you say where it is that you call home."

Grace sipped at her drink. "I guess home is becoming wherever I happen to be. It used to be a town not far from Fort Collins, Colorado. My husband and I worked in real estate, eventually setting up our own business. We ended up building an energy-saving home on land that gave views to the prettiest mountain range you'd ever want to see. The house is still mine, but I haven't lived in it since he died. It's rented to the office manager of Carmona Properties. She'd better take care of it if she knows what's good for her."

Claire looked at Grace. "I'm sorry. I didn't know you were a widow."

"That's all right, Claire. It's been almost eight years now, and doesn't hurt quite so much. Anyway, let's not get dreary. We haven't heard from Hanna. Will you be going straight home when this all winds down?"

"You bet I will. I'm marking the weeks on the calendar: San Francisco, here I come. I can't wait to see Ben. And my father, of course."

Claire put down her glass and sat up a little straighter. "You know, girl, ever since Spring Festival, you've been mooning about and sighing over this Ben of yours. Whatever happened? You weren't like this last autumn."

Both Claire and Grace sent inquisitive glances in Hanna's direction. Hanna took another sip of her drink, not certain of how to reply.

"You know? I'm not sure myself. All I know is that we spent the most heavenly two weeks together and when it was over, I wondered how I could ever have left that dear man behind for an entire year, well … ten months, anyway. This Hanna that sits here would not dream of signing such a contract."

Grace looked at Claire; Claire looked at Grace.

They spoke in unison, "She's in love."

Claire went on. "So, tell us a wee bit more about this wonderful man who is waiting for you all this time. Did you expect him to do that?"

"I guess I didn't give it much thought at the time. One door was opening after another for me and off I went to have my first teaching experience putting that ahead of everything else."

Claire frowned. "Hmm, Grace, whad'ya think? We've got a real risk-taker here, wouldn't you say?"

"Yes, I would. I'd like to know more about the man. Is he as perfect, as compliant as he sounds?"

Hanna got up to refresh their three glasses before attempting to answer.

Once seated, she began."He appeals to me. He's the right age, five years older, and he has a good steady job with a boss who really likes him. He's a family man, loyal to both parents and his younger sister, kind to dogs and little kids. The only slight blemish, if it could be termed that, is that he was married before. There were no children. He has spoken about it several times. His first wife divorced him because of it. I've always told him that it means little to me. Now that we have spoken seriously about spending the rest of our lives together, I do have to wonder to myself if that earlier response is quite adequate to the issue at hand."

The women took a few moments to think about what Hanna had told them. Grace sipped at her drink, then put down her glass.

"Hanna, it's easy to see why this seems to be more of an issue to Ben than it has been to you. He possibly worries about what your response will be if it turns out that you and he end up having no children. So it does beg the question, how do you feel about being a mother? Have you always wanted that for yourself?"

Hanna continued speaking in the same thoughtful manner. "Whenever I thought about it, which wasn't often, I just assumed that some day that would happen. Find the right man, settle down to a life of work and home, and welcome in the newborn when it arrived. Pretty naive, wasn't I?"

"Maybe," Grace said, "but where has your thinking taken you since? You must realize that there are many childless marriages that succeed quite nicely. Mine, for one. And there are plenty of babies born in the world who need a set of parents to tend to them."

Claire nodded her agreement. "So it seems there are some options out there for you and Ben in case the urge to parenthood comes strong upon you. Take it from this Scotish lass, there's more than one way to skin a sheep."

They all had a good giggle over that one.

CHAPTER 37

On Sunday evening, Hanna arrived in the cafeteria a good ten minutes before her dinner companions. When they got there and they each had a tray-full of food in front of them, Milo and Jack began asking her if she had heard about the Trade Fair opening later next week in Guangzhou.

Jack told her, "It's an annual event. Merchants come from all over the world to place orders. All kinds of Chinese manufactured goods are available for export. You may notice a few absences in your classes. The management hires students to work in the booths. Our students are especially valuable to them because they can get by in a second language."

Milo went on to add "Jack's right, Hanna. Don't be surprised if you have a few empty chairs in your classrooms. Sometimes the student isn't called to work until the last minute. No time to notify the teacher ahead of time."

Hanna leaned forward and said, "You know? I was going to ask you guys about that. How are we supposed to handle it when a student fails to show up for class? It just happened to me this past week. First absence I've experienced since the start of the Fall term."

Milo answered. "The student is asked to hand in a note ahead of time to let the teacher know he will be missing class. Or, the student can write an explanation to hand in the next week in case he failed to give notification."

"Okay, thanks, Milo. I'll wait and see what happens tomorrow."

Monday morning, Hanna was in the classroom in time to see the students enter the room. As they filed in, she was hoping to spot Cindy. But when everyone had taken their seat, she saw that empty place yet again.

"Never mind," Hanna told herself. "I'll try to see Silent after class. Perhaps she can explain the absence to me."

The class began with a spelling bee of two teams formed by dividing the students in half. The book of words Hanna used was an old spelling dictionary of hers that she had tucked into the corner of her suitcase at the last minute when she packed for Guangzhou. It had come in handy for this particular exercise. In the second hour, the students worked with song. Hanna had designed this activity and it proved to be one of the classroom favorites. In preparation, Hanna had selected from a list of sing-along songs that the students themselves had decided on. In carefully formed block letters, she wrote out the lyrics of "Leavin' On A Jet Plane", the John Denver song she had selected from the list. She wrote the lyrics out by heart. She was fairly certain she had them right. She made four copies, then took out her scissors and began snipping. Four envelopes received a full copy of the song cut into long, thin lines, six lines to verse one, six lines to the chorus that followed. In class, twenty students were divided into four teams. Each team received an envelope. The lines to the song were a jumbled mess within. Which came first?

"All my bags are packed I'm ready to go," or

"Hold me like you'll never let me go?"

The sorting of the lines led to much discussion, all conducted in English. Students were making use of their already acquired language skills and perhaps picking up a few new words. It was a fun way to learn. Once a team had sorted out the lines and put them in order, it had to prepare to sing out lustily the completed song. Sometimes one team would have the lyrics in a slightly different order from another. When this happened, it would bring on good-humored laughter. In the end, the teams agreed on just one order and sang the song from start to finish. The activity ended with an air of triumph. Just what Miss Hobbs had wanted to see.

Hanna was not quick enough to catch sight of Silent after the bell rang. She stuck her head out into the hallway, but saw no sign of her.

"That's all right," Hanna told herself, "I'll just have to resort to plan B". The night before, she had searched through one of her desk drawers to retrieve the list of students' names for Oral English Class 92.2 that had been issued at the beginning of the term. This morning, she had carried this list with her. Now, removing it from her backpack, she walked down the hall and up one flight of stairs to enter the office of the English Department. She asked to speak to Mr. Zhang, but was told the director wasn't here at this time. So she brought out the list and decided to ask the receptionist her question.

She began by saying, "I'm here because one of the students in this class has been absent for the past two weeks. I wonder if you can tell me anything."

Together, the receptionist and Miss Hobbs bent their heads over the list to read the name to which Hanna was pointing. In the left-hand column, twenty names were printed in Chinese script. Beside each Chinese name, Hanna had written the English name the student had chosen for the classroom. Hanna was pointing to the name, Cindy. The receptionist clearly understood what was being asked of her. They both straightened up and looked at each other.

After a short pause, Hanna heard the woman say, "That student is no longer at the university."

Impulsively, Hanna blurted out, "No longer at the university, but why ever not?"

But the receptionist had nothing more to add. She merely repeated, "No longer a student here," and turned away to speak to someone who had just entered the office.

Today, being Monday, the teacher van would be making its regular run to town. Hanna had planned to go. She had to hurry to get back to her rooms, grab a quick sandwich, and get out in front by one o'clock. It wasn't until she was seated in the van that she had time to think how very odd it was to be told that her absent student was no longer at the university. She really would have to make a deliberate effort to speak to Silent. Now it would be another whole week.

CHAPTER 38

Wednesday afternoon, Hanna received a phone call from Grace who wanted to know if she could come over to talk to Hanna about something. "To vent" were her actual words. Hanna was in the middle of a lesson plan so she asked Grace to give her thirty minutes. When Grace arrived, she and Hanna sat side by side on the spongy brown sofa and Grace started right in.

"Hanna, you are the perfect person for me to speak to about this. I'm so glad you are here. Today in the American Society class a video was shown to introduce the subject, and then I had to talk about it. You know, from past experience, that we have no say or prescheduled showing of the videos chosen by the department, or their superiors. So today, we were treated to a fifteen minute film of the L.A. riots in 1992 on the first anniversary of that event. The acquittal of the defendants in the Rodney King beating is something none of us can justify, but neither can we excuse the rampage that followed. I was somewhat prepared, since, as teacher, I'd been given a syllabus at the beginning of the term. I knew Rodney King was the subject for yesterday's class. I had some remarks prepared. But I feel certain that students paid little attention to what I had to say. The film images were too graphic."

Hanna, recalling her duty as a hostess, offered to put water on for tea, but Grace told her not to, not yet. She wanted to finish.

"You know, Hanna, I've been thinking a lot about it since yesterday. I heard somewhere along the line that the thing the Chinese fear the most is social unrest. They have a term for it, 'dung wa', meaning chaos. What I saw on the screen yesterday was chaos on the streets of an American city. To put this in front of a roomful of young Chinese is to say, 'See? See what can happen if we don't keep order? Maybe we're not so bad. Look at the Americans. They let things get out of hand.'"

Hanna jumped in. "Let me tell you something. Last term, it was my turn to be taken unawares by the preplanned class video. I had to sit through fifteen minutes of drunken student behavior — what you might expect, staggering, slurred speech, vomiting, fistfights — and the film was presented as college life in America. Well … I had no trouble getting across that this behavior did exist but it affected only a very minor part of the student population. I doubt the students will withdraw their applications to US universities anytime soon. But the film was disturbing. They had seen the worst of the college scene. And you and I both know that it does exist. Now that I hear about the video in your class, I wonder if drunken college students wasn't just another form of social unrest to wave in front of Chinese youth."

Grace nodded. "Probably. Guess we've both had our subject run through the wringer. When you think about it, there's really little we can do. When I talk about such things as elections or national parks, or public education it possibly puts some balance into the equation. Lets hope so.

"How is your work going, by the way?"

Before Hanna had a chance to answer, her phone started to ring. The call was from Silent, speaking in a rush. Silent wanted to tell Miss Hobbs that she had a job at the Trade Fair on Friday and three days of the following week. She said she didn't have time to talk, but asked if Miss Hobbs could come to the Fair on one of those days. Hanna agreed to try. She was anxious to ask Silent about Cindy.

Before hanging up, she heard Silent say, "I'll call again on Friday from the Fair to tell you where to find me." And she was gone.

CHAPTER 39

When Hanna boarded the teacher van to town on the following Monday, she saw that Claire and her daughters were already seated. Hanna joined Claire in the empty seat next to her. Claire greeted Hanna with a smile.

"I hear you're going to the Trade Fair."

"Yes, I am," Hanna nodded. "But why should that be a noteworthy item?"

"Oh, you know, anything slightly out of the ordinary is an item around here where we languish in routine. Are you going today?"

"This very afternoon. As soon as I get my copy of the *Herald Tribune* at the hotel, I'll take a taxi from there. And then get home by taxi later on."

"A big spender. You are becoming famous for taking a personal interest in your students."

"I can't help it, I am interested in them and in their lives. One I've known since last Fall has told me where to meet her today. She's working at a textile counter. I'll be able to see her in a role that is new to her, to see how she manages."

"She'll manage just fine, you can be certain of that. Brian tells me that these students love the chance to earn a bit of spending money, an opportunity that rarely comes along. Let me know how it goes," Claire added, before turning her attention to one of her daughters who was hanging over the seat in front of the women, impatient to ask her mother a question.

Hanna's first sense of the scale of the Fair came as she stepped out of her taxi in front of a cavernous warehouse of a building. It reminded her of the Cow Palace in San Francisco. She and Ben went there every year to see the cutting horses weave their magic in tight competition. Or of how she imagined Madison Square Garden might look from the outside. After she bought a ticket and entered the building, she was certain this was the largest room she had ever stood in anywhere in her life. It created a fascination for the casual visitor such as herself. The air was filled with the sound of voices carrying on in so many different languages that it was difficult to identify a simple phrase in one, except up very close to the speaker. The crowds of people were made up of visitors, vendors, buyers, newsmen, assistants to all of the above, and a population of Fair authorities, some in uniform (security), others in dark suits (administrators), there to see to the smooth running of business here. Hanna picked up a guide at a table just inside the door. She moved to the side to find a spot where she could stand still long enough to study it. It was printed in ten languages, English being one of them. The guide included a map of the floor plan; from it Hanna could see that the floor was laid out in three sections, each section laid out in a grid. Thank goodness Silent had been clear in her instruction to Hanna that Hanna could find her at C 11. Without that detail, teacher and student might never manage to meet in this gigantic space.

Passing through the narrow aisles between booths and tables, Hanna had a chance to see some of the goods on display as she made her way to section C. She saw office supplies, clocks and watches, hardware store items, sports equipment, toys, small appliances, and in the distance against a wall, large machinery of some sort. There were tables full of christmas decorations and booths whose shelves were loaded with ceramics of every description. This was Hanna's first visit to a Trade Fair. She hadn't known quite what to expect. The variety of goods was overwhelming to her. After a while, she stopped looking and hurried along to her destination. Afterwards, she would marvel to anyone she told, at how well organized the layout was for such a large undertaking.

Section C had other goods beside textiles, but once Hanna found the orange colored posts that served to set it apart, she had no trouble spotting the rows and rows of flat-topped tables that served to display so many bolts of cloth that it would be difficult to estimate their total. As she walked along, the numbers stenciled on the posts served to inform her that she had reached C9, so C11 would not be far away. She spotted Silent, quietly standing behind a large display table, not busy just then with any buyers. They spotted each other and both broke out in big smiles. Silent called out. "Miss Hobbs, I'm so glad you could make it," her smile had faded quickly. "Stay and talk. We may be interrupted when I have to do some business, but I hope you will not go away."

"Of course not. I find this place to be amazing. So many foreigners, so many goods. It makes you realize what a big world we live in. It also says to me that China is *the* manufacturing giant at this moment. Just look around." Hanna swept her arms wide when she said this, by way of illustration.

When next she looked in Silent's direction, Silent was looking down at some cloth on a bolt directly in front of her, fiddling with the edges, avoiding eye contact. Hanna noticed the evasion. She asked Silent in a quieter voice, "Silent, is anything wrong? Is there something you want to tell me?"

Still, Silent did not raise her eyes to meet her teacher's gaze. Hanna waited quietly. Finally, Silent looked up. There was so much pain in the girl's eyes that Hanna could barely keep her own gaze steady.

"What's happened? Can you tell me? Is it about Cindy?"

"It is very difficult," Silent replied. "It is about Cindy. She's dead. She died in a fire in our dormitory room. It was very terrible." And Silent had to stop.

Hanna wished that such a wide table did not occupy the distance between them. She would like to have taken the girl in her arms, to give her a hug of comfort. Such was not possible, so Hanna tried to sooth the girl by telling her that they could speak of it another time, if she preferred. But the idea did not suit Silent.

She looked up now, as composed as if she had never permitted her distress to show, and told Hanna, "No, we shall never speak of this on campus. We students have been advised to keep quiet about this accident. And we will keep quiet. I only asked you to come here so I could tell you myself what happened."

"Thank you, Silent. I appreciate that. And I really do care about Cindy." Hanna stopped. She felt certain that Silent was going to say more. She didn't have long to wait.

"No one knows for sure, how it happened. We think Cindy was using a lighted candle in bed after hours and that it might have caught the netting on fire. By the time we were awake and had put out the flames, Cindy was badly hurt. She died a few hours later."

"Oh, Silent, that must have been awful for you and the others. I am so, so sorry."

As Hanna spoke the last sentence, she could see two men dressed in well-tailored business suits approaching Silent. Any further conversation would have to wait. Hanna stayed where she was. She let her gaze move idly around, not taking in anything she was seeing. Cindy had died in a fire. How horrible. How could such a thing have happened? With a start, she realized the fire must have occurred more than two weeks ago. Cindy had been absent from class twice. Had there been any kind of an announcement? Had she missed hearing it?

Silent called her back into the present by speaking her name. "Miss Hobbs."

"Yes, Silent." She saw that Silent now stood alone. "I'd like to ask you something, if you don't mind?"

"Sure, go ahead. First, I have something to ask you. Silent, was there an announcement somewhere about Cindy? Do people know about it?"

"No, Miss Hobbs. No announcement. The girls in the dorm know because we all did what we could. But we have been asked not to speak of it. We will do as we were asked."

"One more question. Did anyone come to help you that night?"

"No, nobody came until the next morning at six o'clock. They always come then to unlock the doors."

"I see. No more questions. But you have one, please tell me what it is."

"It's a request, really. Next month there is a contest in one of my classes. I want to be the best. The teacher is strict. It will be difficult. We must recite a story from our life that lasts three minutes. I have my story. I would like to practice it out loud with you. Do you have time to help me?"

"Of course, Silent. It would be a pleasure. Do you want to visit me in my rooms?"

"Yes, that would be best. I will come only one time. You can correct me. When can we meet?"

Hanna and Silent agreed to meet the next week on Tuesday evening. Once again, Silent was being approached by Fair-goers who required her attention. Hanna left the premises barely glancing at the displays on her way out. She was puzzling over the range of emotion she had witnessed in Silent. First, the tragic facial expression of down-cast eyes and down-turned mouth. Her pain had been visible for only moments when Silent finally looked at Hanna. Then the mask of polite indifference returned, the one Silent found useful. Perhaps it was an expressionless look that served Silent here while she worked at the Fair. Still, Hanna wondered.

To herself, she said, "If they've been asked to keep quiet about something that they must feel deeply, then what happens to it? What happens to them?" Of course, there was no answer to these questions.

Thirty minutes passed before she found a taxi that would agree to go out to the campus. When they got near, Hanna had the driver drop her at the main gate, rather than the side gate nearer her building. She wanted the long walk to the Teachers Residence to stretch her legs and settle her mind.

CHAPTER 40

Hanna hummed a few bars, then stopped. She was getting to the part where only Otis should be heard. This was the tape that Ben had selected, volume two of an album called "The Greatest Love." Lately, Hanna had been giving it a complete hearing every evening before going to bed. Her favorite was the one Ben had written about: it was starting now.

> "Sittin' in the morning sun
> I'll be sittin' when the evening comes
>
> I'm sittin' on the dock of the bay
> Watchin' the tide roll away"

> "Someone told me that Otis Redding wrote this song while visiting in Sausalito," Ben had written. "So when you hear him sing it, think of me, sitting by the same San Francisco Bay, seeing it from a slightly different angle."

As Hanna sat listening, she opened the top drawer in the desk and took out Ben's letter, the one that accompanied the tape. It arrived in the mail a month ago. She had read it a dozen times. But Ben's words had the effect of putting her in a receptive mood to take in the messages of the songs.
She read,

> "Hanna, my love.
> How goes it? Have you managed to stay a bit warmer? Spring must get to where you are pretty soon.
> I'm sending you a tape of songs that is such a mixed collection that you are bound to like some of them. Hope it arrives safely. There is one song, the one called 'Dock of the Bay' that I want you to pay special attention

to. I've taken up the habit of going to the Marina in the late afternoon and jogging the mile around the Green. Afterwards, I sit in my parked car and stare out at the water beyond the Golden Gate and think to myself, 'Hanna is at the other edge of that ocean. Someday, she'll be sitting here with me.' And I think of the words Otis sings and I feel close to you.

I'm writing this letter with the Word program on my new Dell computer. I really like the set-up. I have it hooked up to someone's cast-off printer that has been working just fine so far. Becoming computer savvy is really a kick. I've been in touch with David and Ellie by email. They always ask about you. They hope to be down this way before summer's over. We could all go to a new Thai restaurant I've discovered.

I bought a small table for the new Dell. It has a slide-out tray for the keyboard and there are three funny little platforms that rise above it to store stuff. Sita sits on the highest one. The little silver elephant longing for her mate.

I saw your dad at the end of February, just a couple of weeks after getting back. He was in fine form. He really hounded me for news of you, wanted to hear everything about where we went and what we did. And how you were. He came across being quite worried about you. Hope I did something to calm his fears.

We had a good time. I helped him to install his new gas grill out in back on the patio, got it all hooked up and in working order. Tells me he's going to barbecue every Sunday for his golfing buddies. He was like a kid with a new toy. It's really a nice barbecue. You'll see."

Hanna looked up. By now the tape had ended and the player waited to be turned off. Next to it, Hanna's little silver elephant stood ready to be carried with her when she left this room. As was her custom. Later, as Hanna lay in bed, she stared up at the ceiling. She felt close to Ben in spite of the miles that separated them.

CHAPTER 41

The following evening, Milo and Jack were sitting at a table in the cafeteria saving a seat for Hanna. After she sat down with her tray of food, her serving of mixed mushrooms and chicken bits and her bowl of rice, she started right in with the question bursting to be asked.

"Where have you guys been? I've been looking for you."

Jack winked at Milo. "See that? Our girl misses us when we're gone."

"Cut it out, Jack. I am not your girl. And I missed you, not for your clever repartee, but because I want to talk to you about something."

"Well, go ahead and eat your dinner first," Milo ordered, sensibly.

While Hanna maintained silence in order to do justice to her food, Jack and Milo told her about their visits to the Trade Fair, where, like her, they went to visit their students at work.

"Good exposure," one of them said.

"A taste of possible job opportunities in their future," the other added.

Hanna wasn't listening, even though the remarks were being made for her benefit. She was thinking of Silent.

When the dishes were empty and pushed to the side, Jack filled the teacup that stood in front of each one. Then he caught Milo's eye and the two of them turned toward Hanna. She did not have to be asked.

"Listen, have you heard about the fire in one of the girls' dorms? A girl died in that fire. She was one of my students."

"This is the first I've heard of it," Milo answered. "But, then, it's not the kind of thing anyone would talk about unless they had a personal connection like you."

Jack had heard nothing about it, either.

Hanna continued. "Of course I'm sad because I knew the student. She was friendly and doing very well with her classroom work for me. What I don't understand is, why don't you know about it? Wouldn't there have been some sort of announcement? Do the powers that be expect it to remain a secret? How could it, when a building full of her fellow-students know all about it. They witnessed the fire and her long dying afterwards."

Jack remarked, "Too bad. She must have died with her friends beside her having no way to go for help. I wonder if this might lead to some changes," and he glanced at Milo.

Hanna burst in. "What I really cannot understand is how the campus population as a whole is not told about such happenings? Don't they have a right to know? Do you think there was an announcement somewhere, like in one of those Saturday morning classes that we have nothing to do with?"

"What would be the point of announcing it? The university probably thinks the less said the better." Milo was sticking to his particular code of logic.

"I don't get it. If such a thing happened at a college where I come from, the entire student body would be assembled for talks from the most senior administrators and a memorial service would be conducted to honor the dead. That, at the very least, is what we would do."

Jack told her, "But, Hanna, you're not in the States, you're somewhere else right now. This is the way they do things here. That's a mistake we all make in the beginning," he added more kindly. "Thinking that because we would do it a certain way at home, it would be done that way here. Well, it's not. Best to forget that way of looking at it."

Hanna looked at Jack. "Jack, would you do me a favor? I'm really bothered by this. You once told me about the poster board on campus over near the student dorms. You said that was the way the school got information to the students. Maybe they have posted something on the board that relates to this. You read the language. Please, will you walk over there with me sometime to see if anything has been posted?"

Hanna's words spoken, with so much depth of feeling, succeeded in persuading Jack to take such a walk with her. Milo said he would go with them if they went on the weekend. They agreed to do it on Saturday afternoon.

At the appointed hour, Hanna heard Milo's door slam shut before she heard the knock on her door. She was ready to go. It being Saturday, Hanna was wearing her jeans and sneakers, something she wouldn't dream of doing on a day when she had any teaching duties. Milo was similarly attired. They set off down the stairs. There was Jack, in the lobby, looking relieved to see that everyone was on time. As far as he was concerned, this was a wild goose chase. Of course the university was not going to make any public statements about the accident that resulted in a student's death. But Jack could see the best way to convince Hanna of that was to go along with her to the large poster board and let her see for herself.

Chinese teachers and students alike would be accustomed to the use of outdoor poster boards for the display of official notices. Government entities throughout the nation made use of them. Citizens living in large metropolitan areas or the smallest of villages would be in the habit of consulting the notices on the boards to see if some new regulation had anything to do with them. There they could check for news of some up-coming event. Or find calendars giving the dates of festivals or holidays. The notices would be accompanied by banners of patriotic slogans, spread across the board.

As they walked along, Hanna asked Milo a question, one that had been upper-most in her mind.

"Milo, why do they lock the buildings at night? Is it to keep anyone from being able to leave?"

"You could easily jump to that conclusion," Milo responded, without answering the question.

Hanna tried asking Jack the same question. Only this time she added, "You know, if the girls had been able to go for help, the one called Cindy might not have died."

Jack told her, "There is no way of knowing that, now, is there? About the locked doors, I have a guess, but it's only a guess. Not easy around here to figure out why things are done the way they are. You'd drive yourself nuts trying. About the locked doors, not only do they keep people in, but they also keep intruders out. Milo, have you ever walked out on campus after midnight? Do you know what I'm talking about."

"I have and I do. That's why I said to Hanna that is easy to take it only one way."

"Okay, you guys. I'm right here. You don't have to talk around me. Who needs to be kept out?"

Jack continued. "Hanna, this isn't pretty. Are you sure you want to know?"

Hanna nodded emphatically, setting all her curls swirling around her head.

"We all know what the system is for collecting trash. In each building, there is one dumping area from which the trash is removed. Every building on campus gets its trash collected. Then what? No service comes in from the outside to cart it off. No, it all gets dumped on open ground somewhere not too far from our Teacher Residence Building, but well off any walkways. The mounds build up until you have a small hill of the stuff. What happens is, at night this hill of garbage is swarming with homeless people desperate for something to eat. They search nightly. There are too many of them for the police to chase away, so if they are gone by sun-up, they don't get carried off to prison. I'm sorry you had to hear this," Jack added before he stopped talking.

"I'm sorry, too."

They walked on in silence.

The poster board was an attractive sight to the non-Chinese reading observer. It was as wide as the widest of billboards, but not nearly as tall. It was necessary to keep moving along from one end to the other, from left to right, in order to see every posting. There were notices in black calligraphy on white paper, there were poster-size drawings or photos announcing events, there were sheets of red paper with gold lettering painted on them, there were tables with numbers on them, possibly schedules of some sort. Nowhere was there mention of an accident that resulted in the death of a student. Jack pointed to a poster that showed a statue composed of four human figures. He read the caption. "Only socialism can save China. Only socialism can develop China."

Hanna signaled that there was no need to go on. "I'm sorry to have dragged you over here. It all seems so strange and pointless, the way it happened."

Milo spoke to Hanna, his voice less gruff than usual. "That's all right, Hanna. We did what we could to oblige. Are you quite satisfied, that there is nothing more to be done?"

They had already started to walk back across campus to their building.

Hanna hadn't answered Milo's question, a deliberate omission on her part. Instead, thinking of the patriotic posters, she asked, "What do you know about those Saturday morning classes? Didn't I hear one of you mention them?"

Milo answered her. "They're called patriotism classes. Every student must attend, and every student does attend. They are conducted by a number of party officials who live here on campus. These classes are fairly recent. They were put into place soon after the uprising in Tiananmen Square three years ago. I am told they are meant to build national pride."

"I see. And were the monitors in classrooms also put in after Tiananmen Square, or were they used before that time?" Hanna wanted to know.

"Before that time," Milo answered.

Jack cut in. "Hanna, you've been here less than a year. When you've been here a little longer than that, the ways of doing things don't seem as strange. The students are smart and eager to learn. That's the most important thing. That's what keeps us all here. We aren't going to change anything. It is not our place to do so. China is becoming prosperous, lets see what changes that will bring. The death of your student was a tragedy for her and her parents. Just don't think that by itself it will make any difference."

"Right," Hanna snapped. "I won't."

When they arrived back at their building, Hanna and the two men stood in a tight little circle just outside the door.

"Okay, so are we done with this?" Milo asked hoping that Hanna was now ready to set the matter aside.

Hanna knew that was what he was getting at. She answered honestly, "All done except for one more thing."

"And what might that be?" Milo inquired in a solemn voice.

"I'm going to try to speak to Mr. Zhang. I want to write a letter of condolence to the student's parents."

Milo shook his head "no," but it was Jack who spoke out, "That's not a good idea, Hanna. I wouldn't do that if I were you."

Hanna turned and walked into the building without further comment.

CHAPTER 42

On Monday, Hanna stopped by the office of the English Department after her classes were finished.

"I'd like to see Mr. Zhang," she told the woman behind the counter. "Is he here, by any chance?"

"No, he is not here at this time. Would you like to leave a message for him?" Hanna had not expected to be lucky enough to find Mr. Zhang available in his office, but she was disappointed that it would not be as simple as that to get in touch with him. She continued.

"Could you make an appointment for me to speak with him sometime this week?"

The office worker informed Hanna that Mr. Zhang made all appointments himself; none were made through this office. She followed up by asking if Hanna had been given the phone number at which Mr. Zhang could be reached.

Hanna thought back to a printed sheet of telephone numbers that had been issued early in the first term last Fall. She was pretty sure she knew where she had put that list.

"Yes, I have his number," she answered.

As she left the office, Hanna made the decision to try Mr. Zhang in the early evening. The phone number on the list was for a home phone. Her timing was well chosen: Mr Zhang answered at the second ring. An appointment was set up for a time two days later, during the hour break in Hanna's teaching schedule.

"Will you tell me what the subject of our conversation will be?" Mr. Zhang had asked.

"I'd prefer to wait until I see you," Hanna had replied. It was left at that.

At the appointed time, Hanna knocked on the door of Mr. Zhang's office, and heard a muted reply from within that sounded like "come in."

Hanna entered and found Mr. Zhang seated behind his grey metallic desk waiting for her. She noticed that his foot was resting on some sort of box on the floor at the end of his desk. It was bound in layers of wrappings, the toes sticking out for freedom of movement. "Please excuse me, Miss Hobbs. I am having a problem with something you call gout. I am told to stay off my feet as much as possible."

Hanna gazed around and saw a pair of crutches propped up in the corner. "I am sorry to hear of it," she said.

"Take a seat, take a seat," Mr. Zhang urged her. She chose the nearest of the three molded plastic chairs placed on the visitor's side of the desk.

"What can I do for you?"

Hanna was secretly pleased that it was Mr. Zhang to whom she would be making her request. She had found him to be the most pleasant of any one of the officials at this university. In his remarks to the foreign teachers as a group, he expressed real interest in the welfare of the students and their English language studies. He arranged teachers class assignments with the tact of a diplomat, taking into consideration the needs of the school matched to the qualifications of the foreign experts. Hanna had not heard a word of complaint spoken against him. She had high hopes for her chances of obtaining his support.

Hanna was carrying a brown manilla envelope. She reached into it and drew forth the piece of paper it contained. She placed the paper in front of Mr. Zhang and, reading upside down, ran her index finger over the list until she reached the desired name. This was the class list for Oral English Class 92.2, the one in which Silent and Cindy were both students. Hanna's finger stopped at Cindy's name so that Mr. Zhang would be able to see its Chinese equivalent in the adjacent column and know what the subject of this appointment was.

"I'm here to speak about this student," Hanna told him now. She continued. "As you must know, this student died in a fire in her dormitory room. As one of her teachers, I can report that she was doing very well in her classroom work for me. As a token of respect to her memory, I have written a letter to her parents to tell them of her good work in my classroom. It is something I believe they would want to know. I need your help in getting the letter into their hands. Will you do that, please?"

Hanna finished with what she had to say, satisfied that she had managed to word it carefully and not take too long with it. She couldn't help but notice that Mr. Zhang's face had lost its smile of greeting during the course of her remarks. This wasn't the same man who had welcomed her only moments before.

"Miss Hobbs," he replied, "this was a tragic event, the accident that killed this student. We were all saddened by this news. The school has been in touch with her parents, of course. The father has come and gone, there being nothing more to be done about it. He spoke to some of the residents who were there that night. He, like the rest of us, is satisfied that it was a case of a girl doing something after hours that is clearly forbidden because of the very danger it turned out to be. The proper authorities have spoken about this danger to our students in order to prevent such a thing from occurring again. As for your letter, I see no point in bringing word from a stranger to the parents. Let us leave them alone to mourn their loss."

A long pause followed.

The meeting was not over yet: Hanna had more to say.

"Mr. Zhang, I don't know if you, yourself are a parent or not, nor is it my place to ask. But let's say that we could imagine for a moment what this girl's parents are going through. Their only child has done them proud and earned a place at university. In her first year, she writes home with news of her studies, the friends she is making, and the pleasures of life on campus. Then, without warning, comes the news that this daughter has died. Something precious has been torn from their lives. They can't get her back, but don't you think they would want to hear from the people who were around her in her last months of life? I do. That is my only reason for writing a letter to them."

Mr. Zhang spoke in a crisp manner, nearly swallowing the ends of his words.

"Miss Hobbs, you have stated your case very well. What you need to understand is that your letter would not be welcome by the girl's parents, it would be seen as an intrusion, a break with custom. A foreign teacher who had known their daughter for a few months wants to tell her mother and father about her? It is not correct that she do so. It is not anything that I would seriously consider assisting you with. Is there anything else?"

Hanna felt her heart drop. Without help from Mr. Zhang, her letter would never be sent. She couldn't do it alone. Not only was the address unknown but it was unavailable to her from any other source. Besides, she did not know the name of Cindy's parents. Cindy's Chinese name was given on the class-list in Chinese script. Hanna couldn't read that. Even if she asked Jack for help with the name, she still would have no address. There were simply too many unknowns. But her disappointment was not going to keep her from completing what she had to say about Cindy's death while she had this opportunity.

"There is something, Mr. Zhang, if I could just have another minute of your time."

A slight nod from the director signaled his consent.

"The girl's death was a tragic accident. But I understand that the flames did not cause her immediate death. The girls in the dormitory had no way to call for help. The university is generous in its supply of phones to teachers. Couldn't they put a phone in each dorm to be used in just such an emergency?"

"Miss Hobbs," a scowling Mr. Zhang replied. "This university has made a decision not to put phones in the buildings that house students. Much thought has gone into that decision. It is not for you or me to know all there is to know. Put this matter to rest. There is nothing more to be said." And with that, Mr. Zhang gave a wave of dismissal in Hanna's direction, indicating the meeting was over.

Hanna stood up. "Thank you, Mr. Zhang, for your time." Three quick strides and she was out the door.

CHAPTER 43

Silent sat at a desk in an empty classroom. She was getting ready to write her Friday letter home to her mother. Ever since the fire in her dormitory room, Silent had chosen to do all her letter-writing and studying in a quiet spot in the English Building. The only disturbance would come from other students looking for their own quiet place. Sometimes it worked out that two or three spread themselves out in a classroom, each one intent on his or her own project. This Friday, Silent had the room to herself, which suited her best.

She wrote,

> "Dear Ma,
>
> I have been working hard this week. I am preparing for a competition next week in one of my classes, a competition I want to win. You remember I once told you we had a very strict teacher named Mr. Zhu? The competition is in his class. It is on Pronunciation and Intonation. We must write a little story and tell it to the class in three minutes. I wrote a story about the time that monkey climbed into our schoolroom when the teacher wasn't looking and climbed up high on a cabinet. We students could see what was happening but the teacher had his back turned. The monkey grabbed ahold of a pile of papers and began flinging them into the air. The startled teacher turned around and tried to chase the monkey away. Do you remember when that happened? We guessed that it was someone's pet monkey that had gotten loose. We all talked about it for weeks. So I had my story, but I needed practice

telling it. What I did was, I asked our foreign teacher, Miss Hobbs, if she would listen to me and correct me where I needed it. Well, Ma, it worked out really well. Miss Hobbs did more than listen and correct. I went to her building and practiced with her in her rooms. She told me to go over the story twice. Then she told me many new things about intonation and how it is the most difficult part of learning another language. She said my pronunciation was good, but I needed work on my intonation. So what she did was take my story from me — it was all written out in my notebook — and she read it aloud while recording it on a small tape. She gave me the tape and her player to use all week long. I've been practicing each day since Tuesday whenever I get the chance. I listen to her voice and try to copy it exactly. I never expected to get so much help. Ma, if I win, they will award me a framed certificate with my name on it. It can stand on the shelf under the wedding photo of you and dad. I am doing it for you. But I am also doing it for dad; if he were still living, I think he would be pleased.

There are only two more weeks of classes and two weeks of final exams. Then I come home for the summer. My speaking and reading in English have improved during the past months. To keep up practice during the summer, we are urged to continue listening to English-language radio broadcasts. Easy to do if you have a radio that receives them. I did not. But now I do. I'll be bringing it home with me. It is a cast-off from somebody who won't be using it anymore. I'll tell you about it when I get there.

Take care of yourself, Ma. I'm longing to see you.

Your Loving daughter, Ning.

CHAPTER 44

The Three Graces met for their final time on the Saturday evening a week before finals were to begin. This time they met in Claire's suite of rooms. Brian had gone off for one last session at the roulette tables in Macau. Claire needed to be at home to see to the children. It was the girls who greeted Hanna and Grace as they arrived together. No sooner had Hanna given two sharp raps on the door, than it flew open and there stood two first-graders wearing pajamas with panda bears on them, giggling, talking at once, urging the guests to please come in. That was the only time they were to be seen. Once Grace and Hanna were in the living room, seated on the familiar brown furniture, the girls had dashed off to their room. Hanna and Grace could hear Claire speaking to them in there, getting them settled with coloring books and crayons, starting a tape of Hans Christian Anderson stories on the tape player, a tape that Claire had found in a bookstore on her last trip to Hong Kong. Claire closed their door behind her as she came in to join her guests.

"They should be fine for a good long while. I'll just take a wee look in after an hour or so."

When the three women had taken their first sips of the gin-laced orange juice that remained their Saturday Night beverage of choice, they began exchanging news of their immediate plans.

"Guess we'll be the first to go," Claire started them off. "Brian finished work on his project yesterday. We'll be packing our things starting Monday when he gets back. Then we fly to Beijing, and on to London from there. We'll take a few days to be tourists before going to Edinburgh by train. Brian's family have told our tenants to be out of our cottage by the first of July.. Oooo, I can't wait to get my hands in the soil. It won't be too late to do something with the flower beds close to the house, and to get some squash and tomatoes started in the vegetable garden." In her enthusiasm, Claire stood and did a pirouette in the middle of the room before collapsing on the sofa next to Grace. "What about you, Grace? Are you fleeing the country?"

"Only these parts. I'm coming back here in August for the Fall Term. I'm not sure how many more years I have left in me to lead this nomadic life. So for the summer, I'm going to travel within the People's Republic and see what I can see. To start with, a teacher friend from Shenzhen has made plans for us to go visit Xinjiang in the northwest. That's the province where the Uigurs used to outnumber all other minorities. But today they are outnumbered by Han Chinese sent to construct roads and railways and develop the area. They tell me the Uigurs and the Han don't like each other very much. My friend has an invitation to visit the Moslem family of one of her students. We'll go by train to Urumqi, but only to meet our hosts there. They will be driving us to their town in a place four hours away. They live in a home that is quiet and has flowering vines growing on trellises. Sounds good to me." Turning to look at Hanna, she continued, "and what does our junior member have planned?"

"Nothing as exotic-sounding as you two. The exams for my classes aren't scheduled until week two, so I have to wait to give myself a couple of days to get my grades in. I leave two weeks from next Tuesday. The Waiban arranged for my ticket. I'll fly to Shanghai, than immediately on to San Francisco. Ben will meet me at some ungodly hour of the early morning. I'm going to stay with my dad for the first couple of weeks, and simply relax and eat lots of good home-cooking, pot roast and meat loaf and even macaroni and cheese. Don't laugh. Simple pleasures will be my motto. I'll get my car back on the road and go apartment hunting with Ben. We're going to try to find something we both like; two salaries will go farther than one. Then, I'll, quick, have to look for work. It's not been easy getting any appointments set up from here. It should be much easier when I'm on the spot. Other than that, what I most look forward to is looking up and seeing some blue sky once in awhile; that, and fresh popcorn at the movies."

Grace offered to pour them round two of drinks. Claire had left the room to check on the girls. In the silence that followed Hanna's remarks, Claire realized that some loud sounds were coming from the children's room. She had gone to investigate. She found the girl's wide awake and starting to play their favorite forbidden game: jumping off their beds and landing in giggling heaps on the floor. After Claire told them she would have to bring them into the living room where she could keep an eye on them, they went back to their table to finish coloring the pictures promised to their daddy upon his return. Claire left them after saying she would be in soon to tuck in her "little angels."

"Thanks, Grace," she said upon returning to her guests as Grace handed her a freshly refilled drink.

Hanna held her glass and swirled the ice around. She watched it move. She looked up at Claire and then Grace.

"Could I talk to you about something that puzzles me?" she asked.

"Sure. Go Ahead," Grace answered.

"It's about the death of that student in the dormitory fire."

"What about it?" Grace wanted to know.

"I told you I knew the girl," Hanna went on. "I also know one of her room-mates. In fact it was the room-mate, the one who calls herself 'Silent', who told me what had happened. I've seen Silent since then to give her a little help with something she was preparing for one of her classes. At that meeting, in my living room, with no one else around, she no longer would speak a word about the event. I wanted to let her know how sorry I was for the girl who died, but also how badly I felt for her. They had been good friends. I said most of that to her but got nothing in response except a request to return to the work at hand. Do you think she was intimidated by being here on campus or was it talking to a foreign teacher that was keeping her closed up? I mean, death is a startling thing, especially when it happens in such an unexpected manner."

"If you ask me, I'd say you are making too much of an issue of this." Claire's voice had taken on a deeply somber edge. "Perhaps it is you who is not well-acquainted with death. These Chinese youngsters have already had plenty of experience with it."

"That's a good point," Grace joined in. "Hanna, you have no way of knowing what deaths may already have occurred in the life of this student. Nor will you hear anything about it from her. The Chinese are a reticent lot when it comes to the very personal. Most stories remain tightly held within the family. This has nothing to do with you, or your offer of sympathy. It's just the way it is. You'll never know all there is to know. This student will go home and end up telling her mother all about it, if she has a mother. And that will be that. Different strokes for different folks."

Hanna looked up when Grace had finished. In a voice, greatly subdued in tone from her usual cheery manner, she told the others, "Thanks. I needed that. I feel as if I'd just left the principal's office after a good talking to, one that ends with me saying, 'No sir. I'll never do that again. Promise'."

Claire jumped to her feet. "Come on. Let's finish what little remains in this bottle. Hanna, you get more ice, Grace can pour the orange juice, and we'll all have a jolly good blast on our last Saturday together."

The evening ended with a trio of voices singing in harmony at the top of their lungs, the familiar strains of "Auld Lang Syne". From the children's room a sleepy voice could be heard in the silence that followed, "Mummy, is that you?"

===

On Monday morning, the students entered the classroom to find Miss Hobbs writing phrases on the blackboard. It was a short list. Once seated, Miss Hobbs turned and explained that the final would be chosen from among the subjects on the board. She would interview each student in turn for four minutes during which time they would have a back and forth conversation. The phrases contained such subjects as asking and giving directions, rules of football, description of city sights, instruction in meal preparation. Students could prepare by reviewing the vocabulary used in these classroom lessons. When she had finished, Miss Hobbs noticed that Nick had raised his hand.

"Yes, Nick, what is it?" she asked. Nick was one of the boys who had come to Hanna's rooms for tea earlier in the school year. She remembered he had been extremely helpful at the time.

Nick announced, "Miss Hobbs, you need to know that we have a winner in our class. It is Silent. She has placed first in the Competition for Pronunciation and Intonation."

Hanna clapped her hands. "Why, that's wonderful news. She should be very proud. Look class, here's what we can do," and she turned and wrote in big chalk-white letters the word 'congratulations.' "This is what we say on an occasion like this. I'll pronounce it for you, then we'll all say it together. 'Congratulations'" said Miss Hobbs, drawing out each syllable. She followed up by waving her arms like a conductor before an orchestra. The word broke forth in unison from the entire class, including an embarrassed Silent — "Congratulations."

At the end of the period, Silent approached Miss Hobbs to thank her for the help she had given her, and to return the tape player.

"You are most welcome," Silent heard Miss Hobbs say. "Shall we make one last visit to town on Saturday and have a treat at McDonald's?

"Yes, I would like that" Silent replied. The two of them went on to arrange a time and place to meet.

"See you then." And Silent was away down the hall.

CHAPTER 45

One evening during the first week of exams, Hanna went to the cafeteria earlier than usual. She moved along the counter selecting her meal. She collected a bowl of rice, to go with a serving of pork cooked with ginger and bean sprouts that she had developed a taste for along with a large serving of unidentifiable green and gray vegetables. She set down her tray at a table where empty seats meant there would be room for the guys to join her. She was the first one here. As she looked down at the contents on the tray, she said to herself, "After I get home, I never want to see a dish of Chinese cooking again." But then she added, "At least not for six months."

Milo and Jack joined her just after she had finished eating as much as she was going to eat. Hanna was pouring herself a cup of tea as they seated themselves.

"So, how goes it, Hanna?" Jack asked. "Are you busy giving exams?"

"Not yet, I'm busy preparing them for next week. All my exams are scheduled for week two."

"That's a tough break," Jack remarked. "Mine will be over by next Monday, and I'll be away from here by the end of next week.

"Going anywhere in particular?" Hanna asked.

"Yep. Xiaoling and I are going to bicycle west to the lands of fantastic scenery, namely in Guangxi. I want to see those crazy peaks that so many painters have put in their scrolls. And Xioaling knows about a trip through the Li River Valley that you do both by boat and by bike. As long as they employ me around here, I'll be taking in the sights."

Milo looked at Jack and said, "Sounds like a lot of deprivation and sweat to me. But then, you're not as old and cranky as I am."

Jack's retort came quickly. "Yeah, well, when we're done, I'll tell you about the sights and pleasures along the way, paid for by that sweat and deprivation. Then you can be the judge of which basket on the scales weighs in the heavier. You will be coming back in the fall, won't you?"

Milo raised a few mouthfuls of food to his mouth in slow, steady rhythm. He took the time to chew and swallow before speaking again. "I'll be back as long as I keep getting the invitation to teach. So, yes, you'll see me again in August." He turned to look at Hanna. "Guess we won't be seeing you for very much longer."

"Nope. I'm at the end of my tour. It has certainly been educational," Hanna added with a wry grin on her face.

Milo continued. "Will you go on working as a teacher when you get back to California?"

"That remains to be seen," Hanna told him. "I don't know where the openings would be in my part of the world. Before I came here, I worked in Admissions at a college. We had a lot of foreign students applying. Of course entrance exams weeded out the ones who were not really qualified, but my job was to assess the ones who passed. After my time here, I believe I would be better able to distinguish those who were really eager to study for lifetime goals from those who were merely spinning their wheels. I have to think about the teaching. Maybe my first choice will be to do what I was doing before."

Milo continued. "But generally, would you say you had a good experience with your teaching here? I know you managed your share of those Senior Research Papers that are such a pain to us all."

"Oh, sure. The students were the best part, so eager and willing to try. As for the senior papers, it only meant that my night-time reading was devoted to that and not my favorite detective. Besides, a few of the students wrote a really good essay. Too bad the requirements made them so long. Most theses and proofs could have been accomplished in half the space. Ah, but I mustn't tell others how to do things, must I?"

This gave Milo a perfect opening. "Speaking of telling others, Hanna, you've never told us much about your private meeting with Mr. Zhang."

Jack chimed in. "Yes, Hanna, what happened when you went to see him?"

"Nothing much except that I satisfied myself that I had spoken my piece. I let Mr. Zhang know that the student who died had been in one of my classes. I had written a letter to her parents about her good classwork and asked if he would help get the letter to them. He refused, of course. Told me that was not a custom of theirs, that I was interfering."

"Yes, I can see him saying that," Milo remarked. "Anything else?" When Milo said this he looked at Jack and gave a sort of nod with a half-smile on his face.

"Yes, before leaving, I spoke to Mr Zhang about the possibility of placing a phone in student dormitories for use in emergencies."

"I bet that went exactly nowhere."

"You're absolutely right, Milo, but it satisfied me to put forth the idea. You never know."

"Whadya think, Jack?"

Jack surprised them both by telling them, "I'd say we have a real trouble-maker on our hands."

"That's a bit much, you guys. I wasn't out to make any waves. I just thought it a good idea to look at the event, see what went wrong, and possibly make some suggestions about how to avoid similar tragedies in the future. Besides, there are feelings to be considered; the parents and friends of the girl are players here, too. The way the school handled it, with an instant clamp of silence imposed, does not allow for the feelings of these others."

Milo exploded. "Feelings," his voice was reduced to a loud whisper. "Feelings don't count."

"Milo, what do you mean? Feelings don't count?" Hanna was aghast.

Jack cut in. "Look, Hanna. You've been here the better part of nine months, going on ten. Show me a single instance where the feelings of a student or other members of the campus population are taken into consideration by those in authority. They have a different set of criteria to operate from. Feelings would not even be an entry on their list. You'll think about this in your months at home when you look back. But the simplest answer is that this university, like many institutions in China, is governed by a strict set of guidelines to which everyone must adhere. There are no battles here to be fought by us. We serve our students and ourselves. End of editorial."

Next, Milo took a final turn. "Hanna, ask yourself, why did you come here? Was it to help your students to improve their English? Or was it to observe the workings of a foreign university and make so-called 'helpful' hints about changes for the better?"

Hanna looked away across the room. It took her some moments to gather her thoughts.

When she spoke at last, this is what she said. "Of course, it was the first reason that brought me here. The students and the teaching have been a wonderfully rewarding experience. I never thought much about the regulations of this campus until this event occurred. Now, I guess I got caught up in something that has put me a lot off balance. From the school's point-of-view, I am here to teach and that is all. The human element will have to wait and be lived out elsewhere. This is not my place."

"Way to go, Hanna." Jack jumped up from his seat and came around to raise Hanna from her chair so he could give her a hug. They both eased Milo from his sitting position so he could join in.

"One more cup of tea?" Hanna asked.

"Sure. Why not?" Milo answered.

Three cups of tea were poured from a fresh pot. Jack raised his cup in the air. "Here's to the end of Miss Debutant and the beginning of a new Hanna." They clicked cups and drank.

"Here's to Miss Quick Study and her successes ahead." This from Milo.

"And here's to next year's Miss Debutant, the one you choose for your special attention, the one who has the good fortune to come under your surveillance." Hanna clunked her cup first against Jack's, then against Milo's. The three of them were still on their feet.

CHAPTER 46

Silent was facing a dilemma. As she lay in bed just after lights-out, she stared into space, still wide awake, thinking about the decision she must make. Tomorrow, she would go to town with Miss Hobbs for the last time. When they had made the arrangement, Miss Hobbs had said to her, "I'd like to hear from you how you came to choose the name 'Silent'. It is rather unusual, isn't it?"

"Yes, it is," Silent had to agree. But she said nothing about explaining what was behind her choice.

That was what was keeping her awake. She would very much like to please Miss Hobbs. But the story was not one Silent felt she could tell her, or anyone, for that matter. It was far too personal. It was a family story. Any meaning in the story would only be felt by her mother and her father, when he was still alive. It was not for others, and Silent would not tell it to others.

Silent's father had completed two years at a teachers' college before the course of his country's history changed his life. Instead of graduating and going back to his village to start work in the local middle school, he was ordered into a re-education camp. He was classified as part of the bourgeois intelligentsia. Three years of hard agricultural labor undermined his health. He never recovered his strength. He married his childhood sweetheart and lived for seven joyful years after the birth of their daughter. That was all the time that remained to him before he succumbed to the ravishes of ill-health.

Silent remembered her father as loving to tell stories to her, stories about the people who were neighbors, or stories from any number of books he had read. Often there was a lesson to be learned from the story he told her, a lesson he clearly pointed out when he was finished. One of his stories concerned an incident in their village.

There was an old class-mate of her father's who lived by himself a short distance from the village. He was a quarrelsome sort of fellow who found work only periodically as a farm laborer. This man kept a few ducks in a small pen beside the wall of his tumble-down house. The pen was encircled with bamboo poles that were none too sturdy. The ducks often got out, but never went far from home. One day, two of them were run over and killed on the road in front of the man's house, a road that saw little automotive traffic, as a rule. The driver of the car turned out to be a visiting government official making the rounds of this section to collect reports from local authorities on agricultural production. He was an important personage in the lives of many of the residents hereabouts. Nevertheless, the former classmate complained over the loss of his ducks to the village headman. Formality required that the complaint go to the provincial capital. Pretty soon, a summons came to call the ducks' owner to the capitol for an inquiry. He wasn't seen for over four months, and the village speculated on the cause of his prolonged absence. Silent heard her mother and father talking about the missing man's disappearance. Her father told her mother, "Really, it is best to be silent. I learned that in the labor camps." In her child's mind, the words "silent" and "best" would be forever linked. After that, her father would say to her, "Remember what you heard, 'it is best to be silent'" and he'd give a little wink.

And Silent would reply, "To be silent is best."

At last Silent could drift off into sleep. By recalling the details of the incident, the voice of her father had come to help her make her decision. She was right to think of this as a family story, not one to share. She whispered her father's words to herself, as she relaxed into the knowledge of what to tell Miss Hobbs.

PART IV

Summer
2003

CHAPTER 47

"Who wants to ride with Papa?" Ben directed his question to an empty room. But he knew it would not be empty for long. He'd heard the sound of giggles as two dark-haired imps stood just beyond the archway, waiting to make an entrance.

"I do, I do!" came loud, heart-warming pleas as they ran into the room. Here were Ben's darlings, his two black-eyed Susans, his China dolls. One was a head taller than the other, a good thing, because otherwise it would be hard to tell them apart, they looked so much alike. Actually, they were sisters, which explained the resemblance.

"I want to ride with Papa," the taller one said.

"All right, Lila Lee. But what about General Tso, here? What will she do?" As he asked, Ben reached down and put a strong arm around the smaller child and heaved her up onto his knees. He held her securely.

"I'll come with you, too," the little one said. Ben put on a long face. He loved nothing more than play-acting with his girls. "Then who will ride with Mommy?" he asked and used fingers to pull down the corners of his mouth even further.

Before anyone could answer, Hanna strode into the kitchen to find her family gathered there. She had overheard everything. "I'll tell you what. You, Lillian and you, Jennifer, may both go with your father this morning. I need to make a stop at school on the way. I'll be quicker about it if I go alone. Anyway, you'll both be riding home with me because Papa has to do some work in the late afternoon."

"There. It's all settled. See how easy that was?" Ben smiled at Hanna as he eased Jennifer back into a standing position.

Sundays at the Rinaldi's household generally took some strategic planning. There were two fixtures in the day that needed accommodation. The girls went for an hour in the morning to Chinese School. Hanna felt strongly that it would be essential for them to keep up with their Mandarin speaking. Ben backed her up on this. Perhaps, more importantly, Hanna and Ben wanted them to learn about Chinese culture and customs so that they could take some pride in their heritage.

The other Sunday event was a barbecue at the home of Hanna's dad. Mr. Hobbs lived in the same house down the road in Burlingame, the one in which Hanna had grown up. He had been playing golf on Sundays with the same foursome of friends for years. Although he was thrilled over the introduction of two little granddaughters into his life, he hated to break up the foursome. After several weeks of negotiation, the foursome managed to stay together for a Saturday date. They lost one player, but replaced him with the brother of the member who had to drop out. Mr. Hobbs was thus free to play the role of grandpa every Sunday. For Ben and Hanna it was a relaxing half-day away from the city and the girls loved going there.

Hanna and Ben had been together since her return from China in the summer of 1993. One of their first orders of business had been to find a place to live. They were looking at a time when rental fees were rising steeply. It was difficult to know what rate was fair to both owner and renter. Because it had taken over two months to find anything decent that was affordable, Hanna had become discouraged. She'd been living with her father all summer. She managed to find work again at City College, in admissions, but she did not fancy having to commute from the Peninsula to her job in the city. When she spoke to her dad about it, he was of the opinion that she and Ben would be better off trying to buy something with the help of a mortgage, and not paying rent at all. Hanna agreed but had not yet mentioned this to Ben.

Meanwhile, Ben was doing his behind-the-scenes work at the San Francisco Opera. His pal, Louis, was no longer his supervisor: Ben had qualified as a master carpenter and worked in the scenery shop these days. His work continued to take him to the Opera House on performance nights, where he sat in on poker games with the guys.

One evening Ben was telling everyone about the woes of apartment hunting. Louis responded with a suggestion. "I got some friends doing work on a ground-floor flat on Lake Street. Nice part of town. The relatives of the late owner are really anxious to unload this place, so I'm told. Any chance you could pull together all your winnings and make a bid? Or aren't you ready to be an owner?"

"Oh, I'm ready, but I don't know if my bank account is. Still, I'll speak to Hanna, about it. She has a good head on her shoulders."

"Here. I'll give you the construction guy's name and number. Give him a call when you're ready."

"Thanks, Louis. You're a pal." And Ben took the slip of paper that Louis was handing him.

Ben told Hanna about the place, and they both agreed it wouldn't hurt to go take a look. Ben made the phone call. A viewing date was agreed upon. The recent remodeling had included updated cabinets and counters in the kitchen and window replacements looking out into the small garden in back. The quality of the wood flooring used throughout was something that Ben especially appreciated. Hanna liked the open kitchen plan. Best of all was a hot tub discretely placed in a corner of the garden, carefully fenced off from any prying eyes of neighbors. "I love it!" Hanna exclaimed.

When Hanna went back to Burlingame that night, she told her dad about this find. She told him she liked it so much, she would consider cashing in the remainder of her trust fund to be able to make an offer on the property.

"Don't do that," he told her. "Look, I've been meaning to ask you about this for some time. Do you love Ben?"

"Yes, Dad, I love him very much."

"Enough to marry him?"

"Now, Dad, you know that's a tough one for me. I'm one of these modern types who believe you don't need a piece of paper to prove that you are committed in a relationship."

"A marriage certificate does a lot more than that, my darling daughter. That piece of paper gives answers to various legal questions that can arise. Such as property rights, visiting rights, parental rights. It says to the world 'here are two people who agree to live their lives together and care for each other'. Is it Ben, himself, who makes you hesitate? Sure, he may not be the brightest bulb in the pack, but he is one of the kindest, most agreeable men I know. And look at his loyalty to you. Not many men would still be there almost a year later for a sweetheart who picks up and goes her own way. Maybe you hold that against him. I see it as a big plus."

"So do I, Dad. So do I."

Her father continued, as if he hadn't heard her. "You know, Hanna, if you are waiting for someone to be your equal in the brains department, you may have a long time to wait. Couples who complement each other in strengths and weaknesses are the ones who usually do best. That would be the case with you and Ben. I'm tired of telling you all this. My point in delving into it is that if you and Ben came to me with wedding plans, I would like to offer to make a bid on this flat for you. It would be my pleasure to do so."

Hanna was speechless. She nearly asked in a joking way, if this was a bribe. But she held back, sensing the sincerity in her father's expression.

"Dad, you are an old dear. What a generous offer. I'll talk to Ben about it right away." Hanna reached out both hands towards her father's face and tilted his head down to give him a big kiss on his forehead. "Thanks, Dad, for even thinking of it."

In a voice made gruff by emotion, Mr. Hobbs said, "I want some family to live nearby. It was too quiet around here with you gone all year. No wife, no sons within reach, no daughter. What's a fellow to do?"

"Do just what you are doing. Try to fix it." Hanna smiled broadly as she spoke these words.

CHAPTER 48

More than three years after Ben and Hanna moved into their flat on Lake Street, Hanna found the letter in the mailbox that she'd been waiting years to receive. It was a notice from San Francisco State University offering her a position in their admissions department. Hanna was thrilled. This meant a boost in salary and work serving a much larger student population than had been the case at her present job. To celebrate, she persuaded Ben to use up a few days of his leave allowance so they could go visit Ellie and David in Seattle.

Their friends from years ago in Chiang Mai were as ready as ever to get together as a foursome. David and Ellie each had found rewarding work in their home city. David worked for the Port of Seattle on trade development. He traveled for short periods of time, but only three or four times a year. Ellie worked as a resource librarian four days a week at the Delridge branch of the public library. When they felt sufficiently secure in their jobs, they bought a ramshackle house in the vegetation of Vashon Island, located a short ferry ride from Seattle. David began the work of taming the overgrown land, creating lawns of native grasses that didn't require constant attention but did open up views of ocean not seen for several years. Ellie haunted local yard sales on weekends. She succeeded in finding just the right touches to complement furniture accumulated in the past, furniture that had been waiting in storage for a useful resting place. The house was quirky; it was also warmly welcoming to everyone who entered.

The morning after their arrival, Hanna and Ellie sat together in wicker chairs on the back porch of the house. David and Ben were away doing errands. Ellie had shoved a short list of grocery requests into David's hand at the last minute. She felt free to sit with Hanna and get on with the important matter at hand: catching up. They had managed only a few visits in the years since Hanna's return. There was always some new element in their lives that wanted to be aired.

They sat quietly for a few minutes, taking last sips from the mugs of morning coffee each had carried along with her. In the distance, a thin ribbon of ocean was visible above the tree-line. Occasionally, a brown-feathered hen would walk by not far from the porch, clucking and scolding its way along as it searched for possible sources of food.

"Tell me again, why it is that you keep chickens?" Hanna inquired of her friend.

Ellie replied, "You see, David and I talked about it for weeks. We both would have loved to have a dog, but we didn't think it was fair to the poor animal to leave it alone all day long. So we settled on a few chickens. They are pleasant creatures, easy to provide for, and they couldn't care less whether we are home or not. They have shelter; they can take care of themselves. Besides, we both like fresh eggs. By the way, don't let me forget. You must take a box home with you when you go. We're into surpluses nowadays."

"So, Ellie, do you have family in the area? How did you happen to end up on Vashon Island?"

"Good guess. I do have family here. My brother and his wife are only a mile away. They've invited us over for dinner tonight."

"That's great. I'd love to meet your brother. Is he older or younger than you?"

"He's five years older and always lets me know it. You know how big brothers are. Mike's wife is Texan. She takes a little getting used to. But she's a terrific mom."

"So they have children, then? That makes you an auntie."

"Yes, it does. They only have the one. She's a little girl from China, adopted as a baby. You know, I think they went through that city where you did your teaching. What was it called?"

"Guangzhou."

"Yes, Guangzhou. I'm sure that was it. You can ask Mike and his wife, Annabelle. How's that for a name?"

"Very pretty, very Texan. What did they name their daughter?"

"They call her Emmalee."

"Well, I'll be eager to hear about it if they did go through Guangzhou."

"Tonight we can find out. Now I'd better go do something about those breakfast dishes before the guys get back. They'll need the counter space to unload. Come on, you can give me a hand."

CHAPTER 49

That evening, their hostess greeted them by saying, "I told you not to get dressed up. We're having barbecue. You know what a mess that makes."

She was looking at Ellie and Hanna, who had worn cotton summer dresses for the occasion. Annabelle was decked out in denim jeans, not just everyday jeans, but ones with a stripe of rhinestone down the side of each leg.

Ellie introduced her friends, then told her sister-in-law, "Talk about dressing up, you look pretty splendid, yourself." They stood in an awkward cluster just outside the front door until Annabelle ushered them into the house, declaring, "Come in, come in. You haven't met all of us yet."

Standing in the middle of a brightly lit living room, one of spacious proportions in this house of modern design, stood Emmalee in her two-piece red silk pajamas. Hanna said to herself, "I bet her momma shops at Neiman Marcus."

"Emmalee, these are new friends for you to meet. Say 'good evening' to Hanna and Ben."

Hanna hesitated for a second, uncertain of what to do next. Then she leaned over slightly to extend her hand to Emmalee in a polite handshake.

"Good evening," the child said clearly.

"Good evening," Hanna repeated.

Next it was Ben's turn. He stuck out his hand. "Hello, Emmalee. My name is Ben. I'm pleased to meet you."

"Good evening," Emmalee responded as she held her grave expression and placed her hand in Ben's.

If Emmalee had arrived in Seattle as a shy, skinny little girl who spoke no English, remarkable changes had already occurred. Now an eight-year old girl, she was shooting up tall and her body had taken on some becoming weight. Her careful pronunciation revealed some excellent language coaching along the way. And, of course, with a mother as big of heart and boisterous of manner as Annabelle, the daughter had long ago lost any trace of shyness. Annabelle, for all her bluff, had an extremely tender side which she lavished on Emmalee. The only characteristic that the girl retained was a seriousness of manner that gave adults the impression she was mature beyond her years.

Mike spoke up. "That's all for now. Enough of the formalities. I gotta get back to the grill." He went over to Emmalee and bent down to give her a kiss on the cheek. "Give daddy a hug. Night-night, princess." Emmalee hugged Mike as if she weren't going to let go. Then she did. Mike went through the kitchen, which was in plain sight to the left. He opened a screen door, with David in hot pursuit. "Can I help you, Mike?" they heard David ask.

Ellie invited Emmalee to sit on the coach with her while the others went to the bar at the end of the dining area to make some drinks. When they returned, Emmalee and Ellie were deep in conversation.

"Almost time for bed, sweetheart," her mother told her. "Would you like your Aunt Ellie to take you in?"

"Oh, yes, please. And could she read me a story?"

"If it's a short one. Let Ellie choose."

"I will."

"Now say a good-night to our new friends. No, there's no need to shake hands again."

With a wave to Hanna and Ben, Emmalee grabbed ahold of Ellie's hand and the two of them disappeared behind a door at the rear of the room.

Annabelle led her guests back to the center of the room. There, they seated themselves on buttery soft leather and set their glasses down on a glass-top coffee table within easy reach.

"So … Ellie tells me you spent some time in that Chinese city of Guangzhou." Annabelle looked straight at Hanna when she spoke. Before Hanna could answer, Annabelle went rushing on. "Can't imagine spending much time in such a place. Of course, if you have work that interests you, that might make a difference. We could hardly breathe. And you couldn't get anywhere. The Germans were there, putting in a subway system and the whole town was torn up. But our business with the consulate was finished in twelve days, and we were on a plane out of there two days later. And of course we had our darling Emmalee with us, so I'd have to say it was worth all the hassle. Tell me again how long you were there?"

Hanna had finally been offered the chance to get a word in edgewise. She entered right in.

"One full school year, ten months. I read about the city putting in a subway system. That work started after I left. My work was very valuable to me; it's what kept me there to the end. But, Annabelle, you went to China to adopt a baby. Why did you have to spend time in Guangzhou? Is that where you met your baby?"

"Heavens, no. We had to get on some puddle-jumper of a plane and take a short flight to a nearby province to reach the orphanage where we were doing our business. Guangzhou was necessary because that's where an American Consulate is located. We needed to do some official filings there that took some time. Our appointment with the consul had been made months in advance. There were no snafus, but it did take two geniuses like Mike and me to do all the advance paperwork correctly. But why am I making such a big deal of all this? The only memory worth preserving is the feeling I had when I set eyes on our little girl."

The screen door slammed shut. David had been holding it for Mike who entered the kitchen area with a platter heaped high with spare ribs. The host set the platter on a countertop; he called to his wife,

"Time to stir those pots of yours, dearie. We're ready to go."

Annabelle jumped to her feet. Hanna caught a glimpse of high-heeled cowboy boots hiding under the cuffs of the decorated denims. "Finishing touch," Hanna thought to herself.

The dinner was a lively affair. Only the six of them were there, but they made enough noise for a gathering twice that size. Everyone talked at once.

The ribs were truly delicious. They had been cooked slowly so that the meat was tender and practically fell off the bones. Splashes of dark-red sauce had enhanced the flavor. Ears of corn had been roasted in the corners of the grill.

The offering from the pot was a dish of Annabelle's baked beans, "The best you're ever likely to taste," the hostess informed them as she spooned generous servings onto everyone's plate. "I wanted to serve you my special chili, but Mike put the kabosh on that. I suspect he thought it might outshine his ribs."

"Now, Annabelle, I thought no such thing. You should know better than anyone that chili is best served with a side of some form of beef. What do you say, Ben? I hear from David that your family operates a fine restaurant in San Francisco. You must have a pretty good food sense. What's best with spare ribs: chili or baked beans?"

Ben was caught in the middle of spooning beans into his mouth. When he had recovered sufficiently to answer, he came up with just the right response. "I think these beans are best served with these ribs." Everyone agreed with that.

Annabelle looked at Ben and asked, "How long have you two been married?"

"It'll be three years in August. But we knew each other for that many years before we married."

"Ah, ha. Knew each other in the biblical sense?"

"My dear wife. What kind of a question is that?" Mike asked in a mock angry voice.

But Ben remained undisturbed. "I'm not sure I understand the question, so I'll have to pass," he told his hostess.

"Okay. Answer me this," Annabelle went on. "Any little Hannas or Bens running around at your house?"

"Not that I've noticed," Ben kept up the bantering tone.

"Then don't forget. There are plenty more waiting where Emmalee came from. I once told Ellie the same thing and you know what she did? She went out and bought herself a bunch of chickens."

"And I didn't have to make elaborate travel plans to do it," Ellie remarked.

Hanna was seated next to Mike at their end of the table. She turned to him and asked, "Annabelle was telling us about your trip to China and said you had stayed in Guangzhou for formalities regarding the adoption. When you were there, where did you stay? Did you get a travel agent to suggest a place for you?"

"No, we didn't have to," Mike answered. "Our adoption agency here in Seattle made all the arrangements for us. We stayed at a very nice place called The White Swan. It's on Shamian Island. Do you know it?"

"No. I've never heard of it. What is this Shamian Island?" a puzzled Hanna asked back.

"I don't know. It looked like a European section of the city to me. The architecture of some of the buildings was old and colonial looking. Yet I don't believe the British or any other Europeans succeeded in colonizing one square foot of mainland China. I've always meant to look that up, just never got around to it."

Hanna was intrigued by this information from Mike. She had one more question. "Why is it called an 'island'? Is it actually set aside from the city by some body of water?"

"Yes, it is," Mike told her. "It's in the Pearl River. But the side next to municipal land is separated only by a canal . You hardly knew you weren't in the city the whole time."

Hanna placed a hand on the side of her face." I can't believe there was that section of the city that I never heard of."

"Was your school right in town?" Did you know the city well?"

"No, it was on the outskirts and I only went into the city three or four times a month. My surprise comes from my fellow foreign teachers never having mentioned it. Maybe they didn't know, either."

"Maybe it has something to do with the place catering to travelers only passing through. Not exactly the crowd that a bunch of college teachers would be likely to seek out." Mike got to his feet and Hanna quickly followed suit. They joined the others who had already moved to the living room.

Half an hour later, after phone numbers and email addresses had been exchanged, Annabelle saw her guests off at the front door. She hugged each in turn and putting on a strong Texas drawl insisted, "Now, ya'all come back and see us real soon, ya hear?"

They all agreed they would do that at the earliest opportunity.

CHAPTER 50

One month before his and Hanna's fifth wedding anniversary, Ben made a special visit to the post office. He was mailing a thick packet to the China Center of Adoption Affairs. When Annabelle had said it took two geniuses to assemble all the documents required to apply for adoption, she hadn't been exaggerating. Ben and Hanna had worked hard with the San Francisco agency that was ushering them through the process. It had taken months. To begin with, not one but four home visits by a social worker approved by the Chinese had been required. Because Ben and Hanna had staggered working hours, these home visits had been difficult to arrange, but necessary. The paperwork included an application, cover letter, health certificates, tax documents, and criminal background checks. They waited four months for a form signed by U.S. Immigration Services in Chicago that would grant preliminary approval for the child to enter the U.S. as a citizen. That was the most trying part. When it showed up, their work was complete. A quick review by the agent in the San Francisco office, and Ben was off to the post office the next day.

Then began another long wait, the wait for an offer to come from China of a baby chosen for them. They waited more than a year. When Hanna contacted the agency, she was told there was nothing wrong about this. The average waiting time was seventeen months; anything less than that and they would be beating the averages. As it turned out, Hanna and Ben did beat the averages. An official-looking envelope arrived in their mail a day before Thanksgiving in 1999. They carried it with them to the gathering at Ben's parents the next day.

"Look at this! The Chinese want to give us two babies, not one," Ben announced.

In formal language the letter informed Hanna and Ben that their application had been approved. It went on to add that the three-year old girl selected for them had a little sister, also brought to the orphanage. If possible, the orphanage hoped that the agency would arrange for the sisters to go to the same family. Otherwise, the orphanage would wait a little longer to offer Hanna and Ben a different suitable child.

"What do you think, Mama?" Ben asked in front of the entire family gathered there. "We don't want to wait. But two babies sounds like twice as much work."

"Twice as much work and twice as much joy. Hanna, what do you think? Before you answer, I'd like to say something. I'll be thrilled to step in and be a grandmother at home with the little ones anytime you might need me. I can't wait to have a baby to snuggle in my arms, to sing my baby songs to. Papa and I have talked this over. If I have to neglect my duties in the kitchen at the restaurant, I'll hire someone to come in. I'm easily replaced here, but no one can replace a caring grandma. I'll help. I really will."

Hanna walked over to Ben's mother and gave her a big hug. "That settles it, Ben. Wouldn't you say? With Mama as backup, how can we possibly go wrong? Let's send our reply on Monday. We'll do it."

****

"Ben. I must be crazy. Or I'm in a really realistic dream. Tell me the truth. Am I on a plane to Guangzhou with you?"

Hanna was seated with her seat belt fastened, looking straight ahead. She felt certain it was Ben next to her; she had her head on his shoulder.

Ben put his hand on her head and smoothed down her curls.

"You are. You're returning to Guangzhou. Only this time you're bringing me with you."

"Good. See that you don't lose sight of me. I'm definitely in a foggy state. Did you see the airport in Shanghai? That wasn't the same airport I came through seven years ago. There were signs in English. I never saw those before. I suppose a lot of things have changed over the years. Including us."

Ben continued to stroke Hanna's curls as he said to her, "Hanna, relax. We're here for one thing and one thing only. That's to get our girls. Maybe you'd be better off if you didn't think too much about the past."

But Hanna couldn't help it. Everything in Guangzhou 2000 was such a surprise to her. The hotel most of all. The White Swan Hotel was luxury worthy of five stars; their San Francisco agency had reserved rooms for them at a group rate, or they could not have afforded it. The hotel boasted a working waterfall in the lobby. And the two tired occupants were delighted to see fresh flowers and a bowl of fresh fruit in their room.

On their one free day, the day after their arrival, a groggy Hanna dragged a jet-lagged Ben to two of her old haunts.

On taxi rides through the city, Hanna and Ben saw signs everywhere of new construction. Giant cranes spun their arms in slow motion above the crowds, going about their business. Hanna noticed at least a dozen buildings already reaching up to heights not realized by their neighbors. Ben had stared and stared.

"You never told me that Guangzhou had a skyline."

An amazed Hanna replied, "It didn't used to."

Their first stop was the Dong Fang Hotel.

Hanna told Ben, "We'll go there so I can show you where I mailed my letters to you. And bought the newspaper that was my weekly gift to myself."

The hotel was no more than ten or twelve stories high. Hanna noticed for the very first time that the hotel next door towered over it, overshadowing the humble Dong Fang. She wondered to herself, "Why didn't I ever go into that one?" But she didn't wonder for long. The Dong Fang might have been a poor cousin in the neighborhood of hotels, but it had an air of dignity about it once you entered. It felt good. Hanna led them right through the lobby and down a short passageway to the mailroom. There, they stood and watched for a few minutes as people came along to do their business at the counter. Then they stopped in for a short peek at the small room off the lobby that sold local and foreign periodicals. Hanna was swamped with feelings of gratitude for what this small hotel had provided her during her stay at the university.

"Ben," she said, "this place meant so much to me."

"Yeah?" she heard the question in the tone of Ben's voice. "I guess you'd have to have lived it to appreciate it. It all looks pretty ordinary to me."

Of course, Ben was right, and Hanna knew it. She would never be able to share with anyone who had not been there, the strangeness, the homesickness, the difficulties with food and climate, the outright discomfort at times, coupled with moments of triumph in the classroom. Her experiences were hers to keep, but difficult to share with others. She might as well not try. After all, her stay in Guangzhou had been only ten months out of what she expected would be a long life.

Ben perked up when they reached their second destination of the day. This was the original McDonald's. restaurant. Hanna learned from the taxi driver that there were two in town by now. He took them straight to the nearest one which turned out to be the one that Hanna had known. Once seated with their orders on trays in front of them, the Big Macs and milkshakes did wonders to revive two weary travelers. Ben looked around.

"This is the biggest McDonald's I've ever seen."

"I thought the same thing when I first saw it," Hanna agreed.

"So, how often did you come here to eat?"

"Only two or three times a month. It was always a treat."

"Why didn't you come more often, then?"

"Never mind, Ben. It doesn't matter. I don't feel like explaining all it took to get here."

Ben didn't ask any more questions after this reproach from Hanna. Hanna considered, then decided she'd best do something to ease a slight tension in the air.

"What I will tell you about is the last time I was here. I brought one of my students with me, a girl who had won a contest in an English class, not mine. I had helped her study for it. Anyway, this girl chose 'Silent' as her English name, a bit unusual, wouldn't you say?"

Ben nodded his head. "Why did she do that?," he asked.

"Exactly. Why did she do that? That's what I asked her on that last day. She told me it was a saying in their family, that it is best to be silent. She wanted to be best, so she called herself Silent."

A low "hmm" came out of Ben. Then he muttered, "If she wanted to be best, why didn't she just call herself 'Best'?"

Hanna needed to be charitable at this point. "That would have taken care of things, wouldn't it?"

Hanna came away from this conversation more convinced than ever that her Guangzhou past was not meant to be dragged into the present.

As they left the restaurant, she gave it a sweeping look. While doing so, she clung for a moment to the memory of the girl who had called herself 'Silent'. Hanna put her hands on her opposite elbows and gave herself a little hug. She hoped Silent was doing well.

The next day, Hanna and Ben were feeling much better after one long night of solid sleep. They showed up early for their appointment at the consulate; they didn't mind the wait. The consul general had been in Guangzhou for only two years, they learned, as they made their introductory remarks to each other. He was interested to hear that Hanna had worked in this city seven years earlier.

He asked her, "Will you get a chance to go out and visit the campus while you're here?"

Hanna replied that they wouldn't take the time to do that. "Besides," she added, "the place is not the same. I've heard from one of my former teacher friends who did go back, that a whole new division is running the school and the buildings have all been remodeled. He told me he didn't recognize the place."

"Was that Milo?" Ben wanted to know.

"Yes, it was in an email, remember? But we're not here for that. Let's find out what we need to do to bring our babies back home."

The consul thrust a short stack of papers in Ben's direction. These were more forms to fill out and return after the children were in their possession and before they boarded a plane to leave China.

"One thing you'll notice is that a copy of each birth certificate must be attached to the form." He pointed out the place to them. "Are you staying at the White Swan?" He noticed Hanna's nod and went on. "The hotel has copying machines which will make this easier for you. Just drop off the completed forms with any staff member on duty the day you come by. No need to see me again. Good luck. I feel certain your efforts will be well-rewarded."

Handshakes all around. The appointment had lasted all of ten minutes.

CHAPTER 51

On a June Sunday in 2003, the Rinaldi family arrived at the home of Hanna's father in two cars within a few minutes of each other. Hanna's dad led them into his backyard for the afternoon visit. The gas grill standing at one side of the brick patio was doing its work on some chicken legs and Italian style chicken sausages that were a favorite of both Ben's and Mr. Hobbs's. A round, wrought iron table with five chairs occupied a part of the patio nearest the lawn. After tending to the grill, Mr. Hobbs seated himself in one of the cushioned seats to take in the scene in front of him.

Hanna and Ben were tending to their children on the playground set that Mr. Hobbs had installed out on the lawn two years earlier. At that time, Lilian had been old enough to enjoy it, and Jennifer was soon ready as well. Mr. Hobbs had once considered having a putting green built on his spacious back lawn, but he decided that would be a bit self-indulgent, so he held back. Then Hanna and Ben brought two little girls into his life, and he found a much better use for the space. As he watched, Ben pushed four-year old Jen in a swing while Hanna watched six-year old Lillian climb on the junior-sized jungle gym nearby. He saw Hanna say something to Ben, and then leave to stride toward him and take a seat next to him, one that afforded her a view of the activities.

After she was seated, Hanna remarked, "Ben can handle things. In fact, he does handle things and is very happy to do so."

"He sure seems to have taken to his role as Dad. But then, look at those little girls. If they aren't the cutest things I've ever seen, I don't know what is."

As Hanna and her father sat and watched, Jen moved from the swing to the slide, and Lilly sat in the larger of the two swings and began to propel herself. Ben positioned himself at the bottom of the slide to catch a squealing General Tso when she hit the ground. A fourth activity remained; a teeter-totter stood at the end of the swing set awaiting the moment when both sisters would want to go there at the same time.

"Well, Hanna, you really did it, didn't you?"

"Did what, Dad?"

"You went back to that city in China and collected a couple of prizes. Let me ask you something. Do you think things would have turned out this way if you hadn't gone there to teach?"

"Can't say for sure. Seems to me it was more a case of one thing leading to another. Remember, ten years ago, you weren't too happy about my going off to have an 'adventure'."

Mr. Hobbs interrupted. "I remember too well. You were determined to go, and I was dead set against it."

"Yes, Dad. You made that perfectly clear at the time. Can't say why I felt so strongly about going, but doing so certainly satisfied whatever that particular need was. It made me appreciate the possibilities of life for me right here in the Bay Area. I haven't left home since, except to go with Ben to pick up our girls. It's only an irony of fate that to do so meant going to that same place."

"An irony of fate ... I like the way you put that." After a few moments, Mr Hobbs went on, "You know, we sit here on this sunny day in Burlingame, and we all have a lot to be thankful for. If those ten months is what it took to keep you within shouting distance for years afterwards, then it was worth the worry and the loneliness."

"Thanks for saying that. For my part, I experienced terrible loneliness, too. But of course I had the demands of my work and as long as I stayed zeroed in on that, I managed to endure."

Mr. Hobbs gazed at Lilly and Jen, who were moving up and down on the seesaw. Ben sang them the nursery rhyme about Margery Daw as they giggled and pushed, giggled and pushed. Soon they would come running onto the patio, demanding of their grand-dad, "Did you see me swing? Did you see me slide?"

"Hanna, let me ask you this. Do you think it will make a difference to you, as a mother, that you spent that time in China? Do you think it will bring you even closer to the girls?"

"Hey, Dad, you're really digging deep today." Hanna paused. "It has already made a difference, and I know it. These girls are mine. They are mine as surely as if I had given birth to them. I love them like nothing I have known before. There is simply this feeling of belonging that came to me the moment I saw them. If that is because of those ten months, I can't say. But that's how it is. Does that answer your question?"

"It does. It certainly does."

That evening, when Hanna and her family opened the door into their home on Lake Street, a beam of outside light fell on the figures of two small silver elephants standing side by side on the mantle over the fireplace. Two silver elephants waiting together for the time that two little girls would take them down and play with them.

Every person who goes to China to teach an English course has a unique experience. <u>Silent's Teacher</u> describe's Hanna's year at a particular school in one particular school year. It is not meant to represent a picture of university life in a general way in China. The author taught English at this university in the era in which Hanna's story takes place.

Edwards Brothers Malloy
Thorofare, NJ USA
December 17, 2015